UNKNOWN REVENGE
Marshal Series
Book 4

Robin Lyons

COPYRIGHT

ACKNOWLEDGMENTS

Unknown Revenge took me four years to complete. A world-wide pandemic, painful family losses, illness and the construction of a new home derailed my creativity.

During this time, we lost my big sister, Gwen, a fan, and supporter of my writing. To be honest, I'm still in disbelief she's gone. I'll love and miss her forever.

We also lost my mother-in-mother, Ethel, one of my biggest fans. She encouraged me to keep writing books and shared many life lessons with me. I loved her so much and miss her every day.

Last, we lost the sweetest woman I've ever known, Jessie, also a big fan of my writing—she'd always ask when would she be able to read the next book. We will forever love and miss her, too.

I feel blessed to have had these wonderful, supportive women in my life. Somehow, life has a way of righting itself. My creative muse (so to speak) returned and just like that, Unknown Revenge is in circulation and I'm on to the next book.

Special thanks: Proofreading provided by the Hyper-Speller at https://www.wordrefiner.com.

ROBIN'S READER CLUB

What do you get when you join my reader club? Free books, exclusive giveaways, book recommendations, author updates, and behind the scene on what's happening at the ranch, where I live. My weekly newsletter arrives in your email inbox every Saturday morning. It's a great way to start your weekend—your favorite morning beverage, and a glimpse into my country life.

Email addresses are never shared. I value your privacy as much as mine.

Join the club at: https://www RobinLyons.com

INTRODUCTION

Dear Reader,

You can enjoy this novel as a solo read or read the series in order for an enhanced reading experience. In Unknown Revenge, you'll find a few characters from the three previous novels in the series.

I love sharing a famous quote that relates to the overall story in my Marshal Series. The famous quote, "Beware the fury of a patient man," by John Dryden, could be a summation of Unknown Revenge. It's about a killer who has waited a long time to seek revenge for what he feels are crimes against his family.

Thank you for reading Unknown Revenge. I hope you enjoy reading the story as much as I enjoyed writing it—once my muse returned. Be sure to read the important information about Mac at the end of the book.

Best regards and happy reading,

Robin Lyons

UNKNOWN
REVENGE

Chapter 1

Darkness lingered in the shadows of the Sierra Nevada Mountains—it wouldn't be long before dawn. The nocturnal critters busied themselves as they hunted for their last meal of the night. And birds peeked out from their cozy nests. Under a giant pine tree lay a man in sticky, pungent mountain misery shrubs awaiting his prey. The spring morning felt quite different from his home, where the humidity level was already on the rise. He had to admit, the mild temperature and low humidity were a pleasant change.

Hunter wasn't his real name. Years ago, his friends nicknamed him Hunter because he always hit his mark and the name stuck. Now, when introducing himself to a stranger, he called himself Hunter. He didn't mind it, hunting was his passion and profession. Anyone who visited his home could see the evidence of his expert marksmanship by the trophies mounted in almost every room. What friends back home didn't know—he'd done a few hunts that weren't sanctioned by the Department of Fish and Wildlife. In fact, if the authorities apprehended him today, they'd charge him with first-degree murder, California Penal Code 187, with the aggravated circumstance of lying in wait—Penal Code 189. Of course, he knew what the consequences were, but felt confident they'd never catch him—he was that good at what he did.

His father had taught him how to shoot and hunt from a young age. As he became an expert marksman, his father began teaching him how to track animals.

He'd met his wife when they were seniors in high school—their attraction to each other strengthened when they discovered a shared passion for rock climbing. During their final year of high school, her father had been killed in a car accident. Upon turning eighteen, his wife received money from her father's life insurance, and with it, she and he married and purchased a local sporting goods store in their small Missouri town. The previous store owner had gone bankrupt. Together, they turned the store into a successful business.

Unknown to his wife, a few years back, Hunter had received an offer he couldn't refuse. Financial comfort had been bestowed upon them and the true reason the sporting goods store thrived had not been the retail side of the business.

Out of the blue, a man he didn't know had called him. The voice seemed altered, but he guessed the caller was a well-educated, no-named man with a California slickness to his speech. Hunter didn't have a college degree, but he had street smarts and a good gut.

He listened as the stranger told him he'd heard he was an excellent marksman. The man had done his homework. He knew more about Hunter than his closest friends knew about him. His friends knew as much as he wanted them to know. The stranger even knew about his mother's health.

It threw Hunter off to hear so much personal information about himself from a stranger. Still, his gut told him to keep listening, so he did. The man said he'd heard Hunter was also a topnotch tracker. Being curious, Hunter offered to take the man on a hunting trip. That was his legitimate side business, after all. He took hunting enthusiasts on back-country trips.

The man laughed and said he'd never shot a weapon in his life and didn't plan to start now. Instead, the man offered him a job. Kill a specific person for a large sum of money. More money than Hunter had made in three years working as an independent hunting guide.

There were a few rules—he limited Hunter's preparation to what he learned through observation. No Internet searches. Telling anyone anything about their arrangement would end their relationship. And the job had to be clean, discreet, no evidence left behind.

In a split second, Hunter considered his mother's cancer and the fact that she couldn't afford treatment. Her insurance turned out to be crap with enormous co-pays and deductibles. Being a momma's boy, he'd worked hard to provide what he could for her, but he didn't make enough to pay for her treatment. He accepted the job. Before the call ended, he remembered the man on the phone had added, "And don't show-boat, get the job done and get out. This could be the beginning of a lucrative venture."

Since the phone call, Hunter had done six jobs for the man who remained a stranger. He accepted jobs in the continental USA without exception. He always drove—never flew for business. So far, his jobs included a sixty-something banker in Washington, a college professor in Idaho, a social worker in Colorado, an investment broker in Pennsylvania, a Catholic nun in Alabama, a retired con-man in North Carolina, and the California job which had two jobs in one, making them numbers seven and eight. He always stayed in the crappiest motels he could find because they didn't have security monitors or he slept in the back of the rental trucks he used.

His mother's chemotherapy treatments hadn't saved her life. She'd passed away a year ago, but she wanted for nothing. Hunter had provided her with a comfortable end to her life. A life he and his wife had become accustomed to. A lifestyle afforded because of the jobs he accepted.

The assignment which brought Hunter to the small California town of Brookfield included two targets. His employer had apologized for the short notice. The person said it was a job he'd waited years for that had fallen into his lap. Hunter spent a few days studying the targets. Learned their habits. Watched their routines—opportunities to complete the assignment. He calculated the first shot in the three-hundred-yard range.

Many times, in the last two days, he'd been in the woods outside the secluded home of the retired police officer, Bruce Stockford. As with all his assignments, he'd watched his target and wondered what the person had done to his boss for him to pay to have them killed.

One of Hunter's secrets to success was studying his target. Finding the little habitual behaviors, or as he considered them, opportunities for him to complete his job. Everyone has a routine—waking up at the same time, sitting in the same chair, where they enjoyed their first cup of coffee—same activities, same places, same times almost every day made them easy targets once you knew their routine.

Bruce, an early bird, even though retired, woke before sunrise every morning. At close to five in the morning, Bruce sauntered into the kitchen to make a pot of coffee.

This morning, Hunter tracked Bruce using thermal imaging. He watched Bruce's warm body movement until it became stationary. "Morning piss, eh, Bruce?" he whispered to himself.

Next, Bruce made his way to the kitchen. The low wattage hood light flicked on. Enough light to make coffee and still be kind to Bruce's dry, aging, sleepy eyes.

Gretchen, Bruce's wife of forty-two years, was a night owl. She rose closer to ten. Hunter knew today was going to be a bad day for Bruce's wife.

Hunter observed Bruce had allowed himself to get soft during his retirement years. As with many sixty-something, baby-boomer types, he'd put on a few pounds, moved slower, and exercised less.

The heavily wooded, five-acre, Stockford property had been the perfect place for Hunter to set up a few, low-light game cameras and from the comfort of his dirt-bag, motel room, he'd spent hours observing what the family did during different times of the day.

He hadn't expected Bruce and Gretchen to be babysitting their grandchildren all week. Sasha—age fourteen, and Adler—age ten. From a young age, Hunter had taken his children with him on local hunting trips. He wanted them to be accustomed to seeing dead animals. He doubted Bruce's grandchildren had seen anything more than roadkill.

On his first night in Brookfield, Hunter sat with his back to the family in an attached booth at a local diner. He'd overheard a lot about their time together. The children's parents, Bruce and Gretchen's son, Wyatt and his wife Isabel, had gone on a wedding anniversary, seven-day cruise to the Caribbean.

Sasha, a typical fourteen-year-old, spent more time on her cell phone than she did interacting with her grandparents. Adler, at ten, Hunter had observed, spent a lot of his time doodling or drawing. Hunter sensed Adler still enjoyed hanging out and playing board games with his grandparents. He seemed rather close to his grandfather.

Bruce and Adler had a Cribbage tournament going all week— five games each day. Whom ever had the most wins at the end of the week was the winner. Hunter overheard them talking about the prize—an ice cream sundae of the winner's choice at Dad's Ice Cream Parlor downtown. Hunter knew there'd be no winner and there'd be no celebratory ice cream sundae.

Every day, Bruce and his grandson played two games before lunch and three games after. Old folks, Hunter had learned, like to do things in a routine. Bruce's routine would turn out to be unfortunate for him. The routines provided the perfect opportunity for Hunter to complete his assignment.

Hunter wore camouflage from head to toe. For accuracy, he used a short tactical bipod to steady his rifle and improve the accuracy of his shot. The attached suppressor allowed him time to flee the area before anyone would find Bruce. The day before, at about the same time in the morning, he'd gone to a secluded area within the National Forest about fifteen miles east as the crow flew to sight in his weapon and shot several boxes of ammunition.

The dewy scent of mountain misery invaded his sinuses more than on the previous mornings. After enduring the acrid odor for days, he hoped to never smell it again. He stretched his achy muscles without making a single pine needle crack. Over the years, he'd trained himself to be a contortionist, enabling his body to bend in unnatural ways. His learned talent allowed him to stretch without making a sound while he staked out a target.

"Come on, Bruce—time for coffee on the porch," he again whispered to himself.

As if on cue, the front door opened and his target, adorned in a thick, red and black checkered flannel bathrobe and slippers, padded across the porch to the chair where he sat every morning. He held a large steaming mug of coffee in his right hand. The power of Hunter's scope brought the mug's logo into focus. It read, *Brookfield Police Department.*

Bruce took a cautious sip of the coffee and then set the steaming mug on a small bistro table, next to his favorite porch chair. Hunter watched his every move, looking deep into his target's eyes, and watched him blink a few times. Hunter contemplated the shot—through one eye or between the eyes? The average human head measured smaller than six inches wide, whereas the average human eye was about one inch. He liked a challenge, but remembered the warning to not show-boat. It had been a breezy morning. He lifted a dead leaf and dropped it to watch how the breeze carried it.

Before he pulled the trigger, he always considered the person's last moment of life. As with his mother, he wanted his victims to experience a peaceful departure.

With both hands wrapped around his coffee cup, Bruce took his first full sip of coffee. A look of relaxed comfort washed across his face.

After he'd downed several swigs of the coffee, he placed the commemorative cup on the table and watched nature for a few seconds. Hunter slowed his breathing to a purposeful rhythm. Deep breath in, slow quiet release. Deep breath in, slow quiet release.

The distinct sound of the muffled whoosh woke the wildlife sleeping nearest Hunter. They scattered at the sound of the quiet muzzle blast. He watched Bruce's head bob backward and sprang forward. His body slumped. The shot between Bruce's eyes killed him before his brain registered the pain. His bleeding head now rested on his lap.

Hunter waited a moment. Using thermal imaging, he scanned the home for hot spots. The house remained still. He packed his gear, and for the first time, his boss told him to peg a note to a tree. He hiked back to the rental truck. Almost everything went behind the driver's seat, including his well-worn, leather moccasin-type shoes were his footwear of choice for tracking or stalking. He secured his weapon in a locked box under the driver's seat. He'd dump the suppressor as soon as possible. If, for some odd reason, a lawman pulled him over, suppressors weren't legal in California.

* * *

At close to six, Adler Stockford padded into the living room of his grandparents' home, not knowing this day would become one of the worst days in his life. His Pop-pop always sat on the front porch in the morning. He poured himself a large glass of milk and squirted chocolate syrup into the milk, more syrup than his Nana did. Then he stirred the milk until it turned a dark brown and took a sip to see if it needed to be chocolatier before he put the syrup back into the refrigerator. Then he scurried to Nana's chair to grab her throw blanket. After wrapping the throw tight around his body, grasping hold of his chocolate milk, he opened the front door and peered out.

When he saw his grandfather slumped over, the blanket dropped and the glass fell, shattering on the deck. He ran to his Pop-pop, a shard of glass pierced his right slipper. Not registering the pain in his foot yet, he yelled and shook the man whom he adored. Bruce's body slid off the chair and onto the porch. Adler ran to wake his Nana.

Adler threw open the bedroom door which startled Gretchen Stockford, who'd been in the depths of rem sleep. He sobbed and spoke gibberish in between gasps of air. "Pop-pop, Pop-pop. Blood. Fell…." He turned and ran, waving for Gretchen to follow him. She looked down and saw Adler had left bloody footprints on the bedroom carpet.

Seconds later, she called emergency services. They dispatched paramedics to the serene lake house. As directed, Gretchen stayed on the call. She couldn't provide any details about the situation other than Bruce was deceased. She refused to question Adler.

Sasha and Adler were on the sofa. Gretchen had told Sasha to not look outside. The oldest grandchild kept her head down and tended to her brother's foot injury. Again, wrapped in his Nana's throw, he didn't seem to realize he'd cut his foot.

The dispatch operator told Gretchen to hang up after she'd confirmed paramedics were at her home. She could see many vehicles in her driveway, lights flashing.

Two officers had arrived with the paramedics, they entered the home. Gretchen and the kids sat in the living room. Shock had consumed them. One officer called in and asked for a child advocate. He then asked Gretchen to follow him to the kitchen where they could talk without the children hearing. She pulled her bulky knitted sweater tight around her, giving herself the comforting hug, she needed at that moment in time.

"Did you find your husband?" the officer asked while he flipped open his pocket-sized notebook.

"No. My grandson, Adler, found him."

"Did he move your husband?"

"He said he touched him and Bruce fell out of the chair."

"Then what did he say he did?"

"He ran to wake me."

"Do you know anyone who might have had a grudge against your husband?"

By now, the officers responding all knew Bruce had retired from the Brookfield Police Department. When she didn't answer right away, the officer looked up at her.

She shrugged. "A grudge?"

"Maybe someone he arrested while on duty?"

"It was a long time ago." She pulled a tissue from her pocket and wiped her runny nose.

"Did he have any disputes with neighbors?"

"No. Our neighbors are wonderful people."

"Did Adler say he heard the shot?"

"The shot? I thought Bruce had a heart attack and split his forehead when he fell out of his chair."

"No mam. I'm sorry." He grabbed hold of Gretchen's arms as she swayed.

"Dear Lord," she whispered.

"We have a team on the way to search the woods to make sure you and the children are safe." He jotted down something in his notebook. "Did Adler say he saw the blood before he touched him?"

"I didn't ask. It was chaotic."

He nodded. "I understand." He closed his notebook. "Is there anyone I can call for you?"

"No. Thank you."

"If you need me, I'll be right outside. The detectives should be here any minute. They'll want to speak with you."

"A child advocate will be here soon to help you with the children and to question Adler."

She nodded, returned to the living room, and sat with her grandchildren. The reality of her husband's death hadn't set in.

Chapter 2

Police Chief Malcolm Contee, tossed and turned in his sleep, dreaming he and a younger woman were having youthful sex on a tropical beach. His heart pounded in his chest like an athlete in a marathon.

"Oh, Malcolm, you make me feel so good." Her seductive, hypnotic voice swirled in his mind.

He wanted to see her face, but he couldn't focus his eyes. The harder he tried, the blurrier she became. He thought she had long, dark hair. When he blinked, she hovered above him, her hair tickling his face, dangling in a way that kept him from seeing her with clarity.

Malcolm jolted awake when the house phone rang. His brain snapped to attention. Before answering, he knew, when you're the police chief, there's nothing good about a phone call before sunrise.

He wiped the sweat from his brow and blinked several times to improve his vision. The digital numbers on the bedside clock read zero-five-twenty.

"What is it, Malcolm?" Mrs. Contee asked.

He juggled the phone receiver to his ear. "Chief Contee." Sitting upright, he swung his legs off the side of the bed.

"Chief, it's Marten. Dispatch received a call from a retired officer's wife. Bruce Stockford. Someone put a round between his eyes this morning."

"Murder?"

"Yes, sir," Marten paused, "I'm told it looks like a professional hit."

"What the fuck are you saying?"

His wife touched his bare back and whispered in a sharp tone, "Malcolm."

"I'm not at the scene yet, sir. I'm about three minutes out. The officer on the scene said it looked like someone may have shot him while he sat on his front porch having his morning coffee. The deputy arrived and found the victim had slid off a chair and onto the porch decking. He checked for a pulse, saw blood on his face and determined Stockford was deceased, then he stepped away and secured the scene."

"Well, shit. Stockman you say?" The Chief rubbed the graying stubble on his jawline.

"Stockford. Bruce. His grandson found him."

"This is bad. We need to get a handle on this before the media puts a spin on it."

"I'll call you with an update after I get there. I thought you needed to know. We've switched all communication to a secure channel, but the original call went through the standard protocol. Dispatch didn't know it was an officer shooting at first. His wife was pretty shaken up on the call."

"To be expected." He tossed the blanket aside. "I'll be there as quick as I can." He slammed the phone down.

"I'm sorry, Malcolm," his wife said. She rubbed his back. "Were you having a bad dream?"

"What?" He stood and turned to his wife. "No, why?"

"Before the call came in, you were making muffled noises, like someone was hurting you." She flung the blankets to the middle of the bed. "I considered waking you."

He shrugged. "Don't remember what it was."

She slipped her feet into her pink, fuzzy slippers. "I'll put on the coffee."

* * *

On the other side of Brookfield, Mayor Ozzy Eastland walked a brisk pace on his treadmill in the basement gym at his lake house on the shore of Perla Lake, named after the wife of one of the Mormon founders in the 1800s. He'd been walking, listening to music from the 1990s—some Green Day, and Red-Hot Chili Peppers always got his blood pumping and made him think about himself in a more youthful time. Sweat trickled from his temples. He'd been at it for close to thirty minutes when his cell phone rang. He stepped onto the side rails of the treadmill, saw the police chief's number on the screen, and answered. "Yes, Malcolm?" His voice was breathy from exertion.

"We have a situation. It's going to bring Sacramento media to town and may go national."

"What happened?" He flipped the switch and stepped off the treadmill.

The police chief told him what little he knew.

"The name Stockford doesn't ring a bell." He turned his head not to be heard as he breathed in and out a few times, trying to catch his breath. "Is he someone I should know?"

"I didn't know the name either. I'll know more after Marten gets to the scene."

The mayor said, "Pull his personnel file fast before someone lets something slip to the media. The guy must've done something to someone."

"Ozzy, you don't need to tell me how to do my job."

"I'm not, Malcolm. Calm down. Call me when you know more." He tossed his phone onto the towel piled on the floor and turned to see Ann Sawyer, his lover, standing in the doorway, wearing the sheer black negligee he'd given her yesterday.

He met Ann when she was the superintendent at Blackstone Academy. The instant attraction became too hard to resist. Ann was a single woman and could do as she pleased. Ozzy was a married man. He thought his wife suspected he had a wandering eye. From his perspective, if he kept the relationship discreet, his wife wouldn't make a fuss.

"What happened?" Ann asked.

"Someone murdered a retired police officer this morning."

Ann gasped.

"Don't worry, my darling," he purred as he approached. "Malcolm will figure out who did this." He kissed her cheek, then her neck, nibbled on her earlobe. One of his soft hands wrapped around her back while the other glided down the lacy fabric of her teddy, stopping below her waistline to kiss her deeply. As his hand became busy under her nightie, he stopped, pulled back to look into her eyes. "Meanwhile, we can't speak to the press or media about it. Not a single word, to any…."

She pushed him away. "Don't patronize me, Ozzy. I'm not a child. I know not to talk about you or your job." She spun away from him. Her long, black hair slapped him in the face.

He grabbed her thin arm. "I'm sorry, my love." He attempted to kiss the creamy skin on her shoulder, but when she looked at him, he saw anger in her piercing blue eyes. "Don't be mad."

"You better get dressed. They'll be expecting you. You wouldn't want anyone to come here looking for you and find me."

He hustled behind her. "It's going to be a long day. I don't think I'll be back here tonight."

"I won't be here, anyway."

She had a way about her that made Ozzy act like a schoolboy. "Please stay. I'm sure I'll be back tomorrow. We'll make it a long weekend." It may have been their age difference of seventeen years. He longed to please her, or perhaps her fiery temper that made her a passionate lover in the bedroom.

"Forget it. Go do what you need to do. I'm packing my stuff and heading back to town today. If your wife will let you out of the house, you can come to my place tonight." She slammed the bathroom door in his face and clicked the lock.

Chapter 3

Monica and her Maltese, who she'd named Comet because the dog had endless energy, had become regular guests staying overnight at Mac's place. She and Mac had similar lifestyles. They both woke around five o'clock, enjoyed coffee and buttered toast together before they left for their jobs.

Monica had been with the Brookfield Police Department for six years and had her goal set on promoting to a detective.

Mac had all but grown up in the air force, enlisting at eighteen. Now, Mac worked a temporary undercover position as a marshal at Blackstone Academy—it was a favor for the police chief, more of a favor to his best friend, Jason Marten.

Being a marshal at a school wasn't what he thought he'd be doing after the military. He'd served twenty years in the air force. Many of his years were in Special Operations Command—AFSOC. He and Jason Marten, a high school friend who now worked as a detective with the Brookfield Police Department, joined the air force together straight out of high school. In basic training, when asked who will do whatever it took to get to a wounded airman to safety, Jason and Mac looked at each other and both raised their hands. Jason stayed in for eight years. Mac stayed in twenty years, then returned to Brookfield, to be a more present uncle in his nieces' lives, and be a better brother to Maggie. He thought he'd remodel the old Victorian home he'd purchased, and for the first time in his adult life, do whatever he wanted, whenever he wanted.

But Blackstone Academy had a drug problem and the police chief thought the criminals were at the school. It didn't take Mac long to see who the troublemakers were. Since then, Mac had become restless while he waited for the school year to end. He'd promised the school board president, Michael Stromberg, he'd stay for one school year and then consider additional time.

Everyone had become accustomed to a marshal policing the campus, along with Roni Darling, who worked part time with Mac. When he thought about leaving the academy, he felt bad. He knew, even though Roni was working on a college degree in criminal science and she had established herself in the local Brazilian Jiu

Jitsu gym, she didn't have enough life experience to take over as the marshal. He knew, sooner rather than later, as the end of the school year fast approached, he needed to have an honest conversation with the school board.

"Mac," Monica called from the living room. Both dogs rounded the corner from the kitchen. They stopped at her feet and looked up at her.

Mac, wearing a white V-neck undershirt and boxers, poked his head around the same corner. "Yes?"

"Come here. There's been an officer shooting." She pointed to the TV. The scene showed a reporter in a rural area where the agency on scene had cordoned off the driveway as a crime scene.

He said, "Turn it up," as he placed their coffee mugs and a plate of toast on the table in front of Monica. Then he sat next to her on the sofa.

"Thank you. That's Marten and Ruiz." She pointed to the TV as they watched a low-ranking deputy raise the crime scene tape, allowing their vehicle to pass under.

Mac nodded.

Detective Dan Ruiz had been Marten's partner for a few years.

"It must be big if they're on the case," Monica said as she sipped coffee. Noticing the dogs looked like they were on high alert, she realized they were picking up on the seriousness of the situation. She bent down and lifted Comet to her lap. Petting the dog's back side relaxed her. After she calmed Comet, Roxy, Mac's German Shepherd, moved closer to Mac and then sprawled out on the floor.

As 'Breaking News Alerts' scrolled along the bottom of the TV screen, an out-of-breath reporter spoke, "A source informed us the victim is a retired Brookfield Police Officer. The authorities will release the name after they've notified all family members."

"Oh, no." Monica gasped.

* * *

Monica's phone sat on the kitchen counter buzzing. Mac grabbed the phone and tossed it to her. A handful of people could ring through when her phone was on Do Not Disturb. Her parents, her sisters, Mac, her boss, and the emergency services call center.

"Officer Tanner," her voice sounded garbled. She muted the phone while she cleared her throat, then switched the phone to speaker mode as she heard the person on the other end say, "This is Alene at the Emergency Call Center. Detective Marten requested your child advocate services at a retired-officer-shooting crime scene."

Monica looked at Mac with saucer-sized eyes. Both dogs stood next to them.

"What do you mean by my child advocate services?"

Alene, from the call center, took a moment to gather her composure and continued, "Someone shot a retired officer at his home and his ten-year-old grandson found him about forty minutes ago. They want you to work with the boy and find out what he did or didn't see. The chief wants you to be the Family Liaison Officer."

"He does?"

"Yes."

"I'll be ready in ten minutes. Text me the address."

"One more thing."

"Yes?"

"Detective Marten asked for you to wear civilian clothes. The boy's pretty shook up. Marten said street clothes might help calm him."

"Will do." Monica stood, closed her phone, and grabbed her coffee.

Mac took the coffee cup from her hand. "Go. I'll take care of this." Mac swirled his hand around their coffee cups and plate. "Go get dressed."

She took the stairs two at a time, her lightweight bathrobe trailed behind her like a cape.

After cleaning up their breakfast dishes, he joined her upstairs while she finished dressing. She relayed the bit of information she'd received in a text to him while he disarmed the security system at his bedside.

"Sounds awful," he said. "Who is it?"

"Bruce Stockford. The name isn't familiar to me." In the dim light of the room, she saw what she needed on the dresser. She put on her wristwatch, strapped on her ankle holster, and secured her firearm to her belt holster. "Anytime someone kills an officer, retired or active duty, that's as bad as it gets in law enforcement."

Taking one last look in the mirror, approving that her loose, flannel shirt concealed her belt holster over her blue jeans. Seemed like adequate attire for a child advocate—although she had been in her uniform the last time she'd assumed the position of child advocate. She scooped up her cell phone, gave Mac a kiss, and turned to leave.

He said nothing, but he wished he could go with her rather than to the school. He tossed out his thought, "Call if I can help."

She nodded. "I'll let you know what's going on as soon as I can." Then she took the stairs at a fast pace.

Within seconds of her ten-minute estimate, Monica backed up her Jeep to turn it around at the end of Mac's long driveway. She used her free hand to add the address to her GPS system and heard the automated voice estimate an eleven-minute drive. The incorporated city limits had several wooded pockets where developers had built small clusters of homes. The Stockford home was in one of the older developments.

* * *

Officer Monica Tanner saw the metal yard art Marten had described at the end of the Stockford's shared gravel driveway. She also saw media vans parked along the public road—the sign a serious, newsworthy crime had occurred. Officers combed the grounds, looking for evidence. She recognized a few of the guys and waved as she passed them.

Before she put the transmission in park, Marten approached the jeep. He opened the driver's door and stepped into the space between the door and her seat, showing he wanted to speak with her before she hopped off the seat. "The kid's not talking. He's clinging tight to his older sister."

She nodded. "Makes sense. It's a lot for a kid to see." She looked toward the house. "Are they finding any leads?"

"The shooter left a message pegged to a tree where we think he took the shot from. It said, 'You hurt my family, I hurt yours.'" He leaned in closer. "It looks like a professional job."

Her eyes widened. "What the hell? In Brookfield? A professional hit? A retired cop?" Her facial expression showed disbelief. "According to Alene at dispatch, he was a kind man."

"I'm hearing the same." He shrugged. "Still… looks like a hit." Marten stepped back, allowing her room to exit the vehicle. He looked down at her waist. "Button up the flannel shirt. I can see your weapon."

As she buttoned her shirt, they walked to the rear of the jeep, where she kept her go-bag and gear.

"Be delicate, but focus on what the boy did, what he saw, and what he heard before opening the front door, and how he found his grandfather. He called him Pop-pop."

"Got it."

He grabbed her arm to turn her around. "And keep your eye on the wife, Gretchen. We're going to want to speak with her at some point."

"Understood."

When they walked inside the home, Marten veered off to the dining room area. Tanner went toward the sofa where Adler and Sasha, still wearing their pajamas, sat. She introduced herself and shook hands with Gretchen, who sat in a large, overstuffed chair next to the sofa. "I'm sorry for your loss." Gretchen nodded. "May I have your permission to record our conversation?"

"Yes."

Before she sat down, Tanner placed her cell phone on the coffee table in front of the sofa. She sat next to Adler, sitting at an angle so she could see both children. She again told them who she was. Neither child responded. Next, she explained she'd need to record their conversation rather than depend on her memory.

She touched the record icon on her phone and stated into the microphone: "Brookfield Police Officer, Monica Tanner, badge number 715, Wednesday, May 2, 2012, the time is zero-six-seventeen, I'm with Gretchen Stockford, Bruce Stockford's wife, her granddaughter, Sasha Stockford, and her grandson, Adler Stockford." She added the Stockford's address and asked again, on record, if she had permission to record their discussion. When she was ready to talk with the children, she returned her hand to Adler's shoulder as a reminder she was there for him. "I can't sugarcoat what happened here today, kids. It's going to be one of the saddest days in your lives, and I'm sorry this happened to your Pop-pop." After allowing her words to settle for a few seconds, she continued, "You both know your Pop-pop used to be a police officer and if he could, he'd want to do everything possible to find the person who did this. Right?"

Adler nodded. Sasha watched Tanner with widened eyes.

"Sasha, I understand you were asleep. Is that correct?"

Sasha nodded.

Gretchen, the wife, now the widow of a police officer, knew how things worked. For the recording, she said, "Both Adler and Sasha nodded their agreement to your question. She and I were both asleep until Adler woke us."

Tanner said, "Thank you, Gretchen."

They had established a record of whose voice was whose.

"Adler, did you wake up like you do every morning, or were you awakened?"

He nodded.

Gretchen said, "Adler nodded his head yes. He woke up as usual."

Gretchen continued to interpret his body movement for the recording.

"Did you look around inside before you went outside?"

He shook his head.

"Adler shook his head, no."

Tanner had an idea. "Have either of you two kiddos had breakfast?"

Sasha said, "No."

Adler shook his head.

"Are you hungry? We can make you something here, or I can go pick up some donuts for you."

Sasha said, "Donuts would be good. I like maple bars and Adler likes twists with chocolate glaze."

Tanner looked at Gretchen and asked, "Would you like something? A coffee? Cinnamon roll?"

"Nothing, thank you."

Monica leaned toward the coffee table, picked up her phone and said into the microphone, "Brookfield Police Officer, Monica Tanner, badge number 715, Wednesday, May 2, 2012, the time is zero-six-thirty-two, we are taking a short break, end recording," and then she stopped the recorder. "I'll be back in a jiff."

Tanner headed for the door. Marten was on his feet and met her as she walked outside. "I'm going to get the kids some donuts. They haven't had breakfast."

"Good plan. Would you mind getting a couple dozen for the crew?" He pulled out his wallet.

She put up her hand. "No problem. I'll hurry."

On her way into town, she called the non-emergency number for dispatch and asked to speak with Alene. While she maneuvered her way around traffic toward downtown Brookfield to Trav's

Donuts, she asked Alene to tell her everything she could remember about Stockford.

Tanner had spent more time talking with Alene than she had inside Trav's. Three boxes of donuts sat on the passenger seat while she sped back to the Stockford home.

Much like when she had first arrived, Marten scurried to Tanner's car the moment he saw her stop in front of the Stockford home. He accepted the pink boxes she handed him and placed them on the opened tailgate of one of the officers' trucks. The men and women working the crime scene gathered around the boxes.

Tanner took one box of donuts and two coffees into the house and headed straight to the dining room table. She asked the officers inside to clear out. When she caught Sasha's eye, she waved her hand.

Sasha said to Adler, "Let's go eat some breakfast, Buddy."

Adler stood and walked behind his sister. He limped a little because of his injured foot.

Gretchen joined them. Tanner handed her a latte. "I thought you might need something hot to drink."

Tears pooled in Gretchen's eyes. She accepted the coffee and mouthed the words, "Thank you."

Tanner watched as the kids ate their donuts and sat across from them. "I never met your grandfather, but I spoke with a woman who worked with him."

For a nanosecond, Tanner saw Gretchen stiffen.

She continued, "Her name is Alene. She works in dispatching."

Gretchen relaxed and said, "I know Alene. She's a dear."

Tanner continued, "Alene told me your Pop-pop was one of the nicest officers she had ever worked with. She told me about a Christmas Eve when he had to work. I think it was before you two were born. She said it was raining something terrible that night. He saw a young woman walking along the road to town. He pulled over and asked if she needed a ride." Tanner noticed at hearing the story, Gretchen cried.

"I know this story," Gretchen whispered to nobody.

Tanner cleared her throat and tapped into her resolve so as not to cry along with Gretchen. "The woman got in the patrol car. Your Pop-pop asked why she was out on a stormy Christmas Eve when she should be home with her family. The woman told him she worked at the gas station. It was payday and her car had broken down on the way to the bank. Her kids didn't expect Santa would know where they were because they lived in a motel. The owner of their apartment building sold it, giving them short notice to move. She wanted to surprise them with a few gifts from Santa. The woman had been crying. She told your Pop-pop the bank was closed, and she'd appreciate a ride to the motel."

Both kids were chomping on their donuts and watching her as she told the story about their grandfather.

"Your Pop-pop called into dispatch and explained why he needed to be 10-7 for a few minutes." Tanner stopped talking when she saw their questioning looks. "A 10-7 is out-of-service for a few minutes." The kids continued to eat. "He called for a tow truck for her car and then drove the woman to the one store still open. They bought several gifts for each child. Together, they wrapped the gifts and put them in the backseat of his patrol car. The children were already asleep when they arrived at the motel. The motel owner's daughter had been babysitting. He gave the young mother his business card and made her promise to call him if she got into another bind."

Sasha and Adler continued to watch Tanner.

Tanner said to the children, "I bet you can't guess what happened to the woman." She hoped they'd make a guess, or at least say something.

Then Sasha said, "What?"

"She went to the police academy and became a police officer. She's outside. Would you like to meet her?"

Both kids nodded.

Tanner found Officer Maxwell talking to a newbie officer. She explained the story. Maxwell followed Tanner inside. "Before we get in there, refer to me as Tanner. Marten wants me to downplay that I'm also an officer."

"Sure thing."

They found the distraught threesome still sitting at the dining room table where they had been when Tanner went outside. Adler looked at Tanner. The donuts had left a chocolate ring around his lips.

"Officer Maxwell, these are Officer Stockford's grandchildren, Sasha and Adler. And his wife, Gretchen."

Gretchen stood and hugged Maxwell. She said, "I've heard the Christmas Eve story so many times and knew you had joined the force. I'm so happy to meet you."

"Your husband was one in a million. I'm so sorry to meet you under these circumstances." Maxwell extended her hand to shake Adler's, and he accepted the gesture. As did Sasha.

Sasha asked, "How old are your kids now?"

"They're both adults and have kids of their own. Your Pop-pop was their hero. He also bought them birthday gifts until I got back on my feet. He hung with us until we were in an apartment and rebuilding our lives. They say everyone has a guardian angel. He was mine."

She tousled Adler's messy hair and said, "I need to get back to work. You kids are in expert hands. Tanner will stay by your side like your Pop-pop stayed by mine."

The children looked at Tanner. She smiled.

After Maxwell left the dining room, Tanner said, "Adler, I understand you like to draw flip books."

He nodded.

"I've never seen one being made. Would you draw a flip book for me?"

He nodded again and left the table. When he returned, he had a sketch pad and colored pencils.

Gretchen said to Tanner, "Their parents will be here tonight. They took the first plane they could from St. Thomas."

"I'll be here all day. If you need anything, please, let me know."

Tanner went outside, which looked like an ant farm with officers moving in all directions. She searched for Marten.

Chapter 4

After learning about the retired officer's death, although Mac longed to assist the police in some capacity, he muddled through his morning at the school. He planned to talk to Monica or Marten later to see if he could be of service.

He'd seen nothing of importance come from the BAT boxes, also known as Blackstone Academy Tip boxes. During class change, he walked the halls on the high school side of the campus. Mac wasn't a desk job guy.

Most of his years in the air force had been in a pararescue unit. Their unit retrieved soldiers wounded in combat, helped during times of natural disasters, and anything in between. They did a lot of physical activity to be ready when called to duty.

"Mac," Marlene, the superintendent's administrative assistant's voice, came through his walkie-talkie.

He stopped in the corridor between classrooms and leaned against the wall, watching the students hustle past him. "Yes," he responded into the archaic, hand-held piece of equipment still in use.

"Anna Beth Ross would like to speak with you. She's waiting in Dr. Zita's office."

"Be there after the bell rings."

Anna Beth and Mac had a history. She hadn't been in favor of the academy hiring a marshal. When she learned the school board had permitted him to carry a weapon, she ramped up her campaign to circumvent the school board's decision. When that didn't work, she ran for a school board position and won. Since then, she had changed her opinion of the need for a marshal and didn't hesitate to ask him for personal favors.

As the crowd in the hallway dwindled to a few students, the bell rang, announcing the next period had begun. Mac headed toward the front of the school. A few seconds after the bell rang, the PA system crackled to life and two teenage girls began talking.

"Hello, Blackstone Bulldogs, the end of school is near, but we have one more fun activity—Prom!" the girls said in unison, "Prom is this Saturday. Please remember to abide by the dress code. If you're graduating this year, and you haven't already, see Mrs. Weeks in the Administration Office for information about college."

Mac tuned out the rest of the announcement as he rounded the corner into Marlene's open office area. Instead, he heard Anna Beth droning on about her son, Teddy, being bullied.

Marlene rolled her eyes in a crazy gesture and signaled for him to go into the office.

Dr. Zita sat behind his desk and looked relieved to see Mac. He waved. "Come in, come in. Have a seat."

Moving toward the bookcase alongside the large, L-shaped desk, he replied, "I'd rather stand."

Anna Beth didn't skip a beat from her conversation with Dr. Zita. Turning her attention to Mac, "As I was telling Dr. Z., I know we're all still healing from the tragedy we experienced, but Nate bullied Teddy again yesterday. When I picked him up, as soon as we left the parking lot, he cried. Something needs to be done. Can't you expel Nate?" She stared at Mac.

Mac pointed to Dr. Zita. "A question for the boss."

After a harrumph, Dr. Zita said, "I don't believe his offenses warrant expulsion."

"Well then, what do you plan to do about the bullying?"

Teddy was a quirky, fourth-grade student who Mac felt an immediate bond with when he started at the school last August. Teddy, who always had a goofy joke, had become withdrawn. He hadn't shared a joke in some time.

Mac knew Dr. Zita wouldn't do anything about Nate bullying kids. Since he'd started, he'd made few decisions and gave less direction. He'd retired after a long career as a school superintendent elsewhere and had agreed to fill in as the interim superintendent while the school board searched for a suitable replacement for Dr. Sawyer, who the school board had released from her contract for undisclosed reasons.

When Dr. Zita didn't respond to Anna Beth, instead turned his attention to Mac, she followed his gaze.

Mac said, "I'll talk to the boys."

"When?"

"Today." He waited for more from the newest member of the school board to counter his solution. In a nutshell, she was Dr. Zita's boss, or at least one of them. The five-member board couldn't do anything as a single voice.

"I better see a happy ten-year-old when I pick him up today."

"Are we done?" Mac asked.

She waved her hand as if she were the queen dismissing the help.

With three weeks of school remaining, Mac felt as excited for the school year to end as he imagined the teachers and students felt.

* * *

At lunchtime, Mac found Nate sitting at a table next to Teddy. Teddy stared down at his mom-packed lunch on the table in front of him while Nate spoke in a hushed voice near Teddy's ear. Nate's closest pals sat across from the two. When the friends saw Mac nearing their table, one of them kicked Nate under the table.

Nate squealed, "Hey. What'd you do that for?" When he saw they were looking behind him, he turned in time to see Mac straddle the bench beside him. Nate faced Mac. "What do you want?" Nate asked.

"You sure talk tough for a 12-year-old little boy," Mac said.

"Is that why you're here? To tell me I talk tough?"

Nate's friends snickered.

"Why are you harassing Teddy?"

"Who said I'm harassing Teddy? I'm not." Nate spun around to face Teddy. "Did you say I'm harassing you?"

Teddy shook his head.

Mac continued, "I've asked you to stop bullying. From how I see it, the reason you're sitting with someone two grades lower than you is to pick on him."

"We're friends." Nate looked at Teddy once more. "Am I picking on you?"

Teddy shook his head again.

"Lunch started ten minutes ago, and Teddy hasn't eaten a single bite of his lunch. If you were sitting with him because you two were friends, he'd be eating his lunch instead of staring at it."

"It's okay, Mac, we're friends. He's not bothering me," Teddy said.

"See. I told you I wasn't harassing him."

Mac pointed to the two boys seated across from him. "You and you, leave. Now."

The boys hightailed away from the lunch table.

"If I see you sitting next to or speaking to Teddy again, I'll write a citation for bullying."

"But—"

"It doesn't matter to me what Teddy says you are or aren't doing. I see you harassing someone younger than you."

Red tones crept up Nate's neck toward his face, making his red hair look redder and his freckles all but disappeared. "Anything else?"

"No. This is your final warning."

Nate grabbed his lunch tray and left the table.

Keeping his head down and not making eye contact with him, Teddy ate his tuna sandwich with the crust cut off.

"I thought we were friends, Teddy. Why didn't you tell me he was bothering you?"

Teddy took a quick sip from the straw in his juice box and swallowed. "He told me he'd beat me up if I said anything to you."

"Did he say where he'd beat you up? There aren't many places on campus where the security cameras wouldn't catch him. Your mother brings you to school and picks you up."

"He said he'd catch me in the restroom and hurt me like what happened to Theyn."

Mac didn't know how to comfort the boy. He couldn't be everywhere on the campus. He couldn't follow Teddy around as a personal security detail, and all the students knew there weren't cameras in the restrooms.

Teddy added, "I've limited what I drink, so I don't need to use the restroom."

"How about this? I'll check out Nate's class schedule—he has a few class changes—and figure out when he's the farthest away from where you are, so you know you can safely use the restroom?"

He bobbed his head.

"In the meantime, I'm going to monitor him for the rest of the day. I'll have the information for you when school is out."

"Thank you."

"Promise me, if he says anything or does anything to scare you, you'll come to me. He's not as big of a threat as he wants you to believe."

"I promise." Teddy's shoulders sank. He looked over his glasses, which had slipped down the bridge of his nose to see if anyone watched him. "Can I go now?" Teddy asked as he gathered his belongings.

Mac stopped by to see Elsie, the cafeteria supervisor, and asked if they had a leftover apple. She smiled and handed him a red delicious. "For you. I know you love apples."

"Thank you. I can't stay and chat today. I have a date with a bully."

"If anyone can stop a bully, it's you."

Leaving the cafeteria, Roni saw Mac and motioned him to wait for her.

He hadn't seen her since morning when they were together monitoring students as they arrived at the school.

"Where are you going in such a hurry?"

"Nate Collins is still picking on Teddy. I confronted him at lunch and now I want to be sure he isn't retaliating against Teddy on the playground."

Roni hustled alongside Mac. "I'll join you."

As they approached the door to the playground, Mac stuck out his arm to stop her from going outside. "Hang on. Let's find Nate before the kids see us."

They peered out the glass in the door. Students moved past them to exit and enter the building.

"There he is," Roni blurted out as she pointed to the far corner of the blacktop near the tether ball area.

"And he and his pals have Teddy surrounded."

As he pushed open the door, and they walked outside. They said hello to the staff person monitoring the door.

Then they headed straight toward Nate and his thugs. The friends noticed the two adults approaching.

Nate turned in time to see Mac as he grabbed his upper arm. "Come on." Nate squirmed. "You're not allowed to touch me. I'll call my dad and he'll sue you or have you fired."

"Okay." Mac tugged at his shirt. "You're coming with me. We can do this without a scene or you can be the center of attention. But either way, you're coming with me to the superintendent's office."

Nate yanked his sleeve out of Mac's grasp, squared his shoulders, and tromped toward the door.

Mac shook his head with annoyance and wondered if the little twerp acted like that at twelve—how he'd be at eighteen?

After delivering Nate to Marlene, Mac went to his office and texted Monica. *How's it going?*

He watched his phone for a response. Assuming she couldn't respond, he got busy with paperwork—his least favorite part of his job.

Chapter 5

Tanner felt her energy level dropping. She'd been at the Stockford's home for hours. After the children had eaten all the donuts they wanted, Tanner watched Adler draw on his sketch pad. She asked him to sketch any thoughts he had about his Pop-pop.

The first set of drawings were of Adler and Stockford playing Cribbage on the front porch. The drawings were quite similar. Slight variations. In the flip book, the character of Adler shuffled a deck of cards, then the cards were being dealt, and then one player's hand played a card, then the other person played until all the cards were on the table. As if by magic, the pegs moved along the track to keep score. The pages flipped and the entire game came alive.

It had taken him a few hours to draw all the similar but different scenes to create the movement. He'd even drawn his Nana, carrying lemonade, into some of the middle pages. The last few frames showed grandfather and grandson hugging. They both had large smiles on their faces.

Tanner liked that he'd included so much detail in his drawn story.

Adler had spoken very little while he drew the scenes for his book. While he stayed busy sketching, Tanner chatted with Gretchen and Sasha, who'd been on her cell phone most of the day.

Tanner asked if Gretchen had known of anyone who Bruce had disagreed with—she didn't.

Whenever Gretchen asked Sasha who she was conversing with, Sasha ignored her and stayed focused on her device. Gretchen didn't push for an answer.

Tanner watched as Adler cut the pages to about the size of an index card and then assembled his flip book, stapling it several times along the spine.

"Ready?" Adler asked Tanner, surprising her he'd spoken.

"Yes. Yes, I'm ready."

He kept the pages moving at a slow and steady pace as he fanned them, bringing his Cribbage game with his Pop-pop to life.

Tanner, when on duty, had trained herself to tamp down her emotions to a manageable level. She felt herself choking up. "You did a wonderful job, Adler. You're an excellent artist. Do you have other flip books here at Nana and Pop-pops' house that you've made? I'd love to see them."

The boy nodded and left the room.

Sasha spoke up for the first time in an hour. "I have one in my backpack."

"May I see it, please?"

Sasha left the room.

Tanner sipped her water, then asked Gretchen, "Are the children always this quiet?"

"Sasha's a typical teenager—more engrossed in her life and her friends. Adler is a quiet boy, but not this quiet. He's playful and silly and loving." Gretchen pulled her sweater tighter across her chest as if she'd felt a chill.

Sasha returned before Adler. She handed Tanner the small flip book and then turned to Gretchen. "Adler's in his bedroom crying."

Gretchen ran from the room.

As Sasha sat on the sofa, she wiped tears from her eyes. When Tanner and Sasha shared a glance, Sasha looked down to grab her cell phone.

Tanner went to the sofa and sat next to the girl. "It's all right to cry about your Pop-pop."

Sasha's words came out jittery and blunt, "I-want-to-be-strong-for-my-brother."

"He needs to know it's okay for him to cry as well. You hiding your sadness won't help him."

Tanner and Sasha shared a few quiet minutes before Gretchen and Adler returned. Tanner moved to a side chair.

Adler's sweet little face was red and puffy. He handed her two flip books.

Sasha looked at Gretchen. "When will mom and dad be here?"

Gretchen looked at her wristwatch. "They should land in an hour, then it'll be about an hour and a half before they get here."

Tanner flipped through the books Adler had given her, and hearing the timeline for the parents' return, she needed to shift her strategy from flip books to conversation. "Adler, I wanted to ask you about this morning. Are you ready to talk about what you saw?

He shook his head.

Sasha put her arm around him and pulled him tight to her side. "I'm here, Buddy, I'm here with you. Nobody is going to hurt you or any of us. A bad person hurt Pop-pop, not us."

Gretchen sat on the other side of Adler and snuggled him. "I'm here too." She placed a tissue in his hand.

"May I ask you a few questions?" she probed.

He nodded.

She touched the record icon on her phone and again stated into the microphone, "Brookfield Police Officer, Monica Tanner, badge number 715, Wednesday, May 2, 2012, the time is eleven-twenty-five. I'm at the Stockford home with Gretchen Stockford, Bruce Stockford's wife, their granddaughter, Sasha Stockford, and their grandson, Adler Stockford. Adler, do you know what time you woke up this morning?"

"Five-fifty."

"Do you have a clock in your bedroom? Is that how you knew the exact time?"

He nodded.

Gretchen cut in. "Adler nodded his head, yes."

Tanner asked, "Did something wake you up?"

His eyes closed, taking his full attention into the darkness of his mind. He opened his eyes and looked at Tanner. "No."

The front door opened and startled the four of them. Tanner glared at the officer who'd entered without considering what might have been happening inside. Tanner jumped to her feet and bolted toward the door. "Foxmore," she said with a low grumble, "were you told the inside was off-limits? Crime scenes don't have restrooms. Out." She pointed to the door.

The officer, who'd frozen in place the moment he saw the faces staring at him, whispered, "I have to use the head."

"Get in your car and drive to town. And tell Marten to put a sign on the door—everyone needs to stay out."

Tanner turned without waiting for a response. Behind her, she heard the door close.

"I'm sorry about the interruption, Adler." She bent over and patted him on his shoulder before returning to the side chair. "You said nothing woke you up. Do you always wake up early?"

He bobbed his head.

Gretchen said, "Adler nodded, yes."

"Is your Pop-pop always up when you get up?"

He bobbed his head again, then said, "Yes."

"On other mornings, what was your Pop-pop doing when you'd wake up and join him on the porch?"

"He'd be on the front porch drinking coffee." Tears spilled over onto his swollen, red cheeks.

"On those mornings, after you joined him on the porch, would he go inside to make you breakfast?"

"We sat for a while and listened to the birds."

"Do you have a favorite bird?"

"Woodpecker."

"Did your Pop-pop have a favorite bird?"

He shook his head. "He liked them all."

"Yesterday, after you woke, when you joined your Pop-pop on the porch, did you listen to birds for a while?"

"No."

"Why not?"

"The birds were quiet."

"Were the birds quiet often?"

Gretchen and Sasha watched as Tanner and Adler had their conversation.

"No. I noticed the last few days." His lips turned up in a slight smile.

"Did you remember something?"

Looking at Gretchen, he said, "Pop-pop said, the birds must've stayed up late and slept in like Nana."

Tanner felt Adler had nothing to add to the investigation. "Will you excuse me for a few minutes?" She stood, leaned into her phone, and said, "Eleven, forty-two," then shut off the recorder and put her phone in her pocket before she went outside.

She approached an officer standing on the porch. "Where's Marten?"

He pointed toward the woods. "Out there."

She pulled out her cell phone from a pocket and called Marten instead of searching for him.

"Marten," he bellowed in her ear.

"It's Tanner." She covered her mouth, kept it close to her phone, and spoke in a hushed voice so as not to be heard. "I think I'm done here. Other than he noticed the birds were unusually quiet the past few mornings, he doesn't know anything helpful."

"I'll be right there." His connection ended.

Standing on the porch, she looked around the area where the chair had been before the forensic team had taken everything that wasn't nailed down. As the outdoor temperature rose, the large, blood stain darkened on the wood planks. Standing at the porch rail in front of the blood spot, she stared out at all the officers combing the woods for evidence.

Marten emerged from a section to Tanner's right. He waved her to join him at his vehicle.

"Talk to me," he said.

"Adler doesn't seem to know anything. He woke up, found his grandfather, went to his grandmother, end of story."

"He heard nothing? Saw nothing?"

"Not much." She dug in her pocket, found a piece of gum, and crammed it into her mouth. "Like I said, he noticed the birds ordinarily squawked a lot, were quiet the last few mornings."

Marten jotted down the one tidbit of information before saying, "It was one hundred percent a hit."

"Any clues why Stockford?"

"So far, just the message left on the tree."

"What do you think it means?"

"Stockford did something to somebody—the wrong somebody." He looked at his vibrating cell phone. "Ask Gretchen if Stockford hung on to any old case files. If he did, see if she'll let us look through them. Let me know if you are staying to look through the files. If not, you don't need to stay any longer."

When she returned inside, Gretchen sat alone. She looked up when the door opened.

"Adler needed to rest. He's too upset. Sasha is with him. My son and his wife are on their way here from the Sacramento airport. I'm sorry Adler didn't have more to contribute to the investigation."

Tanner shrugged. "I'm glad he didn't know more than he knows." She sat in the side chair. "Did your husband keep any old case files?"

"Boy, did he. He couldn't let go of anything. He filled one side of the basement with boxes. Why?"

"May we look through them to see if any of his old cases have clues to who would've done this?"

She bobbed her head. "Yes."

"Would you prefer we look through them here or take them downtown?"

The question seemed to weigh heavy on her. "To be honest, after the kids all leave, I'd appreciate some privacy. You can have them taken downtown. There's outside access to the basement and a driveway running along the side of the house."

Tanner stood. Gretchen did as well. Tanner went to her and the two women hugged. She whispered in her ear, "I'm so sorry. Thank you for your cooperation. If you need anything, call me."

They stepped apart, but Tanner held Gretchen's shoulders. "There are organizations to help you muddle through the benefits and help with the service."

She nodded.

"Marten and Ruiz will need to speak with you."

"I know. Later, after the kids are gone."

* * *

Gretchen Stockford stood on the front porch of her home, a few feet from where someone had murdered her husband hours earlier, now hidden by a pop-up canopy. She waved goodbye to her grandchildren and their parents, Wyatt—their son—and his wife, Isabel. Gretchen's son and his wife had caught the first flight home from their cruise as soon as they learned of Wyatt's father's death.

Detective Marten and Detective Ruiz stood close to Gretchen, waiting their turn to speak with her.

When she could no longer see her son's car, she said, "All right, I'm about as ready as I'll ever be. Afterward, I'd appreciate having time to grieve." She turned, opened the front door, and went to her favorite easy chair in the living room.

Marten and Ruiz followed her and sat on the sofa.

Gretchen sat with her feet tucked under her and leaned to one side. She pulled a tissue from the box next to her on a side table.

As the guys prepared for their interview, Gretchen looked around the living room. The book shelves held photos of her husband at various stages of his life. One of her favorites—he and Wyatt fishing when Wyatt was about Adler's age. Gretchen wiped her tears.

Marten began, "I'm sorry we have to do this, Gretchen."

"It has to be done. I get it."

"Do you mind if we record our conversation so we don't miss an important detail?"

"Go ahead." She waved her hand at him.

Ruiz pressed the record button and said into the device the pertinent details of the date, time, location, who was present, and why they were there.

Marten asked Gretchen, "The obvious question—do you know of anyone who was upset or angry with Bruce?"

She shook her head. "No."

As usual, when Marten and Ruiz interviewed people, Marten did all the talking, and Ruiz took extensive notes.

"Tell us what you've been doing the last few days."

Gretchen thought for a minute. "Yesterday, we hung out here. Nothing out of the ordinary. Bruce and Adler had been playing a cribbage tournament. They played a few games in the morning and a few more in the afternoon. We watched a movie after dinner and all went to bed after the movie."

"Did anyone call or stop by?"

She took a few seconds to consider the question. "Yesterday was Tuesday?"

"Yes."

"Wyatt and Gretchen had called the kids from George Town in the Cayman Islands. They were in port and preparing to go on an excursion. Their time was two hours later than us—it was mid-morning here."

"Any other calls?"

"Not that I remember. And we had no visitors."

"What about Monday?"

She held up a finger while she looked at her cell phone. "The kids didn't call because they were at sea." She paused. "I don't know. I think it was a typical day. Sasha on her cell phone with friends and Adler hanging with me and Bruce."

"What about—"

"Oh, sorry, I forgot. Sasha helped me bake cookies on Monday." She smiled.

"What about Sunday?"

"The kids got here Friday night because Wyatt and Gretchen flew to Fort Lauderdale on Saturday. Their cruise set sail on Sunday. Sunday..." She tapped her finger on the arm of the easy chair. "We took the kids to Handley's Coffee Shop for dinner. Bruce loves ... loved their meatloaf special on Sundays." She wiped her tears.

Marten leaned toward her and patted her knee. "I'm so sorry, Gretchen."

"I always knew when Bruce worked any day could be the last day I'd see him. After he retired, I let my guard down. I thought we didn't need to worry about that anymore. My concern shifted from him being killed in the line of duty to making sure he ate a balanced diet and took his vitamins to help improve his odds of longevity." She stood. "I need a minute." And then she left the room.

In their bedroom, she buried her face in her pillow and screamed. Tears streamed from her eyes. She mumbled into the pillow, "How do I live without you?"

Ten minutes later or there about, Gretchen returned to the living room and her favorite chair. It was apparent from her puffy, red face she'd been crying. "Sorry."

"Take a break whenever you need one. We want to go at your pace."

"Thank you."

"Sunday. You all went to Handley's for dinner."

"Yes."

"Did you speak to anyone other than the staff?"

"The Handleys."

"Have you had a road rage incident with anyone?"

She guffawed. "I don't think we saw a single car until we arrived."

"Did Bruce talk to anyone in the parking lot?"

"No, he and Adler walked hand-in-hand into the coffee shop."

"Was the coffee shop busy?"

"There were a few customers. Nobody we knew and I don't remember any of us speaking to anyone other than each other and the Handleys."

"Did you go straight home after dinner?"

"Yes."

"What did you do on Saturday?"

"We kayaked on the lake." She focused on the tissue in her hand, then raised her head and locked her eyes on Marten. "We saw a few residents also kayaking and waved to them. It was peaceful."

"I hate to ask, but…" Marten coughed. "Had there ever been infidelity in your marriage?"

Ruiz flipped the page on his notepad.

Gretchen glared at Marten.

"Not on my part. If Bruce cheated on me, he hid it well."

There was an uncomfortable few seconds before Marten continued, "Officer Tanner said you'd be fine with us taking Bruce's old case files in your basement to the station."

"Yes, I don't want them back. I shouldn't have them." She blew her nose. "I don't feel I have anything relevant to add."

"Thank you, Gretchen."

"I'll leave the outside door to the basement unlocked for your officers to access the files. You can't miss them. There are a lot of those Banker-type boxes on one side."

"Why did Bruce have so many case files?"

"Much like Detective Ruiz, here," she pointed at him before continuing, "he was a note taker and thought if he ever had to go to court, he'd have good notes to help recall events and his actions."

They all stood. Marten hugged Gretchen and said, "Words can't express how sorry we are for your loss. I'll check in on you from time to time."

She said, "Thank you."

On the way to the door, Marten glanced at his watch.

Ruiz asked, "What? Do you need to be somewhere?"

"No. What do you think about asking Mac and Nico to help us with this one? The chief wants to keep the case in-house. We don't have enough manpower."

"I'm fine with them helping. Run it by the chief."

Chapter 6

Mac and Roni stood outside the front door of Blackstone Academy, waiting for the dismissal bell to sound. Parents parked along the curb. Some parked in the visitor lot, while others waited along the sidewalk to receive their child.

"Isn't this weather glorious?" Roni waved her hand upward toward the blue sky. "Why can't we have a decent spring with weather like this that lasts longer than a few days? It feels like we have two seasons—summer and winter."

As Roni continued talking about the weather, Mac saw Anna Beth Ross, Teddy's mother, approaching from across the street. He wanted to make a quip about her to Roni, but decided some things were better left unsaid.

"Marshal MacKenna." Repeating herself as she narrowed the distance between them, "Marshal MacKenna."

"Hello, Anna Beth."

Roni added, "Hello."

"Were you able to do an end-run on the bullying today?"

"Nate has been side-lined."

"Good." Anna Beth turned, walked to the main entrance and swiped her card as if she were the queen of Blackstone.

Roni looked at Mac. "Are you two speaking in football code or something?"

"I'm not sure what language we were speaking." Mac nodded to Nico as he headed toward them, and then finished his thought, "I'm trying to keep Anna Beth happy and Teddy out of harm's way."

After Nico, Mac, and Roni exchanged pleasantries, Nico asked, "Did you see the news about the retired cop?"

Roni replied first, "Horrible." She shook her head.

Mac followed. "Monica is helping with the case. She got a call before sunrise asking her to be a child advocate."

Roni's expression looked inquisitive. She tilted her head. "Who's the child?"

Mac wanted to kick himself for saying anything. He'd need to get better at keeping his mouth shut and allow others to do the talking. He responded, "The officer's grandson found him." Mac put his finger to his mouth. "Please don't share that detail."

"Oh, my gosh. I'm even more sad. My lips are sealed," Roni said, as she walked away from the two men.

Nico leaned toward Mac. "I think it was a professional hit."

Mac looked at him, confused. "A professional hit in Brookfield? A retired cop? Why do you think it was a hit?"

Nico explained. "It's not your run-of-the-mill murder." He looked around and continued with a low voice, "It looks like the person was a distance from the house and fired off one hell of an accurate shot to the head. If that doesn't smell professional, I don't know what does."

"Shit like this doesn't happen here," Mac said.

"I was thinking we should start a murder board on the case. What do you think?"

"Sounds like a plan. I'm in."

"Are you available tonight?"

Mac checked his wristwatch, noting the dismissal bell would ring in two minutes. "I think so. I haven't heard from Monica. She'll need to eat at some point. How about when I hear from her we meet for Mexican food at Tres Esposas?"

"Perfect. Let me know what time."

As Nico spoke the word 'time' the dismissal bell sounded and the entrance doors opened.

"Too many kids. I'll see you later." Nico walked back to his SUV to wait for Rae.

RaeAnn Bowen, Rae to her friends, age fifteen, is why Nico moved to Brookfield. Rae has no siblings, her parents were Drey and Sloan Bowen. Life turned upside down for her when a trucker fell asleep while driving and hit her parents head-on, killing both of them. Child Protective Services determined her uncle, her mother's brother, wasn't fit to parent her because he lived in an alcohol treatment facility. They placed Rae with the wealthy DeSalvos— Steffan and Jossalyn. If losing her parents and moving in with a foster family hadn't been traumatic enough as a freshman, because of where the DeSalvos lived, she also had to change schools.

Five months ago, an unknown client hired Nico to be Rae's personal driver. Since then, Rae and Nico had become friends. He was like the uncle she never had—she didn't know her mother's brother because he never came around. Rae would soon have her driver's license, leaving Nico's job in transition.

An explosion of gangly children exited the building. Boys and girls went in all directions to their parents standing along the sidewalk or waiting in their cars parked along the curb.

Roni watched the reunion of children to parents from the sidewalk, where she stood with a small cluster of young mothers.

Mac stayed where he'd been when Nico left. When he saw Anna Beth, her son, Teddy and his first-grade sister, Savannah, passing through the front door, he motioned to Teddy. "Teddy, come here a minute."

The trio maneuvered to where Mac stood.

Teddy walked toward Mac. "Yes, Mr. Mac?"

"First off, how was your afternoon?" Mac slipped Teddy a note with the best times to use the restroom when Nate was as far away as possible.

Teddy accepted the paper and stuffed it into his pocket. "Fine."

"Second, you haven't shared a joke in some time. What's up with that?"

Teddy shrugged.

Anna Beth grabbed Savannah's hand. "Come on, kids."

Teddy planted his feet, looked at Mac, and asked, "What do you get when you cross a fish with an elephant?"

Savannah yanked her mother's arm and pointed. Anna Beth stopped and turned back to look at Teddy.

Mac replied, "I'm not sure. What?"

"Swimming trunks." Teddy smirked, then followed his mother.

Mac felt a twinge of pleasure that the funny, quirky Teddy was still in there, wounded from Nate's relentless harassment, but still there. *Damn bullies*, he thought as he watched the older students piling out the door.

* * *

Later that night, Mac and Nico, already seated in a booth when Monica entered the restaurant. She pointed to the guys in response to the hostess's automated question of how many were in her party. She plopped down next to Mac and gave him a familiar kiss.

"Are you done for the night?" Mac asked as he took a swig of his beer.

"Not even close. Did Marten tell you guys about the note?"

"No. What note?"

She looked around them, lowered her voice and told them about the revenge note pegged to the tree at the Stockford's.

Nico asked, "Do they assume a pro?"

She nodded and put a finger to her lips, showing it's a secret. "They don't want that to get out yet. After the Stockford's son picked up the kids, Mrs. Stockford gave us the green light to comb through Stockford's old case files he'd kept in their basement. I need to help go through those."

The guys looked at each other and then at Monica. "What?" she asked.

Mac responded, "Can we help? We're setting up a murder board on the case. We might be useful."

"Chief Contee is rather fond of you. I'll run it by Marten."

Mac waved at the young male server. "I changed my mind. I'll have an iced tea, no sugar. You can charge me for the beer."

"Was there something wrong with it?"

"No, I found out I might have to work tonight," he said with controlled excitement in his voice.

The server swooped up the bottle and asked, "Are you ready to order food?"

They ordered and as soon as the server left the area, Monica texted Marten, *Hey. Mac and Nico offered to help go through Stockford's old case files at the station tonight. Are you good with that?*

While she waited for Marten's response, she nibbled on chips and salsa, sharing what she knew about the case so far. "As Stockford sat on his front porch enjoying his morning coffee, the shooter shot him from a long-distance, lay-in-wait position, or so we think."

Mac said, "Nico thought the shooter was a pro."

She looked at Mac, then at Nico, and nodded her approval. Turning her attention back to Mac, she said, "The setting is tranquil out there. Not a place you'd expect to find a murder." She shook her head and scooped some more salsa with another chip.

She continued, "Anyway, the shooter had some serious skill. Plus, he had to have suppression on his weapon because the guys went door-to-door and so far, nobody heard anything. Even though the properties are on five-acre parcels, you'd think someone would've heard a rifle shot." After she gulped water, she sat back and relaxed her shoulders. "I didn't have lunch today. I'm so hungry."

Her phone vibrated. She read the text message from Marten aloud. *Sorry, I meant to tell you earlier. The chief would appreciate their help, but nothing gets leaked to anyone. I'll get the process started for Nico's consultant badge.*

Mac already had a consultant badge since he'd been working with the police department since the beginning of school. "I'm offended Chief Contee thinks we'd leak something," Nico said.

"Who knows what the chief meant, Marten's covering his...." Monica stopped talking when she noticed the server nearing their table with a large tray of food.

Mac said, "After dinner, I'll check on the dogs and feed them. Should we meet you at the Stockford's or the station?"

Monica chewed on her bite of taco a few times, then she covered her mouth and said, "We're going to take the boxes to the station. Meet us there."

As the server left the three on their own to devour their dinner, Mac asked Monica, "What have you discovered so far?"

"The grandson who found him didn't hear or see anything." She scooped more salsa with a tortilla chip and took a bite. "They think someone waited in the treed area in front of their house for Stockford to go outside."

Mac added, "The big question is, what did Stockford do to make someone angry enough to hire a professional killer?"

Nico nodded, thinking about what his FBI experience had taught him. "That won't be easy to figure out. How many years had he been retired?"

"Sixteen."

"Too many years off the force." He shook his head. "I wonder if he did something since he retired. And did the hit have anything to do with him being a police officer at all, or had he done something to someone as a civilian?"

"Sixteen years off duty and how many years on duty?" Mac asked.

"Thirty years on duty."

"That's going to be a lot of years to work through." Mac looked at Nico. "I hope you have some efficiency tricks you used when you worked at the FBI."

Nico smiled and pushed his plate toward the table edge. "I might know a trick or two."

Mac turned his attention to his girlfriend. "What else have they learned?"

"They discovered a place on the far side of the woods where someone had parked a vehicle." Her cell phone vibration distracted her for a moment. "Damn spam calls. Anyway, there's a footprint in the area around the vehicle. Not a barefoot, but a smooth sole print. We haven't had rain since last week, so the ground was nice and dry. There was enough of an impression for them to cast the print just in time—it's supposed to rain tomorrow."

"Depending on the price charged, the top-shelf pros don't leave behind prints—boots or tires," Nico shared while he folded an unused paper napkin like one would fold the America flag before handing it off to a military widow.

Monica asked, "How would you avoid leaving tire tracks?"

"Park off-road on the brush, not leave the asphalt, attach a tree branch to the rear bumper so it scruffs up the tracks."

Monica stared at him without expression, then smiled. "You're a genius. But it would've been a long walk to the house if he didn't leave the asphalt."

Mac watched Nico and Monica processing the scene.

"Could be a female," Nico said, creasing another triangular fold on the napkin.

"What do you mean?" Monica asked.

"You said if he didn't leave the asphalt. You'd predetermined the shooter was a man."

"I meant it figuratively," Monica defended her terminology. "But, you're right. I should keep it gender unknown and use 'the shooter' instead." She stretched her arms high and twisted from one side to the other. "This has been fun guys, but I need to get back out there." Turning her attention to Mac. "I'll see you in about an hour?"

Mac nodded.

She faced Nico. "See you then. And bring all your..." She waved her hand in a circle in front of him. "Your FBI mojo stuff with you."

"Will do."

Monica slid out of the booth. Mac scooted right behind. He said to Nico, "I'll be right back." They walked to her jeep. "Did Nico's comment about predetermined gender bother you?"

"Not at all. I'm glad he pointed it out. He didn't come across as a know-it-all. His observations are helpful. I appreciate learning how to be a better officer, and with the added responsibility Marten has given me, I might be a detective one day. It's all good." She leaned into his firm body and kissed him. "Will you bring me a latte from Trav's Donut Shop? The coffee machine in the breakroom is good, but not as yummy as Trav's coffee."

"How late do they stay open?"

"They do coffee and pastries until eleven, I think."

"You got it. One latte coming right up." He kissed her and then waited to wave goodbye from the door.

When Mac rejoined Nico, Nico had finished his military fold on the napkin and was sipping a fresh cup of coffee.

"Were you able to fold your napkin thirteen times?"

"Nah, not even close. Did I offend Monica by correcting her comment to be non-gender specific?"

"I asked her that question. She said it didn't bother her at all. She wants to learn more so she can be a detective one day."

Nico nodded before sipping his coffee. "Will you pick me up at my apartment?"

"Sure. I'll text you when I'm on my way." Mac waved to their server.

Nico said, "I already paid for dinner."

"Why'd you do that?"

"Why not? I appreciate you letting me tag along with you on this case."

"You don't know this, but I also want to learn from your skills." Mac stood. "I need to get home to the girls. I'll see you in about thirty."

"I'll be ready."

* * *

Before Mac walked out the door, he took one last look at the dogs, who sat waiting for permission to eat, then he reset the alarm on his home security system, and said, "Okay." Both dogs began chowing down their food. Roxy always finished first. When Monica and Comet started staying overnight, Roxy tried one time to push Comet aside and eat her food. Comet, one-tenth Roxy's size, growled and snarled at Roxy, who backed off and hadn't tried again—not while Mac was paying attention. Comet might be tiny, but she's a force to be reckoned with in the dog world.

He noticed his neighbor, Mr. Jenkins, and the man's miniature white poodle, Mimi, seated on his front porch. Mac waved first. Mr. Jenkins saluted. Mac saluted him back. Mimi stood and watched

Mac's truck roll by. He liked the retired navy man. They had a mutual respect for one another, because they'd both served in the military. The old guy still had some spunk left in him. Like the time someone lurked around Mac's place and Mr. Jenkins swung his cane to shoo the man off the property. Along with Mimi barking nonstop, they'd succeeded.

When Mac turned into the circle drive in front of Nico's apartment building, Nico stood waiting on the sidewalk.

He climbed into Mac's truck. Mac asked, "Did you bring your FBI mojo?"

Nico laughed. "Sure did."

"I have to stop at Trav's Donuts to get Monica a latte. There's nothing wrong with the coffee in the break room at the station, but she said she needed a latte."

"No problem." Nico stared out the window. "This investigation will require a lot of caffeine."

The two men parked and made it to the donut shop in record time. Downtown was deserted. Like he'd done many times before, Mac ordered two boxes of assorted donuts, for the police staff, and Monica's latte, extra-large.

When Mac and Nico turned the corner to approach the front entrance to the police station, they heard the media before they saw them. A media circus skirted the perimeter.

"Let's go to the back," Mac said as he turned instead of continuing straight. He called Monica.

"Hey. Why aren't you here?"

"We are. A media mob has taken over the front. Can you let us in the back?"

"I'm on my way." She clicked off the phone before he could say goodbye.

Mac looked at Nico. "She's on her way to let us in."

They hurried their pace.

Monica waited at the gate to the fenced parking lot and waved her badge in front of the sensor, which triggered the gate to slide open. She accepted the coffee cup from Mac's out-stretched hand and gave him a quick kiss.

"First stop is the break room to drop the goodies. They won't last long. Then to get you a badge." She poked her thumb toward Nico.

Mac asked, "Is the chief preparing for a press briefing?"

"I don't know." She slurped some coffee. "Why? I've been knee-deep in old case files and haven't paid attention."

"Have you seen the media crowd out front?"

"Yeah, they've been there all day." She swiped her badge in front of the door sensor, triggering a clunk and release of the heavy-duty lock mechanism.

Once inside, the guys followed Monica as she guided them toward the front. After they deposited the pink boxes on a table in the break room, she grabbed two bottles of water, then they headed toward a clerical person who took Nico's picture and made his badge.

The hallways were busier than they had been on Mac's previous visits.

Monica stopped beside a solid door. "We need to check in with Marten and Ruiz. They're leading the investigation."

She swiped her badge at the door. Inside the large room were ten or more uniformed guys going through white boxes. There were ten times as many unopened boxes stacked against a wall.

Marten and Ruiz were talking to each other in the far corner of the room. The door opening caught their attention. Marten nodded.

"I'll be over there if you need me." She pointed to a vacant seat at the table.

Mac and Nico made it to the corner and said their hellos.

Marten said, "You guy's sure you want to spend the night reading old case files?"

Mac said enthusiastically, "We're ready to help in any way we can."

Nico's head bobbed in agreement, then he asked, "Why did this officer have so many case files at his house?"

"He took copious notes, and from what we can tell, he recreated case files and stored them at his home. His wife said he'd been paranoid about lawsuits or false charges since the day he took the oath to serve."

Mac confirmed. "Thirty years of documents?"

"Yup, active duty, thirty years."

Nico choked on a sip of water. With a strained voice, he croaked, "Did he make files on minor infractions like traffic tickets?"

"It appears he did." Ruiz chimed in. "You two can settle in at the end of the table." He pointed. "We're starting with the most recent cases and moving backward chronologically. You each have a box."

They turned to take their seats, then Nico stopped and looked back at Marten and Ruiz. "Retired sixteen years? Are we going to look into what he's been doing all those years?"

Marten answered, "We've got guys looking into that time as well."

Nico joined Mac at the table. Mac began looking at the documents in his assigned box. The numbering sequence on the box matched the department's categorization for March 1996. He did a fast math calculation in his mind. He looked around the room and a rush of relief came over him when he saw there were about one hundred boxes in total and a room full of people going through them. Once his brain relaxed a bit, he caught Monica looking at him. They exchanged smiles like two people in love.

Nico leaned to Mac. "This guy had perfect penmanship, like my third-grade teacher."

Mac whispered, "Is your box by the book?"

"You mean case activity records, reports, printouts, notes, and photographs? Yes. Neat, and thorough."

"Right. He missed his calling—Monica said he should have been a POST Academy (Peace Officer Standards and Training) instructor on proper paperwork." Mac lowered his voice more and leaned closer to Nico. "Do you think his supervisor knew he was recreating his case files?"

"I doubt it." Nico took a swig of his water. "Seems like some paranoia mixed with obsessiveness."

"From what I've read so far, I'm getting the sense he displayed aggressive tendencies on the job. Not the kind and gentle man we're hearing about."

"Most officers back then were aggressive. It's what they were taught." Nico looked around to see who was behind him. "Same at the FBI. Or so I'm told."

Mac pulled a small notebook from his backpack to jot down a note and said to Nico, "We need to have Monica ask his wife about his off-duty personality."

The guys resumed their study of every piece of content in their boxes. There were hushed voices among a few who sat around the table. Shuffling papers and papers being tamped against the table to straighten them had become the white noise in the room.

While the hours passed on the enormous wall clock, Marten and Ruiz remained in the room. They'd post potential clues on their whiteboard, write notes, read over shoulders. One-by-one the crew became smaller, and progress slowed.

It was close to two in the morning when Monica tapped Mac on his shoulder. "I can't keep my eyes open. I'm going home to get some sleep."

Mac looked at Marten, who waved him out of the room. He mouthed, "Go home."

He told Monica, "I'll be home soon."

Mac had been so engrossed in the documents he'd been reading he hadn't noticed Monica had already cleaned her space at the table. He watched her slip out of the conference room.

Nico said, "I need to call it when we're done with these boxes. I can't keep my eyes open."

Mac agreed. "Actually, it sounds like a good idea for me, too." He closed the lid on his box and put a sticky note on it that read, "cleared." He went to his longtime friend, Marten. "How much longer are you staying?"

"Straight through the night." He shrugged. "It's like being on a stakeout. Lots of coffee." He pointed to the large travel mug his wife had given him. "Somebody killed a cop. We need to find the motherfucker."

"I'll be back tomorrow after work. Nico will be here in the morning."

Chapter 7

Music played from Nico's bedside clock, waking him at six-thirty. It had been a long night at the police station looking through the many boxes housing Stockford's police history. He looked outside to find a cloudy day, maybe rain later. Showers weren't good for outdoor crime scenes.

He knew from his experience—every town had a 'watering hole' where the locals gathered in the morning for coffee. Often, it was the older men in the community. They had loose lips and loved to talk. Trav's Donuts wasn't the type of watering hole that interested him. Handley's Coffee Shop on the east side of town pulled in a group of locals, but he wanted a grittier place.

Red's Roadhouse on the west side of town had potential. Nico first learned of Red's when he'd joined Mac on a stakeout to snoop on Mac's sister's doctor-boyfriend. The place had a new owner since then. With the previous owner, it had a party vibe at night. Nico hoped with the new owner it had a slow-to-wake-up vibe in the morning.

He still had his day job, hired by an unknown person to be Rae Ann Bowen's personal chauffeur. Checking his watch, he had about an hour at Red's before he needed to pick up Rae.

When he pulled into the parking area, he saw a few trucks parked along the front of the place. Nico pulled his large SUV in beside them.

He pushed the front door into the dark interior, his vision blinded for a second by the sudden darkness. He shook off the rain droplets from his shoulders and walked careful steps toward the bar, plowing straight into a table with a thud. He rubbed his thigh and took three or four baby steps. Then he saw the long bar with a cluster of men sitting at one end. They snickered—he assumed at his clumsiness.

The barkeep watched him approach the bar. She looked at him and when he moved closer, she said, "Good morning. Welcome to Red's. I've not seen you here before."

He countered, "Do you work here every day?"

Now, the five men seated at the bar turned and stared at him.

"I do," she replied. "I'm the owner." She shook her thick mane of red hair. "Red's Roadhouse."

He smiled and raised his hands. "Guilty. I've not been here before. Drove by with a friend and thought it looked like a decent place—during the day. The night we drove by, it seemed like a much younger crowd."

"You talk like you're a hundred years old."

The local boys chuckled.

"Can I get you a coffee?"

"Bar owner and mind-reader. Yes, please." Nico pulled out a stool, leaving several empties between him and the local boys.

"Cream and sugar?"

"No, just black."

She returned with a big mug filled to within a half inch from the top. She placed it in front of him without spilling a drop and then stepped back to lean against the counter where the cash register lived. "Just black, do you have a name?"

"Nico. Nico Stark." He stretched out his hand to shake hers and she accepted.

"Rinda Tofte. What brings you to Brookfield?"

Nico noticed the conversation among the group of locals had died down when Rinda asked him the question. None of them turned their heads, but they all seemed to turn up their hearing aids.

"I moved here five months ago." He would not make this inquiry easy for her or the cronies down the bar from him.

"And what brought you here from parts unknown?" She smiled and flashed her perfectly aligned white teeth.

He couldn't stop looking at her face. She was a true redhead, creamy white skin, too many freckles to count and vibrant green eyes that sparkled when she smiled. "I own a personal driver type of business."

She moved closer to the bar and leaned her hip toward him. "Like a taxi service?"

He noticed she crossed her feet as she leaned against the bar. He laughed. "Well, yes, except you won't find my phone number listed anywhere as my clients are referrals. I pick up politicians or important muckety-mucks."

"Fascinating. Again, what brings you to Brookfield? I'm not aware of politicians living here or important muckety-mucks."

"Hey, Red. Filler up." One of the older men lifted his coffee mug in the air.

She grabbed the pot of coffee and filled all the guys' mugs. Nico heard her say, "You boys doing all right? Can I get you a muffin or an omelet?"

When the men turned down her offer to feed them, she returned to Nico.

"You serve breakfast?"

She shrugged, "Sorta. I have a cook in the back who does basic breakfast food and basic lunch—burgers, sandwiches, fries. No food after two in the afternoon. Are you hungry?"

"No. Thanks anyway. Should I call you Red or Rinda?"

"Doesn't matter to me as long as you call." She giggled at her own joke.

"Sounds like you've used that line a time or two."

"It never gets old."

"It was nice to meet you, Rinda. I've gotta get going." He stood.

"Oh, yes, to the mysterious and important client who brought you to Brookfield. Come back soon and brighten my day with some more riveting conversation." She flashed her big, toothy smile at him again.

"Will do." He stepped a few paces down the bar to the center of the local boys. Patting one on the shoulder, he said, "You boys have a good day."

They harrumphed and then all said, "You too."

The closer Nico walked to the door; the louder the local boys' conversation became. He hoped he gave them something to talk about. Rinda struck him as someone who'd get a man to talk about his deepest, darkest secrets. Before he left the establishment, he planned to go back and see her again.

Nico pulled into the DeSalvo driveway, where Rae Ann lived, one minute before his scheduled arrival time.

The front door opened and Rae ran to the car before Nico had the transmission in park. Mrs. DeSalvo waved goodbye from the threshold.

Rae hopped into the front passenger seat and slammed the door shut.

"Sorry. I guess I don't know my own strength this morning."

"Good morning to you, too." They smiled at each other. "I wasn't late. What's your hurry?"

"Prom is Saturday. Josslyn is bugging me to go. I don't want to, but she won't stop talking about it."

They proceeded toward the gatehouse of the Blackstone Estates, where the DeSalvos had lived for many years. "Why not?"

"Brandy isn't going. Kevin's still in juvenile lockup. I don't have friends and the Winter Ball was a disaster."

He agreed the Winter Ball had been memorable and not in a good way. He'd volunteered to chaperone with Mac because he had to wait on Rae, anyway. While one boy, Rae's friend's boyfriend, had been in the restroom, someone assaulted him. "Do you wish you were going?"

"No. Dances aren't my thing. I don't know how to tell Josslyn."

"Be honest, but gentle. She loves you and wants you to be happy."

He pulled into the drop-off line at Blackstone Academy, along with the parents. When they arrived at the location where Rae could hop out, Mac waited to open her door.

Nico lowered the passenger window.

"Good morning, Marshal Mac." She smiled at him.

"Good morning, Rae."

Rae continued into the school. Mac shut the door and leaned inside the open window. "Are you headed to the station to go through more boxes?"

"Yes."

"Let me know if you find something good. Marten texted me this morning and said they'd found some possibilities. He also said the mayor is pressuring the chief to find something reportable so the media will back off."

"Sounds like something a mayor would say."

Chapter 8

Brookfield's mayor sat behind his large, polished mahogany desk, dodging calls from the media. Media outlets from across the nation were calling for an interview. With the skill of a megastar's agent, his administrative assistant, Jennifer Carver, handled the bold reporters who'd invaded her office in the city's business complex.

With each phone call she received, she'd buzz the mayor to ask if he wanted to speak with them. So far, he'd said no to everyone except the police chief and his wife of twenty-one years, Leona. She was his second wife. The first marriage ended when an ex-lover had exposed his multiple affairs. When Ozzy thought about his first wife, he felt thankful they hadn't had children. He hoped to never see her again.

He pointed the remote control at the mahogany, built-in cabinet across from his desk, clicked a button, and a panel opened. He tried to remember which button turned on the television, but he couldn't read the small print on the handheld contraption. For a moment, he wanted to throw the remote at the television. Instead, with a huff, he grabbed his old-man reading glasses and put them on. A second click turned on the TV. He muted the volume, hoping the growing crowd outside his door would think he wasn't there.

'BREAKING NEWS' in large, bold letters spanned the screen on the television. A reporter used a live shot of the government building for the backdrop. The mayor planned to keep the TV on all day with the Closed Caption feature turned on and the volume muted. He watched the words scroll by along the bottom of the screen.

"Brookfield Police are investigating an early morning shooting which left a police officer dead in the quiet Lake Woods subdivision. We have a team at the scene and outside the Brookfield Police Department waiting for a press conference with Police Chief Malcolm Contee. I'm outside the mayor's office looking for answers. We're working to find out who this person was and what led to the shooting. We've been told they will release the name of the victim after they notify relatives. Let's go to the scene near Perla Lake. Abby, what have you learned about this shooting?"

Pausing the TV, the mayor crossed the room to fill his cup with more coffee. He contemplated adding a small shot of whiskey to calm his nerves. He needed to spin this in his favor—the election was in six months. The retired police officer's murder had the potential to be the biggest event in his political career.

"We've just learned the victim is a retired police office—not an active-duty officer—but based on the number of officers who've responded to this scene, we suspect there's more to the story." As the cameraman zoomed in on the activity behind Abby, in the wooded area, the reporter said, off-camera, "You can see how the officers are doing a grid search in the woods and we expect they'll be here for several more hours."

Back on camera, the reporter continued, "Here's what we know. Around six this morning, a dispatcher at the 9-1-1 call center received a call from someone at the home requesting help. She'd found her husband deceased. As is customary, they dispatched medics and law enforcement—the officer in charge released the medics. I've asked for details, but they're not giving me anything. This crime scene is being well guarded."

The scene switched to the news team in the station with a small window in the corner showing the on-scene reporter. An anchor in the station asked the reporter, "Has anyone said if there are concerns for public safety?"

Abby, on scene, replied, "The one thing we've been told is they believe this was an isolated event. We've gone door-to-door to see if any of the neighbors heard anything. So far, nobody knows anything. We're going to be live here all morning trying to get answers and information about what happened. Live in Brookfield, Abby Lewis, Sacramento, Channel 7 News." The mayor watched as the live footage at the scene cut out and they were on to the next topic.

Standing in front of the TV cabinet, the mayor checked the time and then buzzed his assistant, Jennifer. When she answered the call, he snapped, "Cancel all meetings today. The murder is my priority."

"Yes, sir."

Next, he texted Ann at his lake house. *Baby, I've tried calling. Are you still at the lake house?*

He tapped his fingers on his immaculate desktop.

To his knowledge, nobody knew about his affair with Ann, except Jennifer, his assistant, and Police Chief Contee.

His attention returned to the TV while he waited to hear from her.

After about thirty minutes, he tried again and listened to her cell phone, voice mail message for the umpteenth time. He said, through clenched teeth, "Baby, you can't still be mad at me. We have a serious situation here. The media stormed Jennifer's office demanding an update. The pressure to have instant answers is tremendous. I could use a few kind words from you. Please return my call. I love you."

He didn't know why he found high-maintenance women attractive. The thrill of the hunt? The satisfaction he felt when they gave in to him. Ann was a hard one to keep happy. He knew a professional hit man killing a retired cop in his community should be his focus, but all he could think about was Ann.

The focus on the news had shifted to an accident in Sacramento where a semi-truck hauling tomatoes took the curve too fast and dropped the load of tomatoes on the highway. He buzzed Jennifer.

"Yes, sir?" Jennifer's professional-sounding voice spoke from his desk phone.

"Please ask Ned to come to my office."

"Yes, sir."

The mayor had employed Ned as his security supervisor for the entire time he'd been the mayor—almost four years. With Ned's colossal frame, bulging muscles, and booming voice, the mayor felt safe in his presence. He suspected Ned knew about his relationship with Ann. He was a smart guy, but they never spoke about it.

From the third drawer down on his left, he grabbed an envelope and his official note pad. On the notepad he wrote, "Please call me. Ozzy." After placing the note in the envelope, he sealed it. Then he wrote on the front of the envelope, "Ms. Ann Sawyer."

On a separate piece of paper, he wrote Ann's home address and the address of his lake house.

A few seconds later, there was a knock on his door. Without hesitation, the door opened.

Ned slipped inside and shut the door behind him. "Yes, sir? Jennifer said you needed me."

"I'm not going anywhere this afternoon. Would you do a personal favor for me?"

"Sure thing. What do you need?"

"This letter needs to be hand-delivered to Ann Sawyer." He held the envelope out as if it were an official document of some sort. "I haven't been able to reach her. She should be at one of these addresses." He handed Ned the notepaper and a set of keys. "Here are the keys to both places. If she doesn't answer, go inside, look around and see if anything looks out of place."

"Are there security alarms at either place?"

"No."

Ned did a quick calculation of time and said, "If she's not in town, I'll be gone close to an hour. You sure you want me to leave this media mess outside?"

"I'll ask the police chief to send a few officers here to handle the crowd."

"Good idea." Ned left as stealthily as he'd arrived.

* * *

At the mayor's lake house, Ann leaned on the granite-topped island in the large, well-appointed kitchen. When not in use, a small television hid inside a cabinet in the kitchen. This morning, Ann had the cabinet open and was watching the local news talk about the shooting. She'd sipped coffee while eating toast and felt a chill run through her. Ozzy's house sat across the lake from where the shooting had occurred. The murder so close in proximity had her spooked.

She hadn't decided whether she'd forgive Ozzy one more time—given the reason he'd had to leave her. At least he hadn't left because his wife summoned him, which happened too often. Ozzy had said he'd make good on his promise to tell his wife he wanted a divorce. Her thoughts took control of her mind for a moment and drowned out the reporter speaking to the viewing audience. She questioned how a spineless man had become the mayor.

As she looked around the lavish, great room, she envisioned it would be hers and Ozzy's one day.

Alone in the house, she gave voice to her thoughts. Her voice spiked with attitude. "The first thing I'm going to do is have this dark kitchen remodeled with white cabinets and marble countertops." Glancing at the stove and oven, she added, "And those outdated appliances need to go."

The reporter continuing to talk about the shooting had become annoying to her. She clicked off the TV and closed the cabinet doors.

After cleaning up her breakfast dishes, she ambled through the house looking at all the distinct design elements which she despised and would change. Standing in front of a large, framed photograph of a giraffe in the library made her scowl. "Why does 'she' have a framed photo of a giraffe? It's not like they go to countries where giraffes roam." She shrugged and moved to Ozzy's desk.

She sat behind the large, dark, wood desk in Ozzy's office and spun around in the chair—looking at everything like a spoiled princess. Saying aloud to herself, "This room is too dark. The paneling will need to be replaced with a light paint or maybe a linen wallpaper. Yes, wallpaper. I should make notes on the changes." She used a feature on her phone to jot down the improvements she'd been talking to herself about. Then she heard a sound outside the front door.

She hurried from the library, down the hall to the great room, and straight to the windows by the front door to look out. There were no cars out there. *There it was again—the garage.* She thought.

Stumbling, she turned and ran to the interior garage door in the mudroom. Before opening the door, she placed her ear against it. A feeling of fright shivered through her. Hearing nothing, she opened the door, flipped the light switch, and asked, "Ozzy, is that you?"

The single car in the garage was hers.

Ann slammed the door, locked it, and turned on her heels. She needed to pack and get the hell out of Ozzy's lake house. She made a vow to herself, and she planned to tell Ozzy—she wouldn't return to the lake house until he left his wife. There were other men in town interested in her.

She couldn't shake the uneasy feeling. It was time to pack and get out of there. She went to the main bedroom and began folding her clothes, stacking them in neat piles on the bed. Busy in the bathroom packing her makeup and hair products, she didn't hear the front door open. There wasn't a security system at the lake house. Ozzy had been quite lazy about facilitating that safety measure.

When Ann turned away from the bathroom mirror where she'd freshened her lipstick, she saw a large black man and screamed.

He stepped back several feet and raised his hands. "It's me, Ned—Mayor Eastland's security supervisor."

She threw her lipstick at him, hitting him in the chest. "Holy Moly, Ned! You scared the crap out of me!"

"I'm sorry. The mayor asked me to deliver this envelope to you. He gave me the keys and told me to let myself in if you didn't answer. I knocked a few times." He stretched his hand out as far as possible, waiting for her to approach him and take the envelope.

"I told him I'd be back in town today. What was so important he had to send you all the way out here?" She grabbed the envelope from him.

"I don't know, Ms. Sawyer." He turned to leave.

"Wait a minute, I might want to send a response." She tore open the envelope and read the paper where Ozzy had written, "Baby, please call me." She folded the paper and slipped it into the back pocket of her jeans. "Thank you, Ned. Nothing more is necessary. You can go." Her dismissive tone would insult anyone she addressed. She all but waved him away.

"Oh, wait." Her tone changed to sweetness. "Would you mind walking around the perimeter of the house and see if there's any sign of someone being out there? Did you see anyone? I heard something. It might have been squirrels. Please check."

Ann returned to the bed to finish packing her garments. She sat on the bed and waited for Ned to return.

"Ms. Sawyer," he said when he returned and neared the main bedroom.

"Yes."

He cleared the doorway to the bedroom and said, "I didn't see any signs of trespassers. Maybe some deer activity."

"Thank you. I feel much better. Can I trouble you to take my luggage to my car in the garage and put them in the trunk?"

"Sure thing, no problem."

She waited in the kitchen at the island. When he found her there. He asked, "Are you leaving soon? Should I leave the door up?"

"Yes, thank you. I'll be right behind you."

"Have a safe drive back to town."

"You too."

As soon as the front door shut, she locked the door and the deadbolt. At a fast clip, she went to each exterior door to check that Ozzy had locked them before he left. One-by-one she closed the blinds and drapes. The rooms became dark. Using the remote control, she closed the shades on the large, two-story windows in the living room. Then she heard Ned knock on the front door.

"What did you forget to tell me?" she said with mild irritation as she opened the door to a man she didn't know.

Chapter 9

Hunter had stayed an extra night at the no-tell-motel. While in the area, he'd split his time between watching Bruce Stockford and Ann Sawyer. She'd been staying at a sweet lake house on the other side of the lake from the Stockford family. He knew as much as he needed to know about his targets. No emotion that way.

When he left the motel, he'd made sure he left nothing behind. He wiped down every surface he'd touched. His standard method was to sleep on his own bedding on top of the motel's bedding. He had shaved his head bald each morning while he was on assignment so as not to leave any hair behind at either crime scene. He even went so far as to not use the bathroom in the motel room, driving to various gas stations to use their facility.

He felt more than ready to head home. Once he crossed the state line into Oregon and then east, he'd relax. He'd had a previous hunting client in Oregon he planned to visit for one night. It felt like the stop solidified his alibi—he'd been in California meeting a client who booked his services as a hunting guide. Because you never know who opposed hunting for sport, he kept his client list confidential and many of his clients had deep pockets. They preferred to keep their extracurricular activities quiet, and he wanted to stay in their good graces. He doubted anyone would connect him to the Brookfield murders. It hadn't happened on any of his other assignments.

From his observations of Ann Sawyer and her lover, he got the sense she was a hellcat to deal with. When the two occupants sat on the deck of the fancy house, drinking wine and talking about their plans, her temper often flared. Her lover calmed her down by telling her his vision for them once they could be together.

He'd seen the lover leave earlier—today had to be the day. She had a negative attitude and a dark vibe about her. Sometimes it was impossible for a target to be in a pleasant state of mind when they drew their last breath. Every rule had exceptions.

As he crept along the side of the house, a deer startled him, causing him to bump into the house. He froze, thinking, *novice mistake*. He wished he could put one between the doe's eyes. The woman inside had to have heard him, so he retreated to the treed area beside the house.

His heart raced for a few seconds as he nestled into a mound of needles next to a large pine tree. About five minutes had passed when he saw a large SUV with dark-tinted windows approach the house.

He watched a large, fit man go to the porch and knock a few times on the front door. When the door didn't open, the man used a key to gain access. Hunter considered the options of who the man might be. Another lover, perhaps? The man stayed inside for a while before he left.

After walking the perimeter of the grounds around the house, the man drove away in the SUV, leaving the garage door up. Hunter knew his window of opportunity was about to close. Once the car was out of sight and he could no longer hear the motor, he neared the house, almost being seen by the hellcat as she closed the living room drapes.

He hurried to the front door, pulled his handgun from the holster, attached a suppressor, and knocked on the front door.

As she approached the door, he heard her ask, "What did you forget to tell me?" She opened the door wide. Before her brain registered that he wasn't who she thought he was, he'd put a round between her eyes. She dropped to the floor with a thud.

He grabbed his shell casing, pushed her legs aside and stepped in, closing and locking the door behind him. Her empty eyes looked up at him, a trickle of blood ran down the side of her forehead and into her combed dark hair. As he so often did, without awareness, he twisted his head one way, then the other, to release the tension in his neck joints with a crack. A bad habit of his that annoyed his wife. Before leaving the scene, he plucked the projectile out of the wall behind the shattered mirror, then hung the mirror back on the wall.

The home was dark with most of the natural light closed off to prepare for the home to sit vacant for a period, which worked well for Hunter. He retrieved everything—the casing, the bullet, then moved toward the garage and found the garage door opener mounted next to the light switch on one side of the door. He hit the button to close the door and hustled to get to the door in time to step over the sensor beam and outside so as not to disrupt the electronic signal.

Once outside, he grabbed the cedar branch he'd left on the side of the garage, turning he saw the garage door connect with the concrete apron. He dragged the tree branch behind him as he walked across the wet pavement to the forest, zigging and zagging the entire trip.

He hiked to where he'd parked the rental truck. The slight drizzle of rain falling made his boot impressions more visible. He couldn't do anything about that, since the boots he wore were a common brand, he didn't worry. As he sat sideways in the driver's seat, he tossed his over-sized boots on the passenger floor, slipped on his sneakers, and drove away.

About an hour on Interstate 5 northbound to Oregon, he decided he was hungry and took an offramp in Red Bluff that showed a cluster of fast-food establishments. He drove through and ordered a bacon cheeseburger, fries, and a sweet tea. He'd almost forgotten sweet tea wasn't a staple in California like it was in Missouri.

Before eating, he retrieved a burner cell phone from his glove compartment and texted his employer, *job 1 and 2 done, wire the funds.*

He turned off the phone, pulled the SIM card from the phone and snapped it into two pieces, tossing them into a cup holder. After he devoured the food, he called his wife.

"Hello."

"Hey, babe." He wiped his mouth with a napkin.

"Are you on your way to Oregon?"

"Yup. Finished the meeting with the new client this morning. He wants to take several executives from his firm on a hunt. It's going to be a big-money trip."

"I like the sound of that. When will you be home?"

"Day after tomorrow."

"Good. Mom and Owen are having a barbecue with his cronies, and he wants us to attend." A year after his wife's father's fatal accident, her mother married Owen Prendergas, a successful investor. Owen kept his investments private. Hunter believed his mother-in-law didn't even know where his wealth had come from, nor did she care—as long as he provided her with the level of comfort she enjoyed.

"Can we leave early? I'm going to be dead tired."

"Yeah, yeah, we'll hang out for a bit, let the kids swim, and then leave."

"I'm going to hit the road again."

"I love you. Be safe."

"I love you too, babe. I'll call you tomorrow when I make my first stop."

After ending the call with his wife, he shut down his phone and slipped the SIM card out of it and back into his pocket.

Back on the highway north, with every clean swipe of his windshield wiper blades, he took in the scenery as he drove toward the mountains. Missouri stayed green year-round, but it didn't have mountains like the western Pacific states did. Somewhere between Red Bluff and Redding, he pulled off the highway, put down the passenger window and tossed one piece of the burner phone's SIM card as far as he could. He did the same after he drove through the small town of Weed. It made him snicker whenever he drove through that part of California. So curious, he once looked up why someone would name a town Weed. He had learned, the town had been named after the founder of a local lumber mill—in 1897.

He waited until he was in Oregon to dispose of the burner phone.

Based on the grandeur of the second lake house, he figured it wouldn't be long before the local officers would discover the woman's body. He didn't relax until he was back in his own truck—halfway to Missouri.

Chapter 10

Mayor Eastland's private phone rang—he looked at his watch. Although it felt like the afternoon, his watch showed ten in the morning. Few people had the phone number of his direct line. Hoping he'd hear Ann's smoky voice on the other end, he answered, "Hello."

His wife, Leona, asked, "Will you be home for dinner?"

"Hello to you too," he sniped. "I can't say. The media are all over the retired officer's murder."

She fell silent. He continued, sounding more like a teenager than the mayor, explaining why he wouldn't be home on time, "They're camped outside the government building waiting for a statement. A few aggressive reporters all but stormed my office earlier. If it hadn't been for Ned and Jennifer guarding my door, they might have gotten into my office."

"Be strong, dear. This is what you excel at—the hard parts of the job. You knew the job entailed more than hand-shaking and baby-kissing when you ran for office."

She knew how to make his chest puff up like a big, old rooster in the henhouse—something he realized at that moment he hadn't considered in a long time. "Thank you. You've always been my cheerleader." He ended the call.

Pulling his cell phone from his pocket, he texted his lover, *Ann. Baby. You're being ridiculous. Please call me. I love you.*

The phone screen sat silent. He'd thought since Ned had hand-delivered his message, he'd have heard from her by now.

He buzzed his assistant, Jennifer.

"Yes, sir?"

"Send Ned in."

"Right away, sir."

Ned arrived within two minutes. He'd been down the hall in the staff lounge having coffee and a pastry with some of the security officers.

The mayor asked, "Tell me again how the conversation with Ann Sawyer went."

"There wasn't a lot of conversation. She didn't answer the door, so I thought she wasn't there. When I let myself in with the key you gave me, I found her in a bedroom packing. When I left, the last thing she said was she'd be leaving shortly."

"Did you wait to see her leave?"

"No. It didn't seem necessary."

The mayor's phone vibrated. He fumbled it to the floor and retrieved it and saw the police chief's name on the screen. He answered the call.

"Malcolm. What do you have for me?"

"Thought you'd want an update. Are you headed to your office soon?"

"I'm at my office now. You can't give me the update on the phone?"

"I'd rather not. Can you stop by my office?"

"I guess I can."

"Use the restricted entrance to the station. There's a deluge of media at the front of the building."

"Will do. Thanks." He ended the call and told Ned, "We need to go to the police chief's office."

In the car, he said, "take Quartz Street instead of Center. The chief said to use the restricted entrance in their parking lot."

Remaining on the highway, Ned passed their normal turn and stopped the car near the handicapped ramp at the rear entrance to drop off his passenger.

The mayor shuffled inside and down the halls in the police department until he arrived at Chief Contee's office.

His administrative assistant looked up. "He's expecting you." She waved toward the large wooden door.

"Would you bring me a cup of coffee, two sugars, and a lot of cream?"

She popped up from her chair. "Sure thing."

Ozzy twisted the handle and pushed the door open, forgetting it was an inexpensive hollow-core door. The door crashed against the wall. He'd opened the door countless times, but he had a lot on his mind.

"What the hell." The chief shook his head. "You've always liked a grand entrance, Ozzy. Would you like some coffee?"

"Your girl is bringing me some."

"My girl, as you call her, has a name. Her name is Belinda."

"I've never been good with names." He dropped his briefcase and plopped himself into an armchair in front of the chief's desk. "What's happening?"

At the same time as the chief opened his mouth to respond to the mayor's inquiry, Belinda tapped on the door and let herself in. She held the serving tray on her arm, as if she moonlighted as a server in a restaurant. She'd brought two cups of coffee, spoons, forks, napkins, a plate with blueberry muffins, a sugar bowl, and a small carafe of cream.

A heavy veil of quiet engulfed the room while she lowered the tray to her boss's desk.

"Thank you, Belinda."

"You're welcome, Chief."

Watching her walk out of the room, the mayor waited until he heard the door latch before repeating his question, "What's happening?"

The chief paused a moment before answering his question. "Between you and me. We don't have shit, except for the revenge message left on the tree. Whoever did this was clean." He slurped a sip of coffee. "Based on the wound, we calculated what we measured the farthest distance an expert marksman could've set up for an accurate shot to the Stockford's front porch. Then we set up the shot for what we considered being the point of angle and entry. Since he slid from the chair he'd been sitting in, we can't be certain. We scoured the area looking for footprints from the shooter, leaving the scene. It's like he flew away. There are no shoe prints." Looking out the window for a fraction of a second, the chief mumbled, "I suppose the shooter could have been a woman."

"Why do you think it might have been a woman? And for God's sake, women leave shoe prints too."

"I don't think it's a woman. Statistically, men carry out kill shots like what we're dealing with—I can't think of a similar killing with a woman holding the weapon. I wanted to be... I mean, I shouldn't have assumed the shooter was a... oh, forget it." He took another sip of coffee. "We found what looked like animal beds, but no tracks. They seemed man-made, errr, umm, or woman-made. Fucking political correctness is clouding my thoughts."

The mayor sat perched on the front edge of the chair, leaning toward the chief. "That's all you have? I had to come here to speak in private to hear you ain't got shit? What the fuck. I've got things to do. You could have told me on the phone."

"Calm down. I think the animal beds are a clue because they were in a half-circle radius of the front porch. All were at the same distance. We had the team measure from the beds to the porch. They found a foot impression."

"One footprint" The mayor arched an eyebrow.

"He's fucking with us. He scuffed out the other prints and left the one to fuck with us. Or she."

"Will you stop with the fucking political correctness? I don't give a shit if the shooter was a man or a woman."

The chief ignored the mayor's short fuse.

The mayor continued, "That's it then? The person is in the wind and this crime will go unsolved?" His voice became low and croaky. "Have you forgotten the election is in six months? If I'm not re-elected, your job may be on the line too."

"Look, we've known each other for many years—I don't want to know what has made you agitated this morning, but you should get your attitude in check. It's going to be a tense day." He paused. Before the mayor could get in another word, he added, "Of course, I know the fucking election is in six months—you remind me every time something hasn't gone your way."

The mayor slumped back in his chair.

The chief continued, "We've put out a BOLO for any unfamiliar vehicles along Highway 12, but we're asking for an onslaught of calls with such a vague request. And we've set up a tip line and asked the community to help with any tips about unusual activity on Wednesday, between five and six in the morning. This shooter's smart. We're checking hotels for anyone staying a couple of nights that coincide with the murders. And combing security footage from businesses that capture the roads leading to the lake."

The mayor shrugged. "Don't." He held up his hand. "I don't want to hear any more. It sounds like you don't have any leads." He paused. "Can you spare a couple of rookies? I need a favor."

"What's the favor?"

"I can't reach Ann Sawyer."

"Did you think maybe she's avoiding you?"

"Yesterday, she was at our lake house. She wasn't happy I had to leave. When she wouldn't return my calls, I had Ned go out there. He said she was packing her stuff and seemed fine."

"I have bigger problems than your love-life. In case your dick has commandeered your brain—I have a high-profile murder case I'm trying to solve."

"Please."

"Two rookies. I can't spare more. They'll check her place in town and your love shack at the lake, and then they're done."

"That's all I ask." He handed the chief a note with the name Ann Sawyer, her home address, his lake house address, and the keys to both homes.

"Call me later and I'll let you know what they find."

The mayor stood.

"Thank you."

* * *

Within an hour of the mayor asking the police chief for a favor, two Brookfield Police Department rookie officers were on the highway, headed out of town to the mayor's lake house. They'd checked Ann Sawyer's place in town, where they found nothing out of place and nobody home.

The driver, Officer Brant Arbuckle, said to the passenger, Officer Oscar Phelan, "This is a shitty assignment. I wanted to get in on the Stockford murder."

Phelan snorted. "We'd be on some other shit assignment if not on this one. There's no way we're getting anywhere near the Stockford murder—in your dreams."

Arbuckle looked in his side rearview mirror as he pulled into the fast lane to pass a slow-moving cargo truck.

The passenger continued, "Did you see who was in and out of the conference room where they're going through the dead officer's old case files?" He didn't wait for an answer. "You didn't see any newbies, did you?"

"No."

"My point. No rookies."

"Lucky us. We're headed to check on the mayor's mistress."

"You better not let anyone else hear you say that."

"Say what?"

"The mayor's mistress. We don't know. She could be his sister for all we know."

"Yeah. Right. Nobody hides their sister at a lake house."

"She might not even be there."

"I hope not. The last thing I want to do is get in the middle of a love triangle."

Phelan reached to turn up the dispatch radio. "Let's see what we're missing."

The Brookfield Police Department hired the two men, boys, to some of the senior officers, and paid for them to attend the Peace Officer Standards and Training Academy (POST). It helped that both of their fathers went to high school with a few of the guys on the force who'd put in a good word for them.

After high school, Arbuckle had worked odd construction jobs, job site clean-up, type work. He still lived at home with his parents. After the construction contractor fired him for poor attendance, his father told him to move out or go to the police academy.

Phelan had taken a few classes at the community college with no career plan or aspirations. He began working nights as a dishwasher at a local restaurant and dropped his classes mid-semester. His parents weren't happy with his decision, but he was a legal adult. When his father pitched the idea of becoming a police officer, at first, it sounded scary. His mind shifted when he heard the county paid their entry-level officers much better than the minimum-wage jobs he'd worked since graduating from high school.

The two rookies met at the academy, where they attended classes Monday through Friday for eighteen weeks. It was physically demanding, mentally exhausting, and emotionally draining. They'd learned about a culture of crime, drugs, death, and worse that neither of them had been subject to growing up in stable homes or had seen in movies—these crimes involved real people.

Had it not been for the pure adrenaline rush he'd experienced on the driving course—zipping across multiple lanes to screech to a stop in the correct lane with the red traffic light and his father helping him study and prepare for exams, Arbuckle might have quit the academy.

Phelan had an uncommon experience. He enjoyed the physical workouts, dazzled the others with his dominating arrest control—thanks to competitive wrestling on the high school team, and he was book smart. Where he'd struggled had been on the driving course. He had a more controlled personality than his reckless partner.

Phelan read the directions to the lake house as they drove out of town.

When they turned on the paved, private driveway leading to the home, they followed the driveway around to the lake-facing front of the house. Arbuckle blurted out, "Get the fuck outta here! Look at that house."

One of the largest houses on Perla Lake, the Eastland home had five bedrooms, seven bathrooms, a library, an exercise room, a playroom with a ping-pong table, billiards, poker table, and a wet bar, a full chef's kitchen with a butler's pantry, dining room that sat twelve, laundry room and a four-car attached garage. The great room's large, two-story windows looked out at the lake and private dock.

They parked in front of the garages. The exterior of the home had a log cabin look—not your typical log cabin in the woods—the last appraisal valued this one at four million.

"Do you think they have servants?" Arbuckle asked. He placed the transmission in the park position and released his seat belt.

Phelan looked at his partner to get a read on if he was serious or joking. "I'm pretty sure people don't refer to the hired help as servants."

"Whatever." Arbuckle said as he exited the vehicle and left the vehicle's motor running—which was standard operating procedure.

As the two rookies approached the front porch, Phelan observed, "The drapes are all drawn."

Arbuckle knocked on the door. Both stepped backward and waited. Arbuckle stretched out his arm and pressed the doorbell button. "Should we go inside? I'm dying to look around."

Phelan said, "No. We check the perimeter first. You go that way." He pointed toward the garage. "I'll meet you back here."

When Phelan had cleared his side of the home, he saw his partner was already waiting for him at the lakefront side of the house.

"Will you look at those windows? They're even bigger up close," he said, staring up at the expanse of glass reflecting a calm lake.

The partner looked where the guy had pointed. "They're impressive," Phelan admitted, losing patience with his partner.

They both heard a voice say, "Hello, officers." They turned around fast and placed their hands on their sidearms. Their movements synchronized.

"Oh, my!" exclaimed an older woman in a kayak at the water's edge next to the dock screeched and thrust her hands in the air. "Don't shoot me."

The officers walked toward the woman, maintaining their position of readiness. Phelan said, "Who are you and what are you doing here?"

"I live on the other side of the lake. The... the... the lake was calm, so I'm out kayaking."

"Do you have identification?"

"No. It's... it's... it's at my house. I never bring my identification when I'm kayaking." Her raised arms quivered.

Phelan pulled out a small notebook from his pocket, told her to put her arms down, and asked for her name, address, and phone number.

"Is there a problem at the mayor's home? I monitor the vacation homes," she said.

Arbuckle spoke up, "There's nothing here for you to be concerned with. You can continue with your kayaking."

The guys stood rooted in place, waiting for her to shove off.

"Okay, I'll go now. You have my contact information if you need me for anything."

"Yes, ma'am. I'm sure the mayor appreciates you watching his property," Phelan said.

The woman pushed her paddle into the shore and moved her kayak away from the bank, then began paddling away, looking back over her shoulder once.

Arbuckle eagerly said, "I'm going inside and look around."

Phelan, more cautious and by the book, inserted the key into the front door. Arbuckle stood behind him, keeping his hand on his weapon. The guys heard the distinct clunk of the deadbolt mechanism as it landed in the open position. When the rookie tried to open the door, it met with resistance.

"What's the problem?" asked his impatient partner, standing at the ready.

"How the fuck should I know?" He poked his head through the narrow gap and peered inside. He saw his face staring back at him, but fragmented and spattered with blood. He jumped backward, crashing into Arbuckle.

"What?"

It took him a fraction of a second to comprehend what he'd seen. A shattered mirror mounted on the wall across from the front door splattered with blood.

"What the fuck's the problem?" Arbuckle asked, as he poked his head inside to see what had freaked out his partner. He saw a shattered mirror on the wall, and a fancy table beneath it that had a glass bowl on it filled with glass balls covered in blood and what he thought looked like brain matter. He poked his head inside, farther to survey the scene, then yanked his head out and faced his partner with a grin. "There's a dead body."

Phelan stood frozen, not excited to be the first officers at a murder scene like Arbuckle was. "No shit?"

Arbuckle sat down next to the door and stretched his arm inside to take her pulse. "Confirmed. No pulse." He also knew it would be years before he or his rookie partner would be the first officers at a homicide scene again. Before his training kicked into gear, he thought about his resume and that this situation bumped it up a level.

Phelan told his partner, "We need to clear the house," then asked, "Is it her?"

"Are you serious? I can't say if it's her, she's unrecognizable. We need to call this in," Arbuckle said, running through proper protocol in his mind.

"No. First, we clear the house. Whoever did this might still be here."

They both looked over their shoulders in all directions. They went inside through a side door to the garage. Then went in separate directions and cleared the massive house.

When they met back at the deceased woman, Phelan said to Arbuckle, "Now we need to call this in." He punched in the non-dispatch phone number to the police station. When the front desk answered the phone call, he identified himself and asked to speak with the chief.

The partner grabbed his arm. "Hang up and call 911."

"No, the chief might want to deal with this his way."

"What's his way?"

"Shut the fuck up for two seconds. I don't know, but the last thing we need to do is screw this up."

The chief's assistant, Jennifer, answered the phone. He explained the chief had dispatched them to do a welfare check but left out the details of whose home they were at and what they'd found and asked to speak with him.

When the chief's voice came through, Phelan, sounding amped up, described the scene.

"Was there a note left at the scene?"

"A note? No note that we saw. Should we go back inside and look around?"

The chief told the two rookies to stay at the scene—outside. Check the area. He'd send people to assist. The call ended.

Phelan told his partner, "He assigned us to stay here, outside, and secure the scene."

Arbuckle grinned. He held out his fist to fist-bump with Phelan and said, "We have a murder assignment."

Phelan shook his head.

Chapter 11

Mac stood leaning against the wall in Blackstone Academy's cafeteria, watching the younger students eat lunch. Kids trying to out-talk one another. The sound of many conversations echoed off the walls, cranking up the volume. As he looked around, planning his escape to a quieter place, his cell phone vibrated in his pocket.

He hustled out of the noisy cafeteria and into the hallway, where he accepted the incoming call from his friend, Detective Jason Marten.

Covering one ear with his hand and pressing his phone against his other ear, he said, "Hey, hang on a second so I can get somewhere with less noise."

When Mac turned the corner to the front of the building where his office was located, he continued, "Okay. Must be something good for you to call me at the school. What's happening?"

Mac scanned his card to open his office door, flipped on the lights, and tossed his lanyard with identification onto his desk.

"Can you hear me now?"

"Yeah, what's up?"

"Nothing on the Stockford murder. They found your old boss, Ann Sawyer, dead this morning at the mayor's lake house."

"No shit? Did the mayor do it?"

"I don't know for sure. The coroner hasn't given us a time of death. There's an eerie similarity to the Stockford killing."

"Gunshot?"

"Dead center between the eyes."

"Same caliber?"

"No, this was up close and personal."

"I'm guessing the location of the wound makes them similar? Was there a message at the scene?"

"They haven't found a message. It looks like the shooter might have knocked on the front door or rang the doorbell. She opened the door, and it was lights out. Another professional hit, to me."

"Dare I ask why she was at the mayor's lake house?"

"All I know is, his private affair isn't so private anymore."

Mac watched the kids on the security monitors. The upper grades filed into the cafeteria as the younger students scampered to the gymnasium. Because of rain, the teachers herded the kids to the gym to play games and burn off some energy before resuming their studies.

"Are you working the cases as two or connected?"

"The department doesn't have the manpower to assign separate teams to the cases. We're forced to work them together. We haven't found a connection between the two at this point. Are you and Nico still on board to help?"

"Hell, yes. Can I tell Marlene or wait?"

"Great, thanks. Sure, you can tell Marlene about Ann. Reporters already know."

"I've been talking to a guy I knew in the air force. Does the name Lang ring a bell?"

"Luke from San Diego?"

"Yeah. We've been talking. He's got nothing going on—I told him my gig at the school was almost over and that they'd be hiring someone else. He sounded interested. I'll see if he can sub for me so I can spend more time on the cases."

"He'd be a good fit. How will the school board react? Do they even know you don't plan to return in the fall?"

"I've reminded Michael Stromberg several times throughout the year that the agreement I made with Chief Contee was for one school year and no more."

"Offering Lang as a replacement will help. I gotta go."

Jason disconnected the call before Mac could respond.

He gave Nico the information Marten had shared about Ann Sawyer. Nico had never met her. Mac promised to tell him about some exchanges he'd had with her when he had more time.

Mac emailed Lang, asking if he'd be interested in filling in for him starting as soon as possible. Eager for a reply, he refreshed his email program several times while he watched the kids on the security monitors play the hot and cold game in one corner of the gym and dodgeball in another. Mostly, the boys played the physical games. The girls sat on the bleachers watching the boys, pointing at them, and giggling. He gave up on receiving an immediate response from Lang, grabbed his lanyard, and headed straight for Marlene's office.

When he turned the corner in a rush, his sudden movement startled Marlene.

Marlene jumped when she heard him approach. "My God, you scared me," she said as she picked up a small notepad and threw it at Mac. Then she sensed his presence as having a serious purpose. "What's happening?"

Mac sat in the chair next to her desk. She was everyone's mother, everyone's shoulder to cry on, and everyone's source for support or guidance. And everyone knew Marlene loved gossip.

"It's about Ann Sawyer."

"Ann?" Her eyebrow arched and her smile turned to a slight frown. "She and I have a lunch date next Tuesday. Is she all right?"

"You heard someone killed a retired police officer, right?"

Tears pooled in her eyes. "Yes."

"She won't make your lunch date. Officers found Ann shot to death."

She gasped. Tears pooled in her eyes. Mac retrieved a tissue box from her credenza. Grabbing a tissue, she caught the tears as they spilled over onto her cheeks and blew her nose. "Did the same person kill her as the officer?"

"They don't know."

"Then why did you include him in the dreadful news about Ann?"

Mac reminded himself, again, he needed to learn from this mistake and never divulge more information than absolutely needed when delivering this type of news—gossip.

"I'm sorry. I'm not experienced at delivering death notices." Mac felt uncomfortable. "Is the boss in his office?"

"Yes."

"Will you let him know? You'll do a better job than me." Mac and the interim superintendent had settled into a mutual avoidance of each other. "Can I give you a hug?"

Marlene stood and allowed him to hug her. She took an extra second to whisper, "Thank you."

As Mac turned to walk away, Marlene asked, "Are you still going to work at the prom tomorrow night?"

"I wish I could say no, but I'll be there—with ear protection and as much tolerance as I can muster."

Chapter 12

Nico groaned when his alarm buzzed at five in the morning. He'd felt bad last night about Mac suffering alone at the Blackstone Academy Prom, so he'd stopped by to hang out for an hour and talk through some of his thoughts about the murders with Mac. He ended up staying longer than he'd planned. Although it had felt like being in a sea of teenage hormones and pubescent testosterone, he ended up staying for the entire event. When he'd gotten home, his ears rang, and he wasn't at all tired. Rather than trying to force sleep, he watched a late-night movie but now regretted his decision.

He knew he shouldn't have gone to the prom. Rae hadn't gone to the dance, which meant he'd had the night off. Rae had finally told Josslyn, her foster mother, who'd been excited to help Rae be the belle of the ball. There was no way she planned to attend.

In his rearview mirror, he saw the sun peeking over the mountain tops to wake the sleepy town of Brookfield. Twice in one week, Nico arrived at Red's Roadhouse for some much-needed coffee. He was there earlier than he'd been previously. The neon OPEN sign glowed in the window.

He recognized two trucks from when he'd stopped by before— it seemed the older men in this area all drove big trucks. He pulled out his notebook and jotted down the makes, models and license plate numbers of the vehicles. Nico pushed open the door, stepped into the darkness, and stood still for a moment to let his eyes adjust. The windows had a dark tint to them, making it darker inside during the daytime than at night.

Sure enough, the small cluster of gray-haired men sat at one end of the long, L-shaped bar, staring at him. Once his vision cleared and he took his first step, they all laughed at him. The one Nico remembered said, "Don't want to walk into a table again, eh?"

Nico laughed with them and replied with a smirk, "Damn straight. They're more solid than they look."

A man, in his late 30s or early 40s, sat in the middle of the bar, close to the bend. He hadn't joined in on the teasing, nor had he looked to see what was so funny. Nico saw the man's reflection in the big mirror running the length of the wall but didn't recognize him.

Rinda, the owner, walked out from the kitchen with plates of breakfast for the group of men. Her face lit up when she saw Nico. He noticed she had braided her hair—the braid went almost to her waist.

He went to the opposite end of the bar from the old guys. Having learned the first time he was there, the old guys pretended to be hard of hearing but had excellent hearing when they wanted to eavesdrop. Plus, from his years in the FBI, he preferred the seat with his back to a wall so he could see everyone and the door.

After Rinda dropped off the plates of food for the old guys, poured them more coffee, and checked on the single guy who hadn't looked up from the newspaper he appeared to be reading, she brought Nico a mug and filled it full of fresh hot coffee before saying, "Good morning. What got you up before the chickens? My excellent coffee? My jovial banter?"

"All of that and I'm making my rounds," he joked.

"Oh, I see. You hit all the bars in the morning?"

"No. I first stopped in at Trav's Donuts."

"So, you'll soon be a regular here. Is that what you're saying? And why do you look tired? Did you pull an all-nighter driving your client around?"

Rather than admit he'd gone to a high school prom to hang out with his friend, he asked, "Do you work every day and always ask so many questions?"

"Yes, and yes." She leaned back against the counter that also ran along the wall and crossed her feet. She had a towel tucked in the waistband of her jeans. Her legs were long and slender. "Do you work every day for the mysterious, important person who brought you to our small town?"

"I have weekends off unless my client needs my services. I'm available seven days a week, twenty-four hours a day, if a client needs me."

The guy at the center of the bar stood to leave. Red hustled to him and thanked him for stopping by and then whisked away his coffee mug.

She checked on the old guys and then returned to Nico. "Where were we?" She tapped her finger to her chin. "Oh yes, you were about to tell me who your important client is." She grinned, which made her eyes squint.

"I thought we were talking about our work schedules."

"True, we were. Learning more about your secret client sounds more interesting."

He made the motion of zipping his lips. "One reason I have to turn clients away is my strict confidentiality agreement." He shrugged his shoulders. "I provide service to one client at a time—I'm always available without a conflicting schedule." She waited for more information. "I might now and then squeeze in an airport shuttle from Sacramento."

"You won't even name-drop an important client from your past?" She put on a pleading facial expression to strengthen her ask.

Changing the subject, he asked, "How about you? Do you have regular customers besides the guys in the corner? Do regular customers show up every day?"

She turned to look at the small group. "They're all widowers. They come in every morning for coffee together. Sometimes they get into some rousing discussions about politics." She turned back to face Nico and dropped her voice a notch, "It's super sad when one of them stops coming in. You know what I mean?"

"I believe I do. But it happens to all of us."

"Aren't you, mister level-headed?"

"I try to be. So, any other regulars?"

"I work the day shift. I'd say 90 percent are regulars. The guy who left...." She pointed to the seat over from Nico. "He's new in town. Comes in for one cup of coffee, reads the newspaper, and then leaves. He doesn't say much."

"How do you know he isn't commuting to and from Lake Tahoe and needs a cup of coffee to wake up mid-route?"

"I read people. He gave me the new-in-town vibe."

"So, it's true you're a mind reader. What am I thinking?" He fixed his stare at her eyes. She did the same to him.

"You're thinking you would like some breakfast?"

"Close enough. I'll take whatever you think I'll like."

Before she walked away, she said, "What does the saying on your T-shirt mean?" She pointed to his chest.

He looked down like he didn't know what his shirt had written on it. "Win some, learn some. It's a saying this brand of jiu jitsu gear uses. In a nutshell, when you don't win, you learn from the loss."

She walked away to place his order, repeating, "Win some, learn some." When she returned, she asked, "Are you into jiu jitsu or like the T-shirt?"

"Both. I have a purple belt in Brazilian Jiu Jitsu and I love this brand."

"I've never heard of Brazilian Jiu Jitsu."

"Have you heard of any jiu jitsu?"

"No." She laughed. "I watched the movie, The Karate Kid. Does that count?"

"Not even close." He laughed. "I work out at a gym by the theater."

She nodded. "I don't get to the theater much."

"What do you do for fun?" he asked, but she had already turned and gone to the old guys to refill their mugs.

"Sorry, where were we? Oh yeah, what do I do for fun? I like to hike and read, although I haven't had time for either in a while. This place has taken up all my free time"

"What do you like to read?"

"Mysteries."

"I do too."

"You like to read mystery novels?"

"I do."

Before they could expand the conversation about books they'd read, she went into the kitchen for his breakfast. At that moment, Nico felt like he was the only patron in the bar.

She placed a wooden, handled, serving board in front of him with a sandwich on it that looked as big as a Frisbee. The mix of grilled, sourdough bread, fried egg, bacon strips, red peppers, and melted cheese overtook his sense of smell. "Wow! Now, that's a breakfast sandwich."

"It's my version of a Denver omelet in a sandwich." She grinned as he sunk his teeth into the masterpiece.

"Holy Mackerel," he said, as best he could without showing her a mouthful of food.

"I told you, that's what you wanted." She winked at him. "What else are you into besides reading novels?"

He swallowed and wiped his mouth with a napkin. Rather than answer her questions, he said, "I know we don't know each other, but I'll be honest with you."

Her face took on a serious focus. "Uh oh."

As Nico considered whether to bare his dark secret, he heard, "Red, more coffee, please." Nico looked at the cronies down the bar, who were all looking at him and the bar owner.

She pushed herself away from the counter and grabbed the coffeepot on her way to her loyal customers. When she returned, she filled his mug as well. "Sorry. You were about to tell me something juicy. I hope the window of opportunity didn't slam shut with the interruption."

"No problem. I'm sure you've heard this one before. I used to be an FBI field agent." He took a swig of coffee.

She said, "Nope, first time I've heard that one, and it doesn't seem too juicy."

"You said my secret was juicy, not me. I agreed to leave the job and get sober because I'd become an alcoholic."

When she didn't respond right away, he wondered if he'd blown the chance to get to know her better.

"I've heard the recovering alcoholic story before. I suspected that might be a possibility. If you aren't over seventy and meeting your posse at a bar for coffee in the morning, then there's a high probability you have had or have a drinking problem. People come here to confront their demons. Is that why you've been here twice in one week—to confront your demons?"

"No. I confronted my demon two years ago. As a side hustle, I work with my friend, Mac MacKenna, the marshal at Blackstone Academy, and the Brookfield Police on complex cases. I have an ulterior motive for coming to the bar, although I hadn't expected to be distracted by the attractive owner."

Her hand covered her heart. "Who me?" She batted her eyes.

The Posse, as Red called them, stirred, stood, then twisted and stretched their backs while the blood once again flowed to their legs. Then they gathered their belongings.

Nico noted the time—eight, forty-five.

"See you tomorrow, Red." They waved and then said to Nico, "Take it easy, young man." One man signaled the peace sign with two fingers, but then moved his fingers toward his eyes and back toward Nico, signaling he was watching him.

Nico smiled and nodded at the man. Red waved as she darted to the other end of the bar to clean up the area.

When she approached Nico again, she said, "Those guys are so sweet. They're all retired police officers or sheriff deputies."

"They are?" Nico turned to look at the closed door as if they were still standing there.

"I'm all ears. Why are you here?" Her tone had an edge to it he hadn't heard before.

"Did you hear or see on the news about someone killing the local, retired police officer?"

She leaned back against the counter and crossed her arms. He'd picked up on it being her comfortable resting spot while conversing with patrons—more than an arm's distance away from the drunks. "Yes, the guys said someone murdered him. It's been their main topic of discussion since it happened. The news said the killer is still at large."

His experience told him she was on-guard now, suspicious of his purpose. She no longer had a flirtatious air about her.

"I'm helping with the case. When I came in the other day, I wanted to talk with the bartender to see if he or she had heard any gossip about someone not from this area stopping by for a beer or," he raised his mug, "a coffee." He took another gulp, allowing her time to respond. She remained quiet.

"When I met you, I had a sudden attraction—sorry. I'm being honest. I thought if I held off on my questions, it would give me a reason to come back."

She squinted and appeared to be considering what to say next. And then she bent forward and slapped her thigh and laughed. "Damn. You scared me. I thought my past had caught up with me and my asshole of an ex-husband had sent you."

"You have an asshole ex-husband?"

"We've shared enough truths for one day. I'll save that for another time."

"Another time? As in, we'll see each other again?"

Her grin widened. "Well, yes, I assume you'll come back. I haven't told you what I heard about the murder. There's one new customer besides you on my shift. A guy who was here earlier. I know nothing about him, but if he comes back, I'll see if he'll open up and share some of his juicy secrets." She winked at him.

Nico stood up. "I've got to go get some sleep. I was up late at the Blackstone Academy Prom. My ears are still ringing."

"Prom? That's where you were last night? Not driving around your client?" she giggled.

"It's true, I went to the Prom last night." He also laughed. "Truthfully, I felt bad for my partner who had to be there, so I hung out with him and we talked business." He raised his hands to surrender. "I know, lame excuse."

"Your partner, as in….?"

"He's my business partner." He left her a generous tip and walked to the door. "Until next time."

Chapter 13

Mac parked his truck in the driveway of his childhood home where Maggie, his sister, and her two daughters, Bella and Lindy, lived. She had called him earlier in the week and scolded him for not stopping by in more than a week. She reminded him they live close to each other, which was her way of saying she wanted to see him more often, and then she'd asked him to have brunch with them on Sunday. He knew his sister expected him to say yes, so he did.

When Roxy saw the girls run outside to the front yard, she made whiny sounds from the backseat, did some high stepping in the small space and wagged her tail with great enthusiasm.

Mac stepped out of the truck and opened the back door. Roxy waited for him to help her down from the seat rather than allow her to jump and possibly injure her hips. Hip injuries plagued German Shepherds. As soon as her four paws hit the driveway, she took off to chase the girls around the yard while Mac retrieved the flowers he'd purchased for his sister that were in the front passenger seat.

When he turned away from the truck with the flowers in hand, he noticed a white panel van idling curbside a few houses down on the opposite side of the street.

The girls and Roxy were still running around the yard. Looking happy and relaxed, Maggie waited on the porch at the front door. "You brought me flowers? You must've felt super guilty about how long it's been since you last stopped by." She gave him a silly smile of triumph.

He went straight to her, gave her a squeezing hug, and handed her the flowers. "What's for brunch? I smell bacon." He rubbed his stomach. "I'm exhausted and starving."

She rattled off the menu while they watched the girls play with Roxy in the yard.

"What's up with the van?" He pointed to the panel van down the street.

Maggie looked and shrugged. "Must be delivering packages. It's been in the neighborhood off and on all week. Somebody's been on a shopping spree."

"It sucks to work on the weekend."

"You sound like a retired military man. I work weekends all the time." They laughed. Maggie, a nurse at Brookfield Memorial Hospital in the emergency room, worked a rotating shift with weekends off every so many weeks.

Mac enjoyed his new life as a civilian, with weekends and evenings spent doing whatever he wanted to do. The van still being parked down the street bothered him. He said to Maggie, "Seems like the van should've left by now."

They both faced toward the van.

Maggie shrugged, unconcerned, and called to the girls, "Come inside. It's time for brunch." She held open the screen door for everyone, Roxy included, then pushed the door closed, which made a loud screech. She twisted the deadbolt into place. After a big, scary guy, who'd worked for a drug dealer, had gone to their house, gave her youngest daughter, Bella, a threatening message telling her to warn her brother to back off or there would be consequences for Maggie and the girls, she'd become better about locking the door.

Mac hung back behind the girls and told his sister, "I'll lubricate your squeaky door after breakfast. Have you been using your security system?"

Looking at the girls, she said, "Wash your hands." Then she turned to her brother. "Yes, most of the time. Have you stayed out of the local drug lord's business?"

"I think I have. Things are settling down at the school. It's been much calmer with Kevin gone. Stu, Kevin's sidekick, hasn't gotten into any trouble that I'm aware of. You need to use the security system all the time." He looked down. "Is this rug new?"

"Yes. Aren't you the observant one?"

They passed by their parents' old, oak, dining room table with four place settings. Mac sat at the bar facing the kitchen. Maggie went to the stove to check on things and then poured her brother a mug of coffee.

"How's it going with 'the doctor' at work?" he asked.

She pulled a quiche from the oven and carried it to the dining room table. "Ehh, we ignore each other. How's it going with Monica?"

"We're good. She's busy working with the grandkids of the murdered officer."

Without facing him, Maggie replied, "Is the superintendent's murder related to—."

Lindy, with her soft voice, asked, "Someone killed somebody's grandfather?" At 11 years old, Lindy had already experienced a lot of death. She'd been four when Mac and Maggie's parents died and seven when someone killer her father, a sheriff deputy, in the line of duty.

Maggie turned. Mac did as well. Mac replied, "Are you sneaking up on me?" He hopped off the stool and chased her out the back door and into the yard. Roxy and Bella ran to the door. Roxy whimpered and then nudged the screen door open with her snout to join them outside. Bella followed.

The three returned after a few minutes. Mac had slung Lindy over his shoulder. "Special delivery," he said as he entered the kitchen.

"Wash up for real this time. Brunch is on the table."

Mac set Lindy down and followed her to the hall bathroom to do as they were told.

When the clatter of them serving themselves quieted, Mac asked Maggie, "When do you want to do a makeover in the hall bathroom?"

She chewed a mouthful of French toast and watched him the whole time. She swallowed and asked, "Is that your way of telling me the bathroom is outdated?"

"Mom's pink tub, sink, and tile were outdated twenty years ago."

Bella and Lindy giggled.

She countered, "Are you offering to help?"

"Sure. You've thought about it, haven't you?"

"To be honest, I haven't thought about it. I think of mom when I'm in there. But I bought some paint and wallpaper for my bedroom."

He mocked applause. "A good start. Next, give the girls a bathroom that makes them think of their mom."

Maggie turned her attention to the girls. They both bobbed their heads in agreement.

"The next time I have a weekend off, we can start. I'll look online for design ideas."

"It's a date." He held up his coffee mug.

After they'd eaten too much, and talked about school with the girls, Mac said, "This brunch has been delicious, thank you. I couldn't think of a better way to start my day." He helped carry dishes to the sink and offered to help clean up. Maggie shooed him away.

He sat again at the kitchen bar and watched his sister buzzing around, cleaning up their dirty dishes and wrapping left overs. "What's the last day of school for the girls?"

"May 16th. What about Blackstone?"

"Same. Will the girls hang out at the Donaldson's ranch when you're at work?"

"Yes. I'm not comfortable with them staying home alone."

"I can help. Take them to see a movie or something."

She looked at her brother with adoration. "Ahh, you're sweet. They'd love it if you took them to a movie." She dried her hands on a dish towel, folded it and hung it on the oven handle. "Where to next?" his sister asked him.

"Mow the lawn, laundry, boring stuff, put in a few hours at the PD combing through old case files from when the murdered officer had been active, and then jiu jitsu tonight. Where's your lubricant spray for the door hinges?"

"Garage."

* * *

That evening, Monica arrived at the gym in her civilian clothes.

Paired by gender and rank, men and women practiced the jiu jitsu techniques Mac had demonstrated at the beginning of class. She knew the drill—during the first five to ten minutes of his class, Mac explained what specific holds they'd be working on.

Mac caught her movement in his peripheral vision and headed toward her, giving praise to the mat rats along the way.

He reached out for her hand. "Hey babe. How'd your shift go?"

She waved at Nico, then said, "I'm happy to report the murders appear to have stopped." She looked at her watch. "Class is running late tonight." She placed her hand on her stomach and, with exaggeration, mouthed, "I'm starving."

Mac needed no further prompting. He thanked everyone for showing up and then, as they detached themselves from each other to stand, he added, "I'm sure you've all heard about the retired officer we lost this week. Keep your eyes and ears open to anything unusual, even if it seems like nothing—report all tips to the police and let them sort out the relevance. Stay safe. See you next Sunday."

Mac, Monica, and Nico walked the three blocks to the Main Street Pub for dinner. When they turned to go down Pike's Alley, they saw Mr. Culver, the owner of Trav's Donut Shop, going inside the back door of the business.

Monica looked at her watch, and said to the guys, "It's kinda late for him to be here."

By the time they were passing his car parked at the curb with the trunk open, he'd walked back outside with his arms full of stuff. Nico grabbed the screen door and held it open for him.

Mac asked, "Mr. Culver. Do you need some help?"

The older man responded without stopping, saying over his shoulder, "No, thanks. I have one more load. Then I have no more room." He tossed his armful of things into the trunk.

Mac, Monica, and Nico gathered around the rear of the car. To Mac, it looked like the trunk had open donut boxes of documents. "Moving out?"

"Yes." He slammed the trunk shut and dug in his pocket for keys to lock the back door.

Nico asked, "Did you sell the place"

Mr. Culver grinned. "We did. An all-cash offer."

"Please tell me the coffee side of the business will continue," Monica asked, which sounded more like pleading. She thought about getting down on her knees. In her opinion, Trav's Donuts had the best coffee in town and it was a short walk from the police station. She could phone in her order and it was ready when she got there.

"That's the plan—the whole thing, donuts and coffee, but you never know. Buyers can be liars—say whatever they think you want to hear, so you'll give them a good deal on the property." He held up his hands. "Quoting my realtor."

Nico held open the screen door for him to secure the business.

"Thank you." Mr. Culver said, "I left all of my recipes for the new owner. I hope they'll keep the business going." He shook each of their hands, hopped into his car, and drove off.

"Is it me, or did he seem on cloud nine?" Monica asked.

They all laughed.

Mac added, "Retirement does that to you. Your last day is the happiest."

Arriving at the Pub, they settled into their seats at a table. Mac and Monica ordered a beer, Nico an iced tea.

After their server walked away, Monica inquired, "Ice tea? No coffee?" Looking at Nico. "You always have coffee."

"I'm still hot from class and I've had plenty of coffee today."

Mac grinned. "He met a lady at a bar this morning for coffee."

"Not quite how it went," Nico clarified. He'd spoken with Rinda at the Roadhouse, and the old guys she called the Posse.

They shared a platter of barbecued chicken wings and a large basket of garlic fries while they discussed the specifics of the two murders that dominated their thoughts.

Nico nodded as he licked the sauce from his fingers. "Mmm. Good stuff."

Mac said to Monica, "Have they figured out a connection between the officer and Ann?"

"No. I checked in before I went to the gym. They're still busy going through Stockford's old case files. Much of it is still in paper form. There's a lot." Monica took the last swig of her beer.

Mac said to Nico, "We need to start a murder board for Ann, and run the two boards side-by-side." He took a breath. "My air force buddy, Luke, will be here tomorrow. We have a meeting with the school board president, Michael Stromberg, to discuss my leave of absence. Then I'll be free to spend more hours on the investigation."

Nico held up his empty glass for their server to get the cue he wanted more tea. "You sound certain the school board will approve your leave, and Luke will step in."

"My commitment to Chief Contee and the school board was for one school year. The last day of school is in nineteen days, with one more school board meeting requiring security. I've been honest about not wanting to renew my contract. I have other interests I'd like to pursue." He clinked his beer bottle with Nico's ice tea glass. "Luke hopes it turns into a continued gig for the next school year. I have high-hopes it all works out and tomorrow will be a good day."

Chapter 14

Maggie had looked forward to her day off for the last week. She'd been feeling down and longed for adult companionship besides her work friends and her brother. The last relationship hadn't gone so well. Glad she found out he was a jerk before their relationship had progressed, she felt more apprehensive about dating than she had before her failed attempt. She hoped a bedroom makeover would bring her out of her funk.

When she planned her day off, she saw herself sipping wine, listening to some of Bobby's favorite records while she painted.

In reality, she had a sweaty water bottle sitting on her nightstand instead of wine, opting for a sober paint job. She had three glorious hours before the school bus dropped off the girls. The windows were the aluminum-framed type, the single-paned ones that sweat in the winter and radiated heat to the inside during the summer. She couldn't remember the last time she'd opened the window over her bed.

Standing on the bed, she tried to open it. Her legs quivered from the springy mattress, or maybe from her lack of exercise. She told herself when she finished her bedroom make-over, she'd start working out. The window had bound up about halfway. She jiggled it back and forth, up and down to level it out and then pushed it open.

She sat on her bed and looked around the room. An outdated, hollow wood door with a splotchy, brass doorknob, with most of the brass finish worn off—the affordable option for whoever had built the home. Remembering the large baseboard, she'd seen in a home decorating magazine she'd bought at the market, she evaluated the tiny baseboard surrounding the room. She knew the old carpet had to go. It also looked like 1980s, builder-grade carpet, which wasn't meant to last. Several shades of variegated brown spanned the room. Thinking about the need for updated windows to make opening a window less frustrating and the house more efficient, a new door, baseboards and carpet made her want to cry. Looking at the ceiling, she said out loud, "Bobby, I miss you."

After she sat on the bed for several minutes feeling paralyzed by how much needed to be done to the whole house she stood up, pulled her ratty, old T-shirt down to straighten it and said to herself, "Music, I need music." Moving to the living room, she turned on her father's old record player. The record player was as old as her house. That thought made her giggle. It had been a while since she'd used it. She sat on the floor to better see the album covers stacked like books on a lower shelf and found one of Bobby's favorites. With the greatest care, she raised the plastic lid and made sure the brace that held it up still functioned. Then, with steady hands, she placed the album on the turntable, lined up the needle on the outer groove on the vinyl, lowered it, and stepped back. The sound brought immediate tears to her eyes. For a moment she stood in the living room, remembering the last time she and Bobby had played that album. The music had to be loud so she could hear it in her bedroom. She sashayed her way down the hall, clapping with the rhythm of the music.

Her pity party had come and gone. She felt happy listening to the music. After she'd moved everything in the bedroom to the center of the room and piled some things on her bed, she was ready to prepare a wall for wallpaper. Soon, stray hairs had escaped her ponytail and were stuck to the sweat on her face—it was going to be a hot day in the small room. Placing the masking tape on the windowsill, she pulled her hair back and re-did her ponytail to be tighter. Next, she covered everything in plastic sheeting and laid out all the tools before she remembered she needed the ladder from the garage. As she went down the hall, singing with the tunes, she glanced out the large, picture window in the living room before turning toward the kitchen and noticed another white, delivery van with some type of logo on the driver's door whiz down the street. She'd seen more delivery vans going up and down the street in the last week than ever before. She felt a twinge of jealousy because she assumed someone in the neighborhood was redecorating their home. With the security system turned off, she went into the garage.

As she carried the ladder through the living room, she noticed it was almost one o'clock. She thought, at the pace she was going, she'd never be done with the wallpaper before the girls arrived home from school.

After she'd hung the first strip of wallpaper, she put down the large, soft sponge and squeegee she'd used to smooth out the air bubbles, and stepped back to admire her handy work—the soft swirls in a faded, copper colored background looked as lovely as she'd hoped. When she picked up another strip to hang, the doorbell rang.

Wiping her hands on a paper towel, as she neared the front door, she glanced out the picture window and saw a delivery van had backed into her driveway and the back door was open. She turned the doorknob, and said, "I think you have the wrong—"

She fell backward with a thud. The jolt of electricity felt worse than the time she'd grabbed hold of an electric fence when she and Mac were children feeding carrots to the nearby cows in a pasture.

The man, dressed like a delivery driver, stepped into her home and shut the door behind him. He looked down at her, smiled and then tipped his ball-cap and yelled over the music, "Nice to meet you, Maggie."

She looked up at him. Every muscle in her body felt rigid. Adrenaline surged through her, mixed with fear. As the electrical current ping-ponged through her body, she thought Mac was going to kill her for opening the door to a stranger.

The man pounced on her, straddling her hips. Images of rape victims on the gurneys in the emergency room cubicles flashed in her mind. He pulled out a syringe from his chest pocket.

Her brain screamed, "No, no, no," but her mouth didn't cooperate. She tried to shake her head—nothing happened. Then she felt the prick to her skin. A sudden wash of limpness overcame her stiffness. "Wha arrr you doin?"

As he bent over to grab her feet, he laughed. "Sounds like you've been drinking, Maggie."

He pulled her across the floor a few feet to the new rug. Placing her at one end, he then rolled the rug with her inside. Her head swirled. The added sensation of being rolled made her want to vomit. She felt him lift her and swing her over his shoulder. It was dark inside the rug. She heard the front door open and close—her mind went to what her brother had said about lubricating the hinges. She could tell by the ting sound the door had made, it hadn't closed all the way. Her body clonked onto the hard surface when he'd tossed her into the van. Next, she heard the metallic sound of what she imagined had been the back door on the van closing. Wiggling her arm, she made little progress in trying to free them from her sides to escape. The van motor started, and then she felt the familiar bump at the end of her driveway.

She heard the man laugh, and then say, "This is going to be fun. Do you like jokes, Maggie? Which came first, the chicken or the egg? Haha, that's an old one. Here's one you haven't heard before, which came first, Maggie's savior or Maggie's death?"

Chapter 15

On the other side of Brookfield, at Blackstone Academy, Mac sat in his office reading each of the slips of paper he'd removed from the BAT boxes located around the campus. His meticulous method of logging every comment into a spreadsheet, noting which BAT box they'd came from, had tightened after what had happened to Theyn Seder before spring break.

He alternated his attention between his spreadsheet and the video screens mounted on the wall, which rotated the view from camera to camera located inside and around the campus. A glance at the clock told him Luke would arrive soon, as would Michael Stromberg. They had an appointment to meet at one o'clock.

Mac read a note from a teacher named Kelly. He didn't recall meeting anyone on staff with the name Kelly. Most of the time, the notes were anonymous. She'd written, "Can we please hang some bird feeders outside my classroom?" Searching his memory, he couldn't place Kelly or picture what she looked like. After he typed her name into the database to refresh his memory, he saw a photograph of a pretty woman with long auburn hair pop onto his computer screen. He read to himself, "Married, four children." When he looked at the security monitors on the wall, he saw Luke nearing the front entrance. He pressed the intercom for Marlene.

"Yes, Mac?"

"Luke is approaching the door."

"I'll let him inside."

He grabbed his walkie-talkie, holstered his pistol, and scooped up his cell phone on his way out the door of his office.

Luke stood near Marlene's desk when Mac rounded the corner to her office area. Luke had a nervous grin on his face, sticking his hand out to Mac as they met in the middle distance between them.

"Hey, brother, how're you doing?" Mac asked as they hugged.

"Can't complain." Luke stepped back. "Beautiful school."

Marlene cleared her throat.

Mac looked at her. "Did you meet Marlene?" He pointed in her direction.

Marlene stood and smoothed her dress. She smiled.

Luke approached Marlene with his hand extended.

As she swatted his hand away, she said, "I'm a hugger." The two strangers hugged.

Marlene said to Mac, "You didn't tell me Luke was a handsome bodybuilder." She turned to face Luke again. "Do you bench press school buses?" She giggled like a schoolgirl.

Mac cleared his throat. "Anyway, Marlene is your go-to gal. She knows everything about the school, the staff, and the students. She's been here since the day it opened."

Beaming with pride, she added, "The founder, Henry Blackstone, hired me."

Luke asked, "Is he still involved with the school?"

"Oh, no, sweetie, he passed away a few years ago." She popped her chewing gum. One of her nervous traits—Mac had learned.

Mac nudged Luke. "I'll show you the Security Office." Mac had already shifted from the possessive tense for the office, and no longer considered it his office.

They walked side-by-side down the hallway a short distance to the Security Office. Mac unlocked the door with his ID badge.

"That's slick." Luke pointed to the lock. "Is everything linked to your badge?"

"Yes, you'll have full access to every nook and cranny." Mac opened the door and the blast of light from the wall of monitors greeted them. He flicked on the light. "You almost don't need the lights on in here." He grinned.

Luke sat across from Mac's desk. "The security system is impressive," he said.

Mac replied, "One of the best in the country. I was told Mr. Blackstone had priorities—the safety of everyone inside, well cared for facilities, and manicured grounds."

Luke pulled his cell phone from his pocket and placed it on the desk. "They sound like good priorities."

"They're great priorities. Yet, we still have our share of students and staff members doing bad things, much like the rest of the country." He knocked on the desktop. "Knock on wood. Blackstone has never had a shooting during school hours."

"Are you saying you've had a shooting after hours?" Luke inquired.

Mac looked up from tidying the desk, then resumed his busy work. "Yes. During a board meeting, which you'll be required to work. They hold their meetings once a month, but certain situations can require the school board to meet more often. Almost always at night." Mac looked at Luke again. "Are you cool with that? You get paid overtime or can accrue time and half compensation leave if you'd, rather."

He shrugged. "I've got nothing else going on."

Mac continued, "You'll need to stay alert. When you get a bad feeling in your gut, go with it. Don't let the students or the adults fool you." He stood. "Ready?"

"Let's do this."

Luke had his hand on the doorknob. "I appreciate you recommending me to replace you."

"You're topnotch. I'm pleased you accepted."

"Thanks for recommending me." Luke twisted the knob and stepped into the corridor. Mac led the way to Dr. Zita's office.

They seemed similar and different. Luke was several inches shorter than Mac. Mac had a full head of hair. Luke shaved his head bald. Mac worked at maintaining a tough-guy attitude. Luke was a natural—he oozed badass without saying a word.

Marlene smiled at them both.

"Michael isn't here yet. You can wait inside or have a seat in my naughty student seats." She pointed to the five chairs against a nearby wall.

Mac said, "We'll wait here." He sat in a naughty seat. Luke also sat, leaving an empty seat between them.

With her chin resting on her palm, Marlene grinned. "Tell me about yourself, Luke. Are you married?"

Mac laughed. "Watch out, Mother Marlene will try to find you a soul-mate."

"I'm divorced."

Marlene's grin faded to a more serious expression. "I'm sorry about the divorce. Do you have children?"

"No kids. Didn't have time to get around to that. It was a good thing the marriage didn't last long enough. She wasn't the type of woman who could handle my deployments, I learned after we married. She also didn't have the right temperament to be a mother. In the end, I learned she wasn't wife material. A bit lost. She didn't know what she wanted out of life."

Marlene noticed movement on her entrance monitor. "Michael's here." She pushed the button to open the sliding door.

Michael strode into Marlene's office with a whoosh.

"You're in a hurry," Marlene said.

"It's calving season at the ranch. Lots going on."

Mac and Luke stood up as Michael entered the building. After explaining his delay to Marlene, Michael had gone straight to Mac, who then introduced Luke. They shook hands and then followed Michael into Dr. Zita's office.

Dr. Zita stood when the threesome entered his office as if he hadn't heard them in Marlene's area. Michael had a booming voice. It would be hard to not hear him. He motioned to his meeting table. "Please have a seat."

Michael started the conversation. "Mac, is there any way we can talk you into staying?" Michael knew Mac had committed to one school year.

Dodging the actual question, Mac patted Luke on his back and said, "Luke is going to surpass your expectations, and he likes kids."

Luke smiled.

Dr. Zita sat with his hands on the table, more focused on picking at his cuticle than on the conversation. He and Mac both knew he had no say in the matter. Dr. Zita was not the one who would decide something as important as the next school marshal. Michael, the school board president, ran the show.

Michael said, "I have a few questions for you, Luke."

"I'm ready."

He proceeded to rapid-fire questions at Luke. "Married?"

"Divorced."

"Kids?"

"No."

"Significant other?"

"No."

"Arrests?"

"None."

"Smoker?"

"An occasional cigar with Mac." He smiled. Michael didn't smile back.

"Drinker?"

"On special occasions."

"Star Trek or Star Wars?"

Luke hesitated, then answered, "Star Wars."

"Pets?"

"None."

Mac wondered if Michael had had a problem with Roxy and didn't like it when he'd brought her to the school with him.

"College?"

"Bachelor of Science in Criminology."

Michael nodded his approval.

"Short-term plans?"

"Get a place in Brookfield."

"Long-term plans?"

"Stick around."

"Where's your family?"

"Parents live in Oregon. Three brothers, one is also in Oregon, one is in San Diego, and one is deceased. I'm the oldest."

"Four boys? Your parents had their hands full."

"Yes, sir, they did indeed."

"Call me Michael. Do you like sports?"

"Football, baseball, and MMA."

"Are you into jiu jitsu like Mac?" Michael glanced at Mac, then back to Luke.

"No, sir. Bodybuilding."

Michael nodded again, as if to say bodybuilding was obvious. "Will you expect to carry a weapon on campus?"

"Yes, sir. From what I've heard, it seems necessary."

"You have a college degree. You have a military background. Why aren't you working?"

"I spent a lot of time over the last year with my parents. My youngest brother had a drug problem. In and out of rehab. They more than had their hands full trying to help him. He drained their bank account and their emotions. Rehab was tough on all of us."

"Will you need to continue to spend a lot of time with them?"

"No, sir. The drugs won. He died in February."

Michael relaxed his shoulders. "I'm sorry for your loss. Please call me, Michael."

"What work did you do after you got out of the Air Force?"

"I did research for a law firm."

"You didn't care for the work?"

"The work was fine. The confinement to an office wasn't."

"When can you start?"

Mac's phone vibrated in his pocket. He looked at it and saw it was his niece, Lindy, calling. "I need to take this." Mac waved his phone and left the room.

After closing the door behind him, he stood in Marlene's office to take the call. "Hi Lindy, what's up?" He could hear loud music playing in the background.

"We got home from school and mom isn't here. She said she'd be here—it's her day off. We found the front door open. Her purse is here, her keys are too, and the van is in the garage."

"I'm on my way."

Chapter 16

Mac did more than a few rolling stops and tromped on the throttle at yellow traffic lights to get to his sister, Maggie's house, as fast as he could. He sped down the familiar street from his childhood. The neighborhood had no activity, everyone was gone or inside. Most of the neighbors were older, their children grown and gone, like Mac.

Lindy and Bella ran outside as soon as his truck screeched to a stop in the driveway. He opened the door, both girls lunged for him. Both crying and frightened.

"Uncle Mac, where is she?" Lindy whimpered.

He scooted them a step away from the truck so he could shut the door. "I want to go inside and look around." The girls clung to Mac's sides as the three of them walked toward the front door.

Lindy reached for the doorknob.

"Stop," Mac blurted out.

He used his T-shirt to turn the knob.

Lindy cried harder at the realization she might've messed up any fingerprints. "I didn't know. I opened the door with my hand and did the same on the inside when we came outside to meet you."

Mac stepped inside and bent down to one knee. "Lindy, sweetheart. You have done nothing wrong. I didn't want to add my prints to yours."

Bella, the more talkative one of the two sisters, had said nothing since he'd arrived.

Staying on bended knee, he turned to Bella and pulled her into a hug. "Are you okay?"

"No. I'm scared." Her words sounded like a whispered secret. "Where's mom?"

Mac stood up. "We're going to figure it out. Maybe she's on a long walk." He looked around the tidy room. "Where's the new rug?"

Lindy and Bella in unison looked at their feet and then at each other. They both shrugged.

Mac noticed one of Maggie's sneakers behind the door. He pointed to the shoe. "Where's mom's other shoe?"

Lindy said, "It was outside on the lawn, so I brought it inside." Her mind processed what she'd said and understood she'd made another blunder. She wept.

Mac patted her back. He took Bella's and Lindy's hands and walked them to the sofa. "You two sit here while I look around. I'll be right back. I'm going to get something from my truck."

They hopped onto the sofa and clung to each other. It took a frightening event to bring an eight-year-old and a ten-year-old to console each other. On a normal day, one tattled on the other and made snide remarks.

Mac returned wearing latex gloves. He saw Maggie's purse hanging from a dining room chair. Placing the purse on the table, he rummaged through it. It looked in order and untouched. Maggie's phone was on the kitchen bar. He tapped the phone, which brought up a pass-code box. "Hey girls, do you know your mom's pass-code to her phone?"

Again, in unison, they said, "No."

Mac thought, knowing his sister, he thought she'd use Bobby's birth date. Looking around the kitchen, everything seemed to be in its place. He tapped the numbers zero-eight-zero-eight and her phone opened to a screenshot of Bella and Lindy in their Halloween costumes about three years ago.

He scrolled through her texts, but found nothing unusual. His finger hovered over her email program. For a moment he thought about his own emails and who he'd exchanged emails with, wondering if he'd feel someone crossed the line to read his private communications. He tapped the icon and her email box opened.

As his finger swiped upward, business emails scrolled by. Clothing stores. Book outlets. Gift stores. News networks. Do It Yourself newsletters. Vacation rentals.

He opened the phone's address section and pressed Thomas Donaldson's phone number.

He heard Bobby's dad's voice, "Hi, Maggie. How're you?"

Turning toward the backyard, he said over his shoulder, "Girls, I'll be in the backyard for a minute. Stay where you are." There was no response, but also no movement.

"Hang on a minute, please," he said into his phone. The sliding door had a gravelly sound to it as he pushed it open and then pulled it closed. He made a mental note to replace the rollers on the door. "Hi, Mr. Donaldson."

"Mac, you need to call me Thomas. Why are you calling me on Maggie's phone? Has something happened?"

"Thank you, sir. I'm at Maggie's house with the girls. They called me concerned because Maggie wasn't here when they arrived home from school."

"Oh, that's not typical for her at all."

He stood on the grass in the middle of the backyard looking at trees that needed to be trimmed. He felt like he'd let Maggie's home slip away. When they found Maggie, he'd do an inventory of needed repairs.

"No, sir. It's far from normal. Her van, purse and cell phone are here. The girls found the front door ajar, and music blaring. Would it be okay if I bring the girls out to you so I can find Maggie without upsetting them further?" He spun around to face the house and saw his nieces standing, holding hands, staring out at him.

"Of course. They can stay here as long as it takes, but you must keep me updated and let me know if I can be of any help. I still have friends at the sheriff's office. After you find Maggie, I'd like to know more about what's happening with Bruce Stockford."

"I'll fill you in when I can. We'll leave as soon as the girls grab what they'll need."

The two men disconnected the call. Mac slid the grinding glass door open and shut again, stepping into the dining room. "Girls, get some stuff packed. You're going to stay out at Grandma and Grandpa's until I can find your mom."

The girls turned toward him with red-faces and tears in their eyes.

Lindy said with a shaky voice, "Where could mom be?"

"I'm going to find out where she is."

Lindy again spoke up. "She wouldn't leave without her cell phone."

Bella asked, "Did the scary man with tattoos who came here come back and take mommy?" She burst into tears and gulped breaths. She remembered the time she had answered the door and a big guy with tattoos gave her an envelope to give to her mother.

Mac pulled both girls into a big hug. "I'm going to find your mom. The big scary man with tattoos did not take your mom. He couldn't have. He's in jail. Go put some stuff in an overnight bag so we can get out to the ranch."

* * *

Mac, Lindy and Bella headed east, out of town, to the Donaldson's ranch. Growing up, Mac spent more time at Bobby's house than he had at his own. Back then, Mac had felt Bobby's parents were normal compared to his. Bobby didn't have an alcoholic father who made home a miserable place to be.

Lindy and Bella sat next to each other in the backseat of Mac's truck.

"How was school today?" he asked, hoping to get their minds off their mother.

Bella looked at him and shrugged. "Okay."

He looked at Lindy. Without looking back at him, she also shrugged. He could see Bobby in Bella's features, and Lindy looked more like Maggie—they had many similar characteristics and mannerisms.

"How about we stop and take a box of cinnamon rolls to your grandparents? I'll call ahead so they have them ready when we get there." Hearing no response, he dialed the number and placed an order for a baker's dozen.

Mac turned off the highway and parked in front of Handley's Coffee Shop. The owner's daughter, Sam, thundered out the front door with a familiar pink box in her hands. Mac passed her two twenties. "Keep the change." He plopped the box onto Bella's lap.

The stop had taken a minute at most to grab the treats. He understood every minute counted in an abduction case. Appearing normal to the girls was also important. As well as keeping them as far away as possible from whatever happened to their mom.

Mac's truck left a swirl of road dust behind them as they barreled down the Donaldson's driveway. "Don't open the doors until the dust settles," Mac said as he brought the truck to a stop.

Thomas and Patti Donaldson stood on the front porch waiting for their grandchildren to get out of the truck. They'd had one child, Bobby. Bobby's children were their last connection to their son, and they adored the girls.

Bella handed the pink box to Mac, then the girls scooted out of the truck and ran to their grandparents. Lindy went to grandpa, Bella to grandma. As soon as they were in their comforting embrace, they cried. After a few moments of hugging her granddaughter, Patti Donaldson took the box from Bella, placing it on a small table.

Bella, the most boisterous of the two, said, "Somebody took mommy."

Hearing Bella as he neared the porch, Mac said, "Bella, we don't know. Mommy might have gone for a walk and fell. She might have hurt herself."

Lindy turned and gave her uncle a stern look. "Mom wouldn't go for a walk without her cell phone."

"Maybe she saw somebody fall in front of the house. Your mom, being a nurse, would run outside to help them and she may have gone to the hospital with them."

Lindy's look showed her mind considered this probable scenario.

"Wherever she is, I'll find her." Mac looked around the porch. "Where's Pepper? You don't want to leave Handley's treats within her reach."

Lindy snapped at him again, "She's in dog heaven."

Patti knelt on the wooden planks to look at Bella from the little girl's height. "Grandpa and I were talking about getting a new puppy. Would you girls like to help us pick out a puppy tomorrow at the animal shelter?"

Bella jumped up a few times. "Yes. I want to go help."

Lindy asked, "What about school?"

Thomas answered his granddaughter, "We know you girls are worried about your mom. Until Mac locates her, you can miss a day of school. The principal will understand."

Bella said, "I don't want to miss school. We're having a test tomorrow."

Lindy concurred, "Same for me. It's almost the end of the year. There's a lot happening."

Mac shrugged, and broke the awkward silence, asked the girls' grandmother, "Do you still have Rhubarb the donkey?"

"Heavens, yes," Patti answered. "I think Rhubarb will outlive us. She's too stubborn to go to donkey heaven." She turned to her husband. "We're going out back to visit Rhubarb." She turned the girls away and led them off the porch.

Thomas looked at Mac and gave a hand gesture to call him. Mac nodded.

"Hey girls," he called out to them, "the next time you see me, I'll know more about your mom, I promise." He hoped his promise wouldn't be a lie.

Lindy turned around, eyes glaring. "You can't promise that." Her words came out angry. Tears spilled over and ran down her cheeks.

He went to her, and pulled her into a hug. Lifting her chin so she could see his face, he repeated, "I'll be back soon. That, I can promise."

Lindy nodded, then headed for the side of the house.

Bella followed her sister, but then turned and ran to Mac for one last hug. She whispered, "I know you'll find mommy."

Once he couldn't see them, he ran to his truck, turned it around and left the Donaldsons. He dialed Nico, whose phone rang twice before he answered. "Hey, are you coming to the station?"

"No. I need your help. I think someone abducted Maggie."

"What the hell? What can I do?"

"Can I pick you up so we can go to her house and figure out a game plan? You know more about this than I do, and my heart has made my thoughts jumbled."

"I'll be waiting outside."

"Thank you. Let Marten know what I suspect about Maggie and that we'll be in touch."

* * *

Mac pulled the truck into the space marked 'No Parking' in front of the Brookfield Police Station long enough for Nico to hop inside.

Nico buckled his seatbelt, then opened the notepad he'd brought with him and clicked the ballpoint pen. "Tell me everything."

Mac ran down the list of what Lindy had told him and his cursory observations. "I didn't want to look around much because the girls were already upset enough. Lindy's old enough and smart. She knows the situation looks bad."

A few minutes later, they parked in Maggie's driveway. Mac held his breath a quick second in hopes she'd walk outside. When she didn't, he let himself inside. Mac turned the key to open the door. He looked at Nico and shared, "Lindy said the front door had been ajar when they got home. Maggie would never leave the front door unlocked and ajar."

Even though the clock showed five o'clock in the evening, the sun still provided a few more hours of daylight, thanks to daylight savings.

Nico sniffed. "Has she been painting?"

"Yes, her bedroom and hanging wallpaper."

"Let's start there."

Mac led Nico down the hall to Maggie's bedroom. The window was open, and Maggie had pushed everything to the center of the room. It looked different from what Mac remembered. In a flash, he thought of his parents in their bedroom and all the whispered conversations he'd had with his mother in there.

Nico interrupted Mac's thoughts, "Looks like she'd hung some wallpaper before being interrupted. There's a piece of wallpaper ready to go up but had dried out. Can you tell if anything looks missing?"

"Not with this mess."

"We'll assume someone either knocked on the door or rang the bell and interrupted her project."

Mac had a flash in his memory. "Wait, when Lindy called me, loud music played in the background, Maggie had had it cranked up. Lindy must've turned it off before I arrived."

"Then it had to have been a doorbell ring." Nico pulled his cell phone from his pocket. "I'll call Marten to ask for someone to come here and see if they can lift a fingerprint from the button."

Mac went to the record player. He looked at it for a second before he lifted the lid to get a better look at what Maggie had been playing. He would've guessed she'd play one of Bobby's favorites.

Nico said, "Marten is sending someone and said we should call if we think this is an abduction."

"What options do you think there are other than an abduction? Her purse and cell phone are here, her minivan is here, she was in the middle of wallpapering, and the girls would be home from school soon?"

Looking around the living room, Nico replied, "You're right, it looks like an abduction. But do you want a bunch of officers here processing the place before we're done?"

"No, I guess I don't."

"You say 'when' and I'll call Marten back." Nico shoved his cell phone back into his pocket. "With the shooting of two prominent people, I think they have so many officers assigned to the murders, we may get rookies."

Mac closed the record player's lid. "Okay, moving on. You make an excellent point about having rookies assigned to help us. Keep going."

"Are you comfortable working on our own until we feel like we've hit a brick wall?"

"Yes."

"Stand for a second and you look around the room. Does anything look off?"

Mac panned the room. "She had a new rug when you walked inside through the front door. It was here yesterday when I came for brunch. I asked the girls where it was and they didn't know."

Nico opened his notebook. "Describe it."

"Damn it. I didn't pay close attention to it. I think flowery and big." He went to where it had been and stretched his arms out. "It was this big by..." He had to walk the space for the longer side dimension.

When Nico looked up, Mac's instincts knew what he thought. "You think someone rolled her up inside the rug, don't you?"

"It's a strong possibility."

"Why would someone do this? Maggie has hurt no one. She doesn't make people angry. She's kind. She's an emergency room nurse. She saves people and..." Mac's voice trailed off.

"It's the worst-case scenario and if the clues lead us in a different direction, it'll be a good thing. If someone abducted her and rolled her up inside the rug—that someone had to have been strong enough to carry her somewhere, or he had an accomplice."

Mac squared his shoulders and his demeanor changed to what the air force had trained him for. Rescue and recovery. "That's a good point—let's go find her."

The two men walked out the front door, locking it for now. They looked up and down the street, Mac remembering it as if he were a child again. He and Maggie riding bicycles, unconcerned about traffic, until the streetlights came on and they had to go inside for dinner.

"Does anything look weird?"

"No. A weird thing, though." He kicked a few small stones off the walkway. "May be unrelated. Yesterday, there was a white, delivery type van parked down the street."

"Did the van have a name on it?"

"No, no markings of any kind that I saw. Weird, right?"

"Sometimes delivery companies rent vans when they've run out of vehicles or one is down for repairs. They don't always have stickers on the doors with the company logo." Nico made note of the van's presence. "I want to look at the neighbors' porch areas to see if anyone has a security camera."

Mac started down the walkway to the driveway. "When I was a kid, an old woman lived there. Mrs. Dearny." He pointed to a house across the street and down a few houses. "She was a human security camera. Not much got past her. She was nosy and sat on her porch all the time. In my memory, if you looked at her house, there she sat, staring at you—day or night. I wish she still lived there, guaranteed she'd know something."

"Every older neighborhood has a Mrs. Dearny," Nico added. "Let's see who lives there now."

As they walked across the street, Mac recalled, "One time, my dad and I were getting into it in the open garage. He, of course, had been hitting the bottle. He freaked out, I think because he thought about me being alone in the garage, and feared I'd find his stash. In the heat of the moment, I noticed Mrs. Dearny and her dog. She glared at us while we screamed at each other. It was the one time I remember her voice sounded kind and concerned when she'd asked me if everything was okay."

"Old people can be grumpy—but most have a kind heart." Nico rang the neighbor's doorbell.

They waited several seconds. As Nico's finger wavered over the doorbell button for a second press, the door opened. A woman in her mid-30s looked at them.

"Hello."

Both guys said, "Hello."

Mac started. "I'm Mac." He stretched out his hand. Noticing her hesitancy, he pointed at Maggie's house and continued, "My sister, Maggie, and my nieces live across the street."

She shook his hand. "Oh, yes, I've met Maggie. Lindy and Bella are so sweet. What can I do for you?"

He jabbed his thumb at Nico and said, "Nico and I work as consultants with the Brookfield Police. Did you notice a white van parked on the street yesterday or earlier today?"

She stretched out her neck, looking both directions on the street. "No. Well, yes, I saw a white van, but not parked on the street. The driver had backed into Maggie's driveway." Her cheeks reddened. "I'm embarrassed to admit I wondered what she had purchased, so I watched."

"Did you see the driver?"

"Yes."

Nico prepared to write what she said, but then spoke up, "Was the driver a male or a female?" Not waiting for an answer, he added, "Was he alone?"

"A male. I think he was alone, but I can't be certain."

She asked, "What's going on? Did something happen?" Her posture stiffened. "We might not want to be involved."

"I'm going to be honest. When the girls got home from school, Maggie wasn't there and we don't know where she is."

"Do you think she left with the delivery guy? Because I watched the entire time he was there and I never saw Maggie."

Mac said, "Do you mind telling us what else you saw? You might have seen something you don't realize is important."

"He appeared to have a clean, shaved head. Caucasian, had a long, bushy beard, and tattoos on his arms, but I couldn't tell what they were. He was a big guy. I work at King's Market. They train us all the time to notice how tall people are when they come into the store in case we're ever robbed." She pointed to Maggie's house. "When he walked on the walkway to the front door, his head bobbed along about an inch or less from the top of the plate-glass window."

Both guys turned to look where she pointed. Nico wrote in his notebook.

Mac continued, "You've been helpful. Thank you. What else can you tell us about him or the van?" Mac tried to sound calm, but his pulse began throbbing in his ears. Feeling a surge of panic, he asked, "Do you have a security camera?"

A man appeared in the doorway. His hair was wet and tousled from a recent shower. "What's this, babe?"

The woman introduced her husband and told him what little she knew.

The husband put his arm around his wife, and asked, "Is the delivery driver a criminal or dangerous? Should we be worried he'll come here because Kara might've seen something?"

"We don't know if the delivery driver plays a role in where Maggie is. We're looking for all leads. For all we know, she may have gone for a walk and a driver hit her." Kara gasped. Mac steamrolled his logic without skipping a beat. "She may have gone for a walk and fallen, she may have injured herself, had a heart attack...." He focused on the husband. "I'm sure you'd do what we're doing—talking to neighbors—if Kara went missing."

The husband's tone softened. "I would do the same thing." He turned his attention to his wife. "Did you see anything else, babe?"

She hesitated. Changing her stance and lowering her voice, she said, "The van had a logo on the door, but I didn't pay attention to what it said. And he delivered nothing. He picked up a big rug. I thought she must've been returning it. He had it rolled up and slung over his shoulder."

Mac looked at Nico, whose face confirmed the two men had the same thought. Remaining calm and controlled, Mac asked, "Is there anything else you might have noticed?"

She shook her head. "No. He drove off after he loaded the rug into the back."

"Which direction did he go?"

She pointed. "Toward town."

"Thank you. If anything comes to mind, call us." Nico handed her a business card.

"Thank you," Mac repeated. "When we solve this mystery, I'll stop by and let you know the details."

Mac and Nico headed for the street. They stopped at the end of the neighbor's driveway. They both blurted out, "Maggie was inside the rug."

Nico added, "Now, we need video footage to see if we can get a license plate or more on the driver. And we need to keep an open mind that she may have been returning the rug, and the driver has nothing to do with where Maggie is. Follow the clues."

"Yeah, yeah. That driver took her. Let's hit up all the neighbors to see if they have any type of security camera." Mac grabbed Nico's sleeve. "What business card did you give them?"

Nico pulled out one from his pocket. It read Two Guys PI - Private Investigations and had their cell phone numbers on it, but no address.

"When did you have these made?"

"As soon as you pitched the idea. I love Rae and I'll always look out for her, but she'll get her driver's license soon, making my services no longer needed. Private investigation sounds way more fun than driving people around. I'll keep the business. Except I'll be more selective with my clients and the jobs."

Chapter 17

Maggie's eyelids felt heavy. She forced them to open. Her wrists and ankles felt bound to a chair. She squirmed and shifted her feet and hands without success. Then her senses rang out like a fire alarm. None of this made sense to her. Her dark surroundings stank like nothing she'd ever smelled before. She had a good sense of smell. She knew when a motorist had hit a skunk on the highway long before the girls did. Right now, she smelled a mix of mildew, earth, dust, something dead, maybe urine and feces. Her stomach retched, but nothing came out. Not wanting to wear her breakfast, she calmed the queasiness.

Trying to determine the cause of the stench gave her something to occupy her mind rather than freak out. "M is for mildew," she said out loud, and then continued analyzing her environment. Again, speaking out loud to nobody, she said to herself, "Decaying something mixed with a back-alley, garbage dumpster smell." She gulped air and held her breath—visualizing an underwater, swimming competition between her and her brother when they were young. They were at the public swimming pool, mid-summer. The pool had many legs to bob and weave their way around as she stroked her arms through the water, trying to get to the other end before Mac—just once she wanted to win. When she couldn't hold her breath a second longer, she gulped air and opened her eyes. Mac was not there. The kids were not there either and wherever she was, still smelled awful.

As she closed her eyes again and held another breath, she heard a noise. Her eyes blinked open, still holding her breath. She filled her cheeks with air. Then she heard footsteps. Unsure what to do, she drooped her head and pretended to still be unconscious.

She heard a metal door scrape along the floor. Heavy footsteps on wooden stairs behind her seemed closer than she realized.

The person grabbed a handful of her hair and yanked her head up. "Wake up," he hissed.

Opening her eyes ever slightly to appear groggy, she looked at him. It was the same man who had rung her doorbell. Lazily blinking her eyes to keep up her charade, she said, "Where am I? Why are you doing this?"

"I do all the talking or I cover your mouth."

She nodded and noticed he had black gloves on and held a bottle of water with his left hand. He was white, bald, had green eyes, red eyebrows, and a long, red, braided beard. He was muscular and tall—close to six feet. Although it was hard to judge his height from her seated position. She saw a black, ornate-looking Christian cross tattooed on his left forearm and an alligator curling around his right forearm arm.

"Open your mouth." He sounded angry.

Doing as he commanded, she tipped her head back, opened her mouth and squeezed her eyes closed. In a fraction of a second, he poured the water into her mouth without allowing her to swallow. And he kept pouring. Water blew out of her mouth and nose as she choked.

"That was stupid. It's all the water you get for today." As he screwed the cap back on the bottle, he added, "I'll leave you an apple on the bottom step behind you. If you can figure out how to get it, it's yours." He turned and walked out of her line of vision.

He said, "See you tomorrow."

"Please, I'm begging you. Please loosen my ankles and wrists." She heard the footsteps clomp up the stairs. "Please!" she yelled, and then heard the door scrape closed.

Maggie wondered what day it was and how long he'd kept her drugged.

She tuned in her senses to what her wrists were bound with. Zip ties. Tight zip ties. Wiggling her finger, she felt thankful she still had blood circulation. Leaning to the right and then the left, she tried to see if her ankles were also bound with zip ties. With her wrists bound to the chair, it kept her from leaning forward enough to see her feet. If he had used zip ties on her wrists, it made sense he'd do the same for her ankles. Curious about why he hadn't gagged her mouth, she feared the answer might mean he'd left her in a remote area where nobody would hear her if she yelled. Grateful he hadn't gagged her, but still curious, she yelled, "Help! Help! Help me!" Exhausted by her effort and looking around, she understood. There wasn't anyone within earshot.

Although it appeared to be evening in the dingy warehouse she'd found herself in, she suspected her concept of time was off because of little natural light. Mumbling to herself, she tried to think, "What time did he ring the doorbell?" Her mind felt fuzzy. "Think!" she tried to scream, then coughed. She wished she'd been able to swallow more of the water.

Staring at an oil smear on the concrete, she ran through her morning. She'd brought in the ladder from the garage. The girls were at sch... Tears trickled down her cheeks. She expected the girls must've gotten home from school by now. Finding her gone had to have scared them. She cried until her nose ran, trying to wipe her face on her shoulder somewhat took care of the mess. As she sat, sniffling like a child, she realized there were no sounds. No traffic, no doors being slammed, no sounds of equipment being used. No voices.

She continued to have a conversation with herself, "Lindy, Bella, mommy is so sorry. First your daddy and now me. You girls don't deserve to lose both parents." Her head felt heavy and sagged forward. She dozed off.

Maggie's entire body jerked and woke her. She wondered how long she'd been asleep. "I'm not in Brookfield anymore. I can't tell if it's daytime or night. The thug drove me hours away from Brookfield," she grumbled. She knew Brookfield like a taxicab driver or a school bus driver—every little street etched in her mind. She'd lived nowhere else. "Where in Brookfield could this horrible building be located?"

Tapping into her deep conscious mind, she almost went into a catatonic state cruising the streets, the roads, the industrial areas, the back roads. First, as a child riding in the backseat of her parents' car, then as a teenager with Bobby scouting places they could park to make-out, and as a nursing school student still living with her parents. Then as a wife. She mentally drove around as a wife and mother admiring the familiar sights and sounds of Brookfield, then something darted out in front of her, she slammed on her brakes— her right arm tried to hold her children in place beside her but her arm felt stuck to the steering wheel. When she looked, the girls weren't next to her. She'd felt a moment of panic, then looked in the rear-view mirror. Their smiling faces met her gaze. When she looked again, they were crying and dressed in black. She looked down and saw she also had on a black dress. When she looked up, she'd parked the car along the curb at a cemetery. Everyone at the graveside turned and looked at her. They were at Bobby's service.

Her mind had become a blank screen—gray and fuzzy. She hated that her brain felt weird. Either the drugs or the fight-or-flight response to her situation had ratcheted up her stress level. She feared the man planned to leave her there to die. From the look of her surroundings, she knew they wouldn't find her body for a long time. She couldn't think straight. It's the damn drug he gave me.

Her feet were cold. In May? She remembered she had on sneakers when she answered the door. The concrete beneath her felt cool. She continued to babble to herself, "Maybe it's late. The nights are still cool in May. Maybe it's nighttime. The girls must be freaking out. I'm sure they called Mac. He'll find me. Lindy, Bella, Uncle Mac will find me."

She fell asleep thinking about her girls.

* * *

Maggie said as she awoke, "I'm here." She looked around and then remembered her current predicament—it was a nightmare, a living nightmare.

A shiver ran from her head to her toes. Her toes. She focused on her toes. At least she still felt her toes. Creating a mini-version of a workout routine she wiggled her toes, spread her knees out-and-in, wiggled her fingers, flapped her elbows as best she could, lifted her butt from the hard seat, tightened her thighs, and then rolled her head from side-to-side. Exercising her limbs and torso was all she could do to keep her blood circulating and stay awake. Plus, it was a way to generate body heat. She did the routine several times until warmth spread through her.

If she knew her brother, and she felt she did, by now, he'd be mad at her for having dropped her guard. The girls had to be frantic with worry. And Bobby's parents must, by now, fear their granddaughters might lose their remaining parent. Would they miss her at the hospital? Nobody else cared about her. But if nobody else cared, she wondered who did this.

She pondered those thoughts for a while until she felt cold again and began her routine. Bare feet on concrete any time of the year felt cold. While stretching and bouncing and rolling her head, she thought about Peyton. As an ER nurse, she'd assisted in many emergency cases. Peyton, 22, out for a night with friends to celebrate a birthday. A man abducted her from a nightclub in Sacramento. Her abductor lived in Brookfield. As her friends said goodbye, she went to the restroom—he snatched her when she came out. He bound and gagged her and put her in a makeshift, human-sized dog kennel and kept her in a dark room to keep her disorientated as to the time of day.

When Peyton arrived at the ER, she had bruises on her sides, on her back and legs that resembled a grilled steak. She told Maggie, 'he' had wrapped a chain around her ankles and the ends connected with a padlock. Her hands had been loose and her mouth uncovered as long as she remained quiet. One time she yelled out. Her captor made good on his threat. After a period, with her mouth gagged and her hands restrained, he allowed her to try again to behave as he expected. She'd followed his rules from that point forward.

She'll never forget the day an ambulance arrived at the ER with Peyton—her ankles still chained together, bruised, and dehydrated with a uniformed officer accompanying her, Maggie thought she'd never recover, never be the same young woman she'd once been.

Some trauma victims didn't speak, some cried a lot, others were afraid to be left alone. Peyton had shown Maggie she had an old soul in a young person's body. She'd been wise beyond her years. Peyton had told Maggie she tried to be a friend to the man who'd taken her.

An officer had told Maggie the man had made Peyton's kennel out of hog panels like you see in the livestock area at a county fair. Because of her five-foot, seven-inch height, she'd been unable to stand in her five-foot box. As she lay in the box, she'd used her feet to push with all her might. After repeating this over and over, day-after-day, she'd popped a few of the welds loose, then a few more. She'd pull the panel back into place before she fell asleep in case he came into the room. When she'd popped enough welds free, she pushed the panel out and waited behind the door. As the door opened and the man stepped inside, she'd jumped on his back and put her arm around his neck—a rear-naked choke jiu jitsu technique she'd seen on TV. He wasn't much bigger than her and flailed about, trying to get her off his back. He slammed her into a wall—she hung on and squeezed tight until he'd passed out, or so she'd thought. She'd hopped until she found an unlocked door and then hopped outside. Knowing she had limited time, she hopped into the street of a normal-looking neighborhood and flagged down the first car she saw. A mother and child drove to their house while calling for the police to respond.

Maggie's thoughts shifted to her worsening plight. Her bladder felt full. Her shoulders slumped at the realization of needing to urinate. Looking around the cavernous place she'd been in for what felt like days, but to be real, she doubted it had been over twenty-four hours. She wanted to channel Peyton's inner strength, Peyton's resolve, Peyton's determination. Warm wetness seeped into the chair seat. The sound of her urine trickling off the chair brought tears to her eyes.

Once her ego had reset after the traumatic reality of urinating in her pants, she looked around again, hoping to see a tool, any tool, a pair of dikes would be perfect, scissors, even a rusty, dull knife could be helpful. Using all the energy she could muster. She bounced her chair twice counterclockwise and spotted the apple sitting on the step where the man had left it. She considered, was she hungry enough to get the apple? Not yet. She felt certain Mac would find her soon.

Chapter 18

Mac stood in Maggie's kitchen hoping she'd walk through the front door while he waited for the coffee machine to finish trickling coffee into Nico's mug. He'd given the girls' grandfather, an ex-law enforcement officer, the bleak update that he knew of no other conclusion than Maggie's absence appeared to be an abduction.

The more he thought about her abduction, the more puzzled he became about why Maggie. An emergency room nurse, widowed with two daughters. She seldom stepped outside her circle of life and people. Since he'd been back in Brookfield, he had already gotten under the skin of a few locals. Nobody came to mind who would be angry enough with him to hurt his sister. Randall Jackson and Mac had had a rocky start, but since then, they'd stayed in neutral corners. Now, Randall's father, Randall Senior, seemed unscrupulous and, being an ex-con, he had connections to people who'd do bad things. Mac and the senior didn't know each other. But, thanks to Mac, his grandson, sat in a juvenile detention center. He may blame Mac for his grandson's arrest.

Nico sat at the dining room table scribbling on a piece of paper. As Mac placed the coffee mug in front of him, he said, "We have a long night ahead of us."

"We do." Nico drew in a long, hot sip of coffee. "Have you thought about who might have a grudge against your sister?"

"Yes. Nobody. She's your basic soccer mom, except the girls don't play soccer. They go about their ho-hum life, work, school, homework, grocery store—rinse and repeat."

"Do you think it has something to do with you?"

"Yes. Except, I can't think of anyone I've done anything to that warranted abducting my sister. Not since I retired and came back home. My life is boring and basic. I wake up, go to work, come home… on Sunday, I teach a jiu jitsu class. B o r - r i n g," he emphasized. "If someone is trying to get my attention—they've got it."

"Someone from your military career?" Nico asked.

Mac sat up straight and tried to rub the kink out of his back. "My job was to retrieve injured soldiers in combat and treat them on the way to the hospital. You don't anger people doing what I did." He stretched his arms above his head, then sipped his coffee.

"Anyone you worked with come to mind? Women you wronged? Baby mommas you don't know about?"

Mac choked and almost spit his coffee back into the mug. Once he'd calmed the sudden irritation to his throat, he said, "No surprise baby mommas and no angry ex-girlfriends." He tapped his fingers on the table.

"Other airmen, you angered?"

"I can't think of anyone."

Nico retrieved the flip chart he'd stashed by the front door. "Let's start with a timeline. What time did the girls leave to catch the school bus?"

"I don't know. I'll text and ask Mr. Donaldson."

"Until then, what's the next thing you know about? She planned to stay home and paint?"

"Yes."

"What time did Lindy call you and tell you Maggie wasn't home?"

"One thirty-three. They'd had a minimum day."

"Good." He wrote the time on the chart paper.

Mac looked at his cell phone. "Lindy told grandpa they left for the bus at seven forty."

"We need to fill in the gap between seven-forty and one-thirty. Five hours and fifty minutes."

When Mac dropped off the girls, he'd assured them he'd know more about what happened to their mother. Mac felt less certain with every passing hour. Mac thought about the girls and hoped picking out the new puppy cheered up Lindy. He feared, her being an old-soul, so to speak, she might not fall for that type of juvenile, bait and switch-trick. Her grandparents were concerned about Lindy's level of angst with her mother's disappearance.

Nico continued, "We didn't have a solid window of time earlier. I think we should go back to the neighbors to see if we missed anything earlier and see if we learn something new." He looked at his notepad. "Do you remember what time the neighbor said she saw the delivery guy take the rug to his van?"

"I don't think she said, or we didn't ask." Mac slammed his fist on the table. "Rookie mistake."

"For you, but I'm no rookie. I guess I'm rusty."

"Do you have more of those business cards?" Mac asked before he drained the last of his coffee.

With a sheepish grin, Nico replied, "About a thousand."

* * *

Nico pulled a handful of the business cards from his pocket. He turned to Mac. "Here you go," he said, as he handed them to him. "Here are a few. The box is in my SUV. Have you heard how the investigation is going?"

"Thanks." He stuffed the cards into his shirt pocket. "I haven't talked to Monica or Marten." Mac pointed. "Let's go the direction the neighbor said the van headed after he nabbed Maggie. If anyone has security cameras, we can ask to see what they have recorded. I know the rat-bastard parked on the street yesterday. I knew something was off with that van. Damn it. I should've gone to the van and asked what the driver was up to."

Nico said, "That way of thinking won't help. Coulda, shoulda, woulda—forget it. Stay focused on the now."

"You're right."

Nico nodded. "You on the right, me on the left. We'll cover more houses if we go alone."

They split apart when they were in front of the house next door to Maggie.

Mac looked around the front as he neared the porch and then saw a camera mounted on the railing. He thought about ringing the bell, but knocked instead. It felt like a more casual approach. He didn't know why, but he also didn't want to leave his fingerprint on everyone's doorbell button.

An older man opened the door, in his mid-fifties, with a well-groomed black mustache, wearing a plaid shirt tucked into blue jeans. He had a dish towel slung over his shoulder. Smells of a fragrant dinner being prepared wafted out at Mac, making his stomach growl—memories of his mother's marinara sauce came to his mind. "Hello, I'm Mac MacKenna. My sister, Maggie, and her daughters live next door." He pointed toward Maggie's house.

As the man opened his mouth to respond, his garage door started to climb upward, and a car pulled into the driveway. He said, "My wife." The man waved at the woman. "Yes, we know Maggie and the girls. What can I do for you or them?"

"I'm pressed for time, so I'll get straight to the point. Someone abducted Maggie today between seven-forty and one-thirty. I believe the man drove a white, utility-type van." The man's mouth gaped open. "I noticed you have a security camera. May I have a look to see if I can get a license plate on the van?"

"My God. Of course. Hang on, I'll get the memory card for you."

Mac overheard the man tell his wife what he'd been told about Maggie. The wife gasped. The man had left the door open a crack— a sign of trust. When the man reappeared in the doorway, he handed Mac the card.

Mac said, "Thank you. Do me a favor. Never leave your door open like this again for anyone. I get you trusted me, but I didn't show you any identification and with what I told you happened to Maggie—I could have been the bad guy looking for another victim."

The man opened his eyes wide with shock displayed on his face. "You're right. It was careless of me. Thank you for pointing that out. May I see your ID?"

Mac showed him his driver's license and his consultant badge with the police department.

"When I find my sister, I'll be back to let you know what happened. I appreciate your trust and letting me use the card." Mac handed him a business card. "If you think of anything you might have seen, a white van on the street yesterday or today—call me."

The man nodded.

Mac spun around and headed for Nico.

Nico appeared stuck talking with an older woman. He turned to see Mac approaching. "Thank you for your help. Call me if you remember anything."

"Wait, wait. You boys look like you need some cookies. They're fresh baked." She left the door wide open and returned with peanut butter cookies mounded on a paper plate.

"Thank you," Nico said, accepting the plate.

She closed her door and then watched from her living room window while the two men walked away from her house.

Mac shook his head and grabbed a cookie then took a huge bite, held it up and nodded to the lady looking out the window, before saying to Nico, "After we find Maggie, remind me to do a personal safety seminar for her neighbors. They're all too trusting."

Nico said, "On the plus side, we've got two memory cards from the trusting neighbors. On our way to the police station, I'll make a list of the businesses we pass with security cameras. The guys in the tech department can look through the recordings and isolate everything with the white van."

Mac remembered something. "Oh, and I stopped back at Kara's. She said she didn't remember the exact time she saw the van at Maggie's. She guessed around noon."

"Too bad. Do you think she didn't want to be more involved than she already was?"

"Hard to say."

They checked to see if they needed to take anything else with them and were on the road to downtown. Nico jotted down business names as Mac blurted them out. They parked in the visitor parking lot and sprinted to the main office. The on-duty officer greeted them by name and released the locked door for them to enter the back area.

They found Marten in the conference room, where a team of officers and detectives were busy combing through documents related to the shootings.

Mac said, "Hey, we have some memory cards we'd like the guys in tech to go through."

"You got it." Marten turned and walked toward where Mac remembered he and Marlene had spent the night looking through school recordings trying to determine what had happened to Theyn Seder.

Marten unlocked the door, and the three men walked into the cool, darkened room with many glowing computer monitors. Yazi stood up and approached them.

"Hi Mac, Marten. Whatcha got for us?"

"Yazi, this is Nico," Marten said, pointing to Nico. "He's on hiatus from the FBI and helping with the murder investigation. He and Mac are side-lined looking for Mac's sister, who has been MIA since this morning."

As Yazi shook Nico's hand, he said, "Sorry about your sister." He shook his head. "We'll do whatever you need."

Mac handed Yazi the plastic baggie with flash drives, then told him about the white van on Sunday and in the morning.

Marten asked Yazi, "Have you found anything helpful for either of the murders?"

"Not yet. Officer Stockford wasn't big on technology use until toward the end of his active duty. We're going through old case files and transferring everything to microfilm."

"Call me if you find anything out of the ordinary."

"Will do."

The three men left together. In the hallway, Marten asked, "Do you want the search for Maggie to be official?"

Mac asked, "Is the chief in?

"He is."

"Nico and I will see if he has time to meet with us first."

"Call me if you need me."

Mac and Nico made the trek to the chief's office. The door was closed and his administrative assistant's desk was empty and buttoned down for the night. Mac knocked on the door.

The mayor opened the door and threw Mac off for a second. "I'm Mac MacKenna, is the chief in? I need a few minutes with him, if possible."

They heard the chief say, "Come on in, Mac."

To Mac, the mayor didn't look too broken up about Sawyer's murder. Nico followed Mac inside.

The mayor said, "I'm going to get a soda. Would you like anything?" He glanced at them both.

They responded with, "No, thank you."

"What can I do for you boys?" the police chief asked from his desk.

Mac told him what he knew so far and added it was time to file a missing person's report. He asked if he and Nico could lead the search since he had so many assigned to the murder cases.

"I'm sorry about your sister. You've got my full support. Let me know what we can do to assist with her search. The murders are our number one priority, but a missing person case is also important. The officer at the front desk will take down the information about your sister. Keep me posted."

"Thank you, sir." Mac stood and shook the commander's hand. Nico did the same. As they approached the door, Mac turned around and asked, "Where'd all the reporters go? They've been in front of the station since the shooting happened."

"They're camped out by Stockford's home, hoping to get a scoop."

As he went to open the door, the mayor opened it and re-entered the office.

"Goodnight, mayor." Both guys replied.

Walking toward the front of the police station, Mac said to Nico, "I'll request a leave of absence from the school in the morning."

"Will that be a problem?"

"Not for me. I'll resign if it's a problem for them. I've given nobody the impression I'd stay longer. Luke already interviewed— he can stay with me until he can get a place of his own."

"They're lucky you provided them with a capable replacement. Most people submit a letter of resignation and leave without looking back. You're a nice guy, Mac."

"Don't tell the students," Mac replied with a grin.

Chapter 19

The next morning, Mac met Luke in the staff parking lot across from the school. "Are you sure you're ready for this?"

He shrugged. "It beats doing nothing."

Mac reached for something in his pocket. "Here's a key to my place and the code for the gate and security system. Have some dog treats on the ready to give to the mutts until they get to know you. The way to their hearts is through their stomachs." Mac stopped his friend. "If you ever need me or my help with anything, call me. I'm sorry to throw you to the wolves like this."

"It's cool, man. Like old times, we never knew when we were going to be called to action." As they approached the main entrance, he patted Mac on his back. "You need to find your sister. These kids won't get the best of me."

"I like your optimism."

Mac passed his ID badge over the scanner, which triggered the door to slide open. He led the way to Marlene, who stopped talking to a woman when she saw them round the corner to her office area.

"Mac." She popped up from her desk and gave him a tight hug. "I'm so sorry about Maggie. If I can help with the girls, let me know."

"Thanks, Marlene."

Marlene looked at Luke. "Nice to see you again."

Marlene plopped onto her desk chair, causing the spring inside the hydraulic mechanism to groan. "Mac, have you met Kelly? She's the temp replacing Crosby Nash in ninth grade English."

Her name didn't ring a bell for him. Then it hit him—a BAT Box note. He extended his hand to shake. "Nice to meet you." He turned toward Luke. "This is Luke. He's replacing me"

They shook hands.

Mac added, "I received your bird feeder request and will pass it on to the right person."

Kelly blushed. "Thank you. You're leaving us?"

"I'm not going far. I'll be working as a consultant with the police department and a friend and I are starting a private investigator business."

Marlene interjected, "Michael isn't here yet. Dr. Z. doesn't want to be disturbed until he arrives."

Mac felt his disdain for Dr. Zita, building inside him. He had things to do. Every minute Maggie was gone was a minute closer to not being found.

Marlene added, "Kelly was telling me she and her husband are taking their children to Disneyland this summer."

Kelly said, "We have two weeks until school's out." Sounding too excited, she gave them a shy grin, then asked, "Have either of you been to Disneyland?"

Marlene noticed movement on the front door monitor, then she blurted out, "Michael's here."

Kelly scurried down the hall. Marlene buzzed her boss. "Everyone is here for your meeting."

He said nothing. Marlene shrugged. Then his door opened. "Come in, come in. Marlene can get you coffee and muffins."

Mac wanted to get down to business so he could get out there and look for Maggie.

When the door shut behind them, Michael said to Mac, "I'm sorry about what's happened to your sister. I'm available 24/7 if there's anything I can do for you. Family is what's most important."

"Thank you," Mac replied.

As the men sat around the familiar, round table, Mac flashed back on the times he'd been in the office with Dr. Zita and his predecessor, Ann Sawyer. So far, his experience in the 'boss's office' hadn't been pleasant.

Michael began, "Luke, it looks like we'll need your services sooner than we had expected. When can you start?"

"I'm prepared to start today, sir, if that's acceptable."

"More than acceptable, also appreciated. Is it your intention to return when school starts in the fall?"

"If you'll have me, I look forward to it."

Dr. Zita sat, appearing uninterested and excluded from the decision-making process.

Michael said, "As long as you don't turn into a pedophile or abuse a child, you'll be a part of the Blackstone Academy family. We put a lot of faith in Mac's recommendation."

In his peripheral vision, Mac thought he saw Dr. Zita roll his eyes.

Michael stood. "We're done. Mac, you go find your sister. Luke, you call me if you need anything and you have Dr. Zita here to help as well."

Dr. Zita smiled.

"Sorry to rush out, but it's a busy time at the ranch." Michael grabbed his cowboy hat and moved toward the door.

Luke said to Michael's back, "Thank you for the opportunity, sir."

Michael turned around. "There's no sir here, I'm Michael. And we thank you for your previous service to the United States and now to Blackstone Academy."

When Mac opened the door to leave Dr. Zita's office, Marlene appeared to be waiting for someone who'd been in the room. She had the look of an expectant child waiting for a treat.

"Thank you, Michael. I'll be in touch," Mac said, as he and Luke turned toward Luke's office and Michael turned in the opposite direction to leave the building.

Mac and Luke walked to the technology office. "First, you need an ID badge." He swiped his badge across the scanner and heard the lock release. The staff inside looked up as Mac opened the door. Felecia, the supervisor, and sole female tech with the school, made her way to them.

"Hey, Felecia, this is Luke. He's taking over my position, and he needs an ID badge ASAP."

"You're leaving us?"

"Sorry, it's a long story." He jabbed a thumb toward Luke. "He can tell you all about it another time. I'm in a hurry."

"Sure, come on." She waved her hand for Luke to follow her.

"Luke. Come to my office... I mean ... your office when you're done."

"Will do."

Mac hadn't prepared to hand over his job so soon. He thought he'd stay through the end of the school year. As he looked around the office and began tossing personal items into a plastic bag, he realized how few things he'd brought to work. He wondered if he had not taken the job, would Maggie be home wallpapering her bedroom instead of at an unknown location? He shook his head and reminded himself to stay in the present, like Nico had told him.

There was no 'how-to' manual for his job. He logged into the security system and looked for Roni, then he buzzed her on the walkie-talkie.

"Roni, can you come to the security office?"

"On my way."

Roni arrived before Luke. Mac told her about Maggie's abduction, Ann's murder—which she'd already been told by a friend at the police department—and he told her about Luke.

When Luke let himself into the office, he looked surprised to see Roni.

Mac introduced the two, telling Luke that Roni was his go-to gal and she'd been with the school a long time. She knew the students better than anyone. When Roni reached for the door handle, Mac said, "Roni, do me a favor and ask Rae to keep an eye on Teddy for me. Nate's harassment of Teddy is escalating. She can ask Stu to talk to his little brother about leaving Teddy alone."

"You got it." She stepped part way out of the office, then turned around and stuck her foot in the room to keep the door from closing. "Come here and give me a hug. I'm going to miss you, and I'm freaked out about your sister."

Mac hugged her. "I'm not moving. I'll still see you at jiu jitsu, right?"

"Yes, I'll see you at the gym. One last question before I go."

"What's that?"

Looking at Luke, she asked, "Are you into Brazilian Jiu Jitsu?"

"No."

"Somebody with less training than me. Yes." She raised her arms in a touchdown fashion.

After Roni left, Mac looked at Luke. "She wants to be a policewoman. She's taking criminal science classes at the college. Her full name is Veronica, but everyone calls her Roni."

Mac spent thirty more painful minutes showing Luke how to use the security camera system, told him about the BAT boxes and how the notes had been instrumental in the Theyn investigation. When he walked out of the office that had been his for ten months, he felt an unexpected tug on his heartstrings.

Marlene stepped into the hallway before he reached the front door. "Hey, you, I'm going to miss you." She held out her arms for a hug.

"I'll miss you too. I promise to stop by to say hello now and then."

They hugged.

Stepping outside, he felt like his decision to leave the academy had lifted an immense weight from his shoulders. Then Maggie came to the forefront of his mind. His phone vibrated. It was Yazi, the media technician from Brookfield P.D.

* * *

Mac stopped outside the school's main door to answer the call from Yazi. The warm, humid air smacked him in the face. He felt like he was in the south, not Northern California. "Hey, Yazi. What'd you find?"

"The flash drive from across the street from your sister's place. When I magnified it to see the detail of the rug…"

"Yeah." Yazi was taking too long to say what he found. Mac felt impatient with the tech.

"You could see strands of hair hanging out from one end of the rolled rug. I'm sorry, man."

"Fuck." Mac looked around to see if anyone had heard him curse. He hustled to his truck in the parking lot and started it. "Anything else?"

"Oh, yeah."

"Hang on, so I can write this down." He put down his window until the air conditioning cooled down the cab. He grabbed the pen and notebook from his glove box, pushed the speaker button, and placed the phone on the dash of his truck. "What else?"

"The license plate is off a Honda Odyssey van."

Across the street, Mac saw Elsie, the food service manager, headed his way. She had a smile as wide as her face. "Yazi, can you hold a minute?"

"Sure."

Mac pressed the mute button on his phone and stepped out of his truck.

"Mr. Mac, you're not leaving without a hug. Marlene told me we have replaced you. Promise me you'll stop by now and then."

He hugged the sweetest lady he'd ever met. "I promise."

She pulled away from the hug. Her smile had vanished. "You better not be telling me a lie. People who leave always say they'll come back and see us, then they never do."

"I'll come back to see you, Elsie."

Her smile returned, causing her eyes to squint.

"I'm sorry to rush you, but I've got a lot going on."

"Marlene also told me about your sister. Go... Go... Find her and make your world right again." She fanned her hands like shooing kids outside to play.

Mac pushed the mute button on his phone again. "Yazi, you still there?"

Halfway across the street to the school, Elsie turned and blew him a kiss.

Mac waved.

"Yeah. So, I have the name and address of the Honda owner if you want to follow up on the plates."

"I sure do, because the van that pulled out of Maggie's driveway was not a Honda."

Yazi rattled off the information. "The guy has no hair. He wore a ball cap, but you could tell he was clean shaved. He had a tattoo on his right arm of what looked like the bottom portion of an alligator."

"An alligator?"

"Yeah. The video is poor quality, and the image gets grainy when you enlarged it—it looks like the tail end of an alligator. Maybe he's from Florida."

"Anything else?"

"There was a tattoo on his left forearm, but there wasn't a good enough angle to make it out. He's a stocky guy, and has a long beard. He wore an uncommon brand of steel-toed work boots." Yazi told him the brand and approximate shoe size. "When we mapped the van's direction after leaving your sister's based on the recordings, see if any businesses on the east side of town have cameras."

"All helpful, Yazi. Thank you."

"When you get more for us, we'll drop what we're doing. Of course, unless we're onto something related to the murders."

Mac speed dialed Nico. "Can you meet me at Maggie's house—I'm checking on some leads."

Chapter 20

The late morning sun radiated warmth through the windshield of Mac's truck as he and Nico sped to the address Yazi had given them. Mac had never been to that area of Brookfield.

The neighborhood sat quiet, children were in school and working folks were already off to their jobs.

The homes were small, and most lacked regular maintenance. They parked across the street from a home that looked somewhat cared for compared to the ones on either side of it. Somebody had mowed the lawn in the last few days. And the front porch looked tidy, with two well-worn lawn chairs and an upside-down apple crate as a makeshift table between the chairs. An older woman wearing a housecoat sat on one of the lawn chairs, holding a mug of something. Mac assumed coffee.

Before the guys got out of the truck, Nico jotted down the Honda's license plate information—it didn't match the plate on record for the vehicle and address. They approached the woman.

She eyed them with suspicion, but didn't move.

On the other side of a screen door, the front door was open. They couldn't hear any sounds from inside the house.

"Good morning, are you Glenda Mullis?" Mac asked.

"Who wants to know?"

Mac introduced himself and Nico. "We're working with the Brookfield Police Department on a missing person case."

"Okay." She sipped from the mug.

Mac put her age at around sixty-five, guessing she lived on Social Security. She looked friendly, the type of woman who'd get on the floor to play with her grandbabies, but she came across surly.

"Is that your silver Honda parked in the driveway?" Mac jabbed his thumb toward the van.

She looked at the vehicle. "Yes."

"Does anyone else drive it?"

"My grandson does when he shops for me."

"Anyone else?"

She straightened her back and crossed one leg over the other, then winced in pain, and uncrossed her legs.

"Are you alright?" Mac asked.

"Peachy. I have a pinched nerve in my lower lumbar—it gives me trouble now and then. What's this about?"

"The license plates from your vehicle were on a vehicle involved in the missing person case we're investigating."

She looked at the vehicle, then back at them.

"How did that happen? The car's been here for days. My grandson hasn't shopped for me since..." Her eyes looked up toward the porch cover. "Is today Sunday?"

"It's Tuesday," Mac said, growing impatient. "We don't know how your plates found their way to the vehicle we're looking for. That's why we're here."

"Anson, my grandson." She snickered. "Did you catch my rhyme?"

Both men starred at her, unamused.

The old woman continued, "He usually shops for me on Friday because the market has sales on Fridays."

"Where can we find Anson?"

"If it was Sunday, he'd have been at work. He works at the Burger Stop. He's a cook," she said with pride.

"Since it's Tuesday, where is he?"

"I don't know. He was already gone when I woke up."

"What days and hours does he work?"

"Sunday through Thursday, six in the morning until two-thirty in the afternoon."

"He's at work today?" Mac wondered if the lady was all there or trying to be confusing. "Does he have a cell phone?"

"Yes, I guess he is at work. Of course, he has a cell phone, doesn't everyone?"

"What's his number?"

She shook her head. "He told me to never give out his phone number."

Mac handed her a business card. "Please tell him we have questions for him and ask him to call either of us."

Accepting the card, she said, "I'm not sure when I'll see him, but when I do, I'll give this to him."

As they were leaving, Nico turned around. "Why does he use your van to shop for you instead of his car?"

She laughed. "He doesn't have a car. He has one of those motorcycles you lay down on. You couldn't fit a jug of milk on that thing."

Back in the truck, Mac said to Nico, "She wasn't super helpful, but gave us something to go on."

"It's early, but I might be ready for lunch. Let's grab something to eat at the Burger Stop."

"Great idea." Mac smiled. "First stop is Handley's Coffee Shop, to see if their security camera pointed at the parking area near the front door is real or fake. If it's real, they may have caught the van headed out of town since the guys tracked the van headed east."

* * *

A short time later, Mac parked the truck in front of Handley's Coffee Shop. "Good. It looks like there aren't many customers. We hit them before the lunch crowd."

As soon as Mac and Nico stepped inside Handley's, the family-owned coffee shop, Tammy Handley, the co-owner, waved at the guys from the kitchen. They went to a corner table. Tammy's daughter, Samantha (Sam) arrived with two coffee cups and a pot of black coffee.

Sam plunked down the cups and filled them before they could decline.

"Two days in a row, aren't I the lucky girl?" She looked at Mac, then turned her attention to Nico. "I haven't seen you in a while. How've you been?"

Before Nico had time to respond, Mac said, "Thanks for the coffee, Sam. Sorry, today, we don't have time to stay for more than coffee. We need to speak with your mom and dad. It's urgent."

"Oh. This sounds serious." She waited a moment to hear what they needed to talk to her parents about, but neither Mac nor Nico said anything. She turned and went straight into the kitchen.

Tammy wiped her hands on the stained white apron tied around her waist as she approached the table, followed by her husband, Joe. Joe had inherited the business from his father, James, at 25. His father had died in a freak accident on his way home from the restaurant during a storm when an old oak tree fell on his vehicle.

Tammy grabbed a chair back and dragged it the few feet remaining before reaching their table. "I needed a break. What's going on?"

Joe arrived a few steps behind his wife. He stretched out a hand to shake both Mac and Nico's hands while he remained standing.

He had a reputation for being a grump. Mac, so far, had not seen that side of his personality.

Mac leaned toward them and lowered his voice, telling them what had happened to Maggie. "I'm hoping the security camera aimed at the highway works and, if so, could we look at the recording from yesterday?"

Tammy looked at Joe.

Joe said, "Heavens, yes, you can look. No good having a security camera if it doesn't work. Follow me." He looked at his wife. "Mother, can you handle things while I show them to the system?" He often referred to his wife as Mother.

"Of course, shoo. These boys are in a hurry." She leaned in to Mac and kissed his cheek, whispering, "I'll pray you find your sister safe and unharmed."

He thanked her and promised to let them know as soon as they found Maggie.

Joe led the guys through the kitchen to a small back room. "It's not much bigger than a shoe box, but it's our office." He unlocked the door, opened it, and stepped aside.

Joe hadn't exaggerated. The office held one desk, one chair, a four-drawer, a tall filing cabinet, and a shelf above the desk held the security hardware.

"If it's alright with you, Joe, I'd like to download a copy of yesterday's recording so I can give it to the technicians at the police department to review."

"Fine by me. You do whatever you need to do. We're happy to help in any way we can." Joe turned and left the boys to download the copy.

After Mac and Nico had loaded the recording onto a flash drive, Mac closed the office door. As they passed through the kitchen, Mac said to Tammy and Joe, "Thank you again. We'll stop to let you know how Maggie is."

Tammy grabbed a big pink box and hurried to the guys. "You can't go to the police station without taking the officers some treats." She held out the box.

Nico accepted the pastries. "I hope it's allowed for us to have our treat on the way." He smiled.

Tammy placed a white bag on top of the box Nico held. "These are for you two." She smiled back at him.

When they re-entered the restaurant, Sam stood at a table taking an order. She turned when she saw movement. "Bye, guys. Don't stay away for so long. We've missed you."

Mac waved as he said goodbye. Nico smiled and nodded—his arms were busy holding the treats.

Mac looked at Nico. "You know she's flirting with you, right?"

"She's not my type."

"What's your type?"

When they were back in the car, ignoring Mac's question, Nico said, "We can drop these off at the station on our way to the Burger Stop. Do you want one now?"

"Hell ya." He shrugged. "I eat a lot when I'm stressed. I'll go for a run tonight."

Chapter 21

Approaching footsteps woke Maggie, louder with each step. She tensed and opened her eyes. Then she thought better, closed her eyes, and began taking slow, deep breaths to appear asleep. The air felt warm and moist and still.

A packed key ring jangled as the person looked for the correct key. After a second of fiddling to insert the key, the door scraped open.

She sensed the person standing in the doorway staring at her. Her back was to the door. She wished she could figure out a way to attack or break free. She lifted her head. "Why am I here? Who are you? I think you have the wrong person. I'm a nurse at the hospital."

Heavy footsteps plodded down the stairs.

The man stood in front of her. She could tell he was the same man who rang her doorbell. "Why am I here? I have no money, and nobody to pay a ransom, if that's what you're after."

"I ain't after jack-shit. And I don't want nothing from you. You're a job to me. Until I'm told what to do with you, you stay here."

"Who hired you and why me?"

He laughed. His stout body bounced as he laughed.

Maggie didn't smile at whatever he thought had been funny. "Please, can you tell me anything? I have daughters at home, I'm sure they're worried to death about me. I'm a widow, I'm all they have."

His smile turned serious. "Ain't how I hear it. You have a brother."

"If this is about my brother. Why am I involved?"

He shrugged. "Like I said, I'm doing a job, lady." He reached into his pocket.

Maggie flinched.

From his pocket, he pulled out a hamburger wrapped in foil paper from a fast-food place and from the other pocket, a bottle of water. "You hungry? Thirsty? I'm supposed to keep you alive for now." He grabbed a bucket from behind her and flipped it upside down in front of her, then sat on it.

She observed, this time, he didn't wear gloves, and his green eyes looked softer. She wasn't seeing the fury in his eyes like she'd seen the last time when he'd almost water-boarded her. "Of course, I'm hungry and thirsty. How long have I been here—24 hours?" She looked at her empty lap. "How do you expect me to eat with my wrists bound to the chair?" As hard as she tried to maintain her cool, her voice sounded too sarcastic.

He opened the bottle and approached her. Like a baby bird in a nest, she tipped her chin up and opened her mouth as he poured. The refreshing cool water trickled into her mouth. She swallowed as fast as could. She burped and automatically said, "excuse me," then silently chastised herself for showing manners to this thug. He set the water bottle on the floor. He then unwrapped the burger and held it to her mouth.

She noticed he was lefthanded. She hadn't seen the tattoos before because of the gloves, this time she saw the letters J E S U S tattooed on the topside of the fingers on his left hand, including his thumb, the word was for him to see, when he looked at his hand. Ornate lettering, black ink.

"Are you religious?"

He snorted. "No. Why?"

"The word Jesus tattooed across your knuckles."

He glanced at his hand. "Stop talking."

She also noticed he had what appeared to be a full-size, poorly drawn alligator curling up his right arm. She wondered, *"Prison tattoos?"* Although disgusted by his grimy hands and fingernails filled with black gunk, she took a big bite of the burger. They continued the feeding in silence.

After he shoved the last bite into her mouth, he wadded up the wrapper and tossed it over his shoulder. She felt she should say "thank you," but told herself manners were not happening again in this twisted situation. Instead, she said, "Please loosen my hands. Please. Just a little. They're so tight they hurt." She tried to sound desperate.

He stood in front of her and appeared to think about her request.

She watched him wrap the tie around her wrists, then ratchet it tight, but not as tight as the other. When the switch blade snapped open, she sucked in her breath. She knew the sound too well from the experiences she'd had in the emergency room with drug addicts high on the drug of choice. He cut the tight tie, and it fell to the floor. She knew then her captor had compassion. It seemed his kindness was present when he wasn't high, despite that, it was in there somewhere.

She felt manners might help her connect with her captor. This time, she said, "Thank you."

Confident Mac would find her, she took in all she could of his appearance, hoping if she said her observations in her mind, they would stick in her memory. "Tall"—or so she thought, not sure if her perception was off because of the drugs and looking up at him.

"Green eyes, green eyes, green eyes." She remembered a friend had told her about the Rule of Seven—if you need to remember something, say it in your thoughts seven times. She closed her eyes and thought, *green eyes, green eyes, green eyes, green eyes, green eyes, green eyes, green eyes*. He wore a dirty gray T-shirt with a hot rod graphic on it—the ironed-on decal cracked and peeling, dirty blue jeans, boots—like a mix of part work boot, part cowboy boot.

The space fell quiet. She opened her eyes and saw him pull a syringe from a pocket.

Panic surged through her. "Please, please don't give me another dose."

He moved closer.

"I'm begging you, please. If I'm going to die, I want a clear mind to remember my daughters. Please."

Ignoring her plea, he jabbed the needle in her squirming arm and released the drugs into her system.

Saying nothing else, he left. The keys clanked against the metal door as he locked it from the other side.

Alone, with her thoughts, she whispered, "Rule of seven—Jesus tattooed on fingers, Jesus tattooed on fingers, Jesus tattooed on fingers, Jesus tattooed on fingers, Jesus tattooed on fingers, Jesus tattooed on fingers, Jesus tattooed on fingers." Her thoughts shifted to Lindy and Bella. Tears stung her eyes and overflowed. She again whispered to herself, "I know the girls are scared about where I am. I'm scared too…"

She felt the drug take control of her. She forced her eyes to stay open. With hazy vision, she looked around for anything that might help her escape. Her wrists were looser, but still tight. Even though he'd kept her ankles secured to the two front legs of the chair, they weren't uncomfortable as much as cramping from lack of movement.

She tried her exercises again. Swirling her hands in circles, next she lifted her toes then heels, sat up straight, rolled her head to one side then the other, took in a slow deep breath and held it to allow her breath to oxygenate her blood. Her movements sped up the distribution of the narcotic throughout her body. She stopped moving.

She thought about Peyton. She'd told Maggie she became a friend to her captor, showed she cared about him. He became more trusting of her and allowed her more freedom as time passed. But it had been a slow journey. Maggie felt there was no way the man's boss would allow him to keep her for long.

A streak of sunshine on the concrete caught her attention. Then the streak began to swirl and reflect light like a disco ball. She stared at the disco ball—the lights were pretty colors. No longer in control, her eyes drifted shut. Knowing Mac, he'd have taken the girls to Bobby's parents straight away. In her heart, she knew the girls were safe, frightened, but safe. She had confidence Mac would find her. And because he also had Nico and Monica on his team, she knew the three of them together would sort this out.

She woke some time later. The streak of sunlight was gone. Closing her eyes again, she thought of her late husband, Bobby. Her feeling of euphoria halted when a fly landed on her nose. She shook her head, but it persisted to torment her by landing in various places where she had exposed skin. "Ahhhhhh! Leave me alone!" she yelled. Flailing as much as possible, she felt the zip ties on her ankles slice the skin beneath them. She thought again about what Peyton had said. "Befriend your captor," she whispered. The fly had moved on to some other object of interest. Her thoughts went back to her late husband. *Bobby, I miss you so much. Please guide Mac to me. The girls need me. They can't live their best lives without both of us. Please, baby, give Mac the guidance he needs to look here for me. Show him where I am.* Thinking of Bobby and talking to him brought her a sense of peace. She drifted to sleep whispering, "Befriend my captor, befriend my captor, befriend my…."

Chapter 22

As Mac put the transmission into park, his phone rang. Monica's photo appeared. He answered it on the first ring. "Hey, hang on a second." Mac turned to Nico. "Go grab us a table. I'll be a minute." After Nico shut his door, Mac said into the phone, "How're you?"

Monica said, "Forget about me. How're you? Have you found out anything?"

Mac shared their activities. "We dropped off some memory cards from neighbors and some businesses to the tech guys. They called with the license plate on the van, which turned out to be stolen—the plate, not sure about the van. We talked with the owner of the vehicle the plates belong to—it sounds like her grandson is involved somehow. We're at his work, Burger Stop, for lunch and to talk with him."

"Those are good leads. I snagged a cinnamon roll from the break room. Thank you."

"Don't thank me. Tammy sent them."

"I didn't know you were here."

"Nico dropped them at the front desk. I'm not in the mood for chitchat with the guys."

"Finding Maggie is taking too long. I'm sure the girls are freaking out and Maggie's got to be scared. Hell, I'm freaked out and scared. Who would do this and why? I don't get it."

"There's something going on. It doesn't feel random. Random criminals don't stakeout your neighborhood or have a vehicle with stolen plates at the ready. This was purposeful."

"Right. But why? I'm going crazy trying to figure out if it's about me. Did I do something to someone, and they took Maggie to get back at me? If so, who? Who did I hurt?" He paused for a moment. "Is it about Maggie? She's as gentle as a butterfly, she has a heart of gold, she helps people. Who would want to hurt her?"

Mac gazed out at the people entering the burger joint, which was bigger than he'd remembered from the few times he'd driven by.

"You'll figure it out. Stockford's death is equally puzzling. He retired so many years ago. Why would someone from an old case wait so long to exact revenge?"

"Maybe an ex-con?" he suggested.

"Possible. I'll look into that. We can talk more about it when I see you. Can you and Nico meet me for dinner tonight? I think I can get away for an hour."

"Yes. Pub food or tacos?"

"Tres Esposas. How does six o'clock sound?"

"Sounds good. I miss you, babe."

"I miss you too. I went to your place and checked on Roxy and Comet. They're good. Don't worry about them. Find your sister."

When Mac pushed open the door, the smell of fried food slapped his senses. He stood in the entryway for a second, scanning the place for Nico before he found him looking his way. Nico bobbed his head toward the kitchen. Mac looked and saw a young man with a partially shaved head—and a tall Mohawk—pushing plates of food through the window.

He sat across from Nico. "Looks like our boy is here."

"I ordered you an iced tea."

"Thank you."

Nico closed his menu. "I'm going for a bacon cheeseburger with fries. Is everything alright with Monica?"

Mac closed his menu without having looked at it. "A bacon cheeseburger sounds good. She's fine, checking in on us. I told her we'd meet her for tacos tonight at six."

"Does that work for you?"

"You ain't getting rid of me until we find your sis."

Mac felt his emotions bubble up inside. He tamped them down. "Thank you. I appreciate your help and friendship. Monica said she'll bring us up to date on how the murder investigation is going."

"Works for me."

Their server arrived, gave them their drinks, took their order, grabbed the menus, and left with no interest in idle, friendly banter which suited Mac. He wasn't in the mood to chat.

Mac took a long drink of his tea. "I continue to have a nagging thought that whoever killed Stockford and Sawyer has something to do with Maggie's disappearance."

"How so?"

"I think what's happened to Maggie has something to do with me. I'm connected to Sawyer through the school." He fiddled with the salt shaker. "I can't connect Stockford. But I also can't imagine Maggie has ever made anyone in her life this angry."

Nico thought for a beat. "It's weird how cases can seem disconnected and then you get one clue and suddenly there's a connection. There's also the possibility they don't connect at all, and Maggie is an isolated case."

Mac shook his head. "My gut says they're connected. Or why would this all go down within a few days?"

They were both quiet in thought and said little while they ate.

After the server removed their empty plates, Nico asked, "Do you remember I told you I stopped at Red's Roadhouse and talked with the owner about whether she'd overheard any interesting conversations about the cop's murder or if there was anyone new in the bar she'd never seen before?"

"I remember."

"I'm going to stop by and see if she's learned anything. She'd told me retired cops and sheriff officers meet there in the morning and she said she'd tune in to what they have to say about the murders."

"Sounds good. You never know what they might have said about it. And if the guys are there, let's straight up ask them what they know." Mac signals for the bill, then glanced at his watch. "But first we need to speak with a guy who rides a crotch rocket."

* * *

Mac and Nico walked behind the restaurant, noticing someone had propped open the back door with a brick. The back of the building lacked maintenance and could use some trash removal. Mac hoped the kitchen had a cleanliness rating better than what he thought it did based on the amount of crap piled up against the back wall.

As if reading Mac's mind, Nico said, "Looks pretty trashy back here."

"I guess you shouldn't judge a restaurant by how the back of the building looks." He half laughed. "I hope we won't be sick later. My burger tasted great."

"Yeah, mine did too."

They walked up to the motorcycle and looked closely at the decals. Nico texted the license plate number to a friend at the FBI Sacramento Field Office. "I'm going to see whose name is on the registration of this slick little toy."

"Good idea," Mac said, as he picked up the helmet the driver had left unsecured on the seat. "Have you ever ridden one of these?" He swung his leg over and straddled the motorcycle.

"No, and never plan to," Nico replied.

"Jeez, this feels like a bicycle with training wheels compared to mine."

"HEY! Get off my bike!" someone yelled from behind them.

Mac turned to see the guy with the mohawk-styled hair and said, "Chill out, dude. We're admiring your ride." Mac stood beside the motorcycle. "Is it for sale?"

"No, it ain't for sale. Get the fuck away from it." He eyed them with suspicion.

"Or what?" Mac said, placing the helmet back on the seat.

Anson stopped five feet short of his ride. Mac and Nico stood between him and his way out of the situation he found himself in. "What do you want?"

Mac asked, "Who'd you give your grandmother's license plates to?"

"Fuck off. You got the wrong guy."

"Oh, we have the right guy," Mac replied.

"Dude, get away from my bike." He took a step toward the guys.

In a move so fast the young guy didn't see it coming, Mac reached out and took him down to the ground.

"What the fuck?!"

Mac held him down with a lumberjack-sized palm on his sternum, enough to keep him where he was but not enough to block his airway. "I asked you who you gave your grandmother's license plates to?"

The kid said nothing.

Mac added, "Look, kid. We don't have a problem with you. We want to know who you gave the plates to. I'm a patient guy. I can stay here all day if that's what it takes to convince you to give us the name. My friend," he glanced at Nico, "is not a patient guy and he's got somewhere to be soon. Unless you want him to stomp on your throat, tell us what we want to know."

"A guy I work with asked if he could borrow my grandma's plates for a job. He said he'd give them back."

"Why hasn't he given them back yet?"

"Don't know."

"Is the guy working now?"

"Yes."

"Go get him."

Mac allowed the scrawny guy to stand and go into the restaurant. When he reemerged from the back door, a few guys flanked him. One guy picked up the brick that had held open the back door.

Nico spoke up. In his slow, calm manner, he said, "Guys, this ain't your fight." The four guys stopped short. "We're both masters in Brazilian Jiu Jitsu and we won't hesitate to break your elbows. You won't be able to work or drive." Nico took a step toward them. All but the grandson turned to go inside the restaurant.

Mac said to Anson, "Was one of them the guy who wanted the plates, or are you bullshitting us?"

Anson ran away from them. Mac took off after him and again tossed him to the ground, this time in the dirt beside a mature pampas grass bush causing the white plumes to rain down on them. "What the fuck?" The blades from the bush cut like a straight-edged barber's razor. Pampas grass is a weapon of its own.

Mac grabbed the kid by the shirt and yanked his slight body to his feet. "Tell us what we want to know and we're done with you."

"His name is Tay."

"Where can we find Tay?"

"He hangs out at the Pool Room bar."

Mac pulled Anson close. "You'll regret it if you've given us a bogus name or a bullshit story." He shoved him away.

Mac and Nico were in the truck and on the road, headed to the Pool Room bar before the punk started his motorcycle.

Mac looked at Nico. "We're masters in Brazilian Jiu Jitsu, says the purple belt." They both laughed.

"You're almost a black belt. I figured we could hurt them if we had to and they wouldn't know the difference between a lower belt and a black belt," Nico added, "do you still want to swing by Red's and talk to the owner?"

"Yeah. Let's see if this 'Tay' dude is at the bar and then we can stop by Red's."

* * *

Irritated that the grandson had given them false information—nobody named Tay hung out at the Pool Room bar—Mac parked the truck in front of the Red's Roadhouse. The owner, Rinda Tofte, stopped sweeping the walkway in front of her business and looked at Nico, then Mac. Her eyes went back to Nico, and she smiled.

Nico opened the door and heard her say, "It's about time you stopped by. I have information for you."

Mac rounded the front of the truck with his hand outstretched. "Hi, I'm Mac."

Rinda reciprocated the introduction, then she swept the last of the debris into her pile and into the dustpan. "Let me get rid of this." She lifted the dustpan. "I'll be right in."

She approached the guys from the barkeep's side of the bar, having come inside through the back door. "Coffee? Bourbon? Iced Tea? What can I get you boys?"

Mac ordered an iced tea. Nico, coffee. They were alone in the bar. They could hear someone in the kitchen clanging pots and pans. The busy hustle of finishing a shift.

After serving them their beverages, Rinda asked Nico, "You know the guys who sit at the end?" She jabbed her thumb toward the far end of the bar.

"Yes."

She removed her hair band, shook out her long, red hair and bunched it back up into a ponytail as if she needed an extra minute to choose her words. "They were going on and on about the retired cop's murder this morning like they were back in uniform and trying to solve the case. One of them worked with the guy, not his partner, but same time-frame. He shared that, back then, there were rumors of him and an emergency operator having an affair."

Mac and Nico waited for a more explosive revelation than an old affair.

She added, "Sex, drugs, money. Take your pick. Any of those will get you murdered."

Nico asked, "Did they drop the woman's name he had an affair with?"

"No. And I felt I couldn't ask, or they'd have known I was eavesdropping."

Mac asked, "Why would an ancient affair be the reason to murder him now?"

She looked at Mac. "The way they were going on about the affair, the cop's wife found out and the guys at the time were all gossiping about him and betting on what his wife would do about it. They made her sound like she had an explosive personality and kept him on a short leash. Their words, not mine."

Mac took a long drink of his tea, then asked, "Did you pick up on anything else, something more recent?"

"Nope." She looked at Nico.

"Thank you. We'll pass along the information to the investigators." Nico drank the last of his coffee. "Has the new guy in town stopped by since I was here?"

"He stops in every morning for coffee. Keeps to himself. Stays about thirty minutes. Says little to nothing. He's an odd duck, to be sure."

Nico asked, "Do you know his name?"

She bobbed her head as she said, "His first name. It's Albert. He pays with cash or I could look on a credit card receipt."

"What time does Albert stop in for coffee? I'll come in and try to strike up a conversation with him?" Nico slid his coffee cup toward her.

"Around seven o'clock."

Mac stood, signaling to Nico it was time to leave before turning his attention back to the bar owner. "Thanks for the information. Please let us know if you hear anything else. Even what may seem like an insignificant tidbit may be a big clue." He handed her one of the business cards Nico had given him. "Call anytime."

In the truck, Mac said, "School will be out soon. I should check on the girls. Where can I drop you?"

"At my SUV, I need to pick up Rae. Are you alright?"

"Nope. My mind is stuck in a loop thinking about what Maggie is going through. Hearing about the dead cop's affair from twenty-plus years ago wasn't as helpful as she thought it was. Or is it? I can't see the connection." His tone sounded agitated.

"After I take Rae home, I'll go to the station and look into the affair and we'll see if there's a connection or not. Go check on the girls."

Chapter 23

Thomas Donaldson waited in his restored 1950s pickup truck at the front of the school for his granddaughters, Lindy and Bella. He put the truck in park and turned off the engine. Hoping to distract the girls from the obvious concern about their mother's whereabouts, he turned up the volume a few clicks on his favorite, 80s radio station.

He'd arrived at the school a few minutes later than normal, which put him ten or more cars back in the line of parents waiting for their children.

The bell rang, children poured out the doors and headed in all directions.

Bella smiled when she saw him and walked toward the truck. Thomas stretched over and pulled up on the door handle, then pushed the door open for her.

"Hi grandpa," she said, as she climbed up onto the seat. "Is mommy at the ranch?"

"Hi, sweet pea. How was your day?"

"Fine."

"Fine? What does fine mean?"

"Nothing different from yesterday. Did mom call?"

"Not yet. I'm sure we'll get some good news soon."

Bella asked, "Can I turn off the radio?"

"Sure."

They sat in silence, waiting and watching for Lindy.

When Lindy emerged from the building, her grandfather watched her turn toward them and walk down the sidewalk. He saw a man. And wrongly assumed the man was a student's father, dressed in athletic clothes, say something to Lindy. She looked up at him while he spoke.

Being a retired sheriff deputy himself, and suspicious of everyone, he started taking photos of the man with his cell phone. When the man handed Lindy something and she accepted it, Thomas's warning bells went off.

The man turned around and went in the opposite direction from Lindy, blending in with the crowd of students and adults clogging the sidewalk. Lindy pulled open the heavy door and stepped up to the seat.

Thomas asked, "Who was that man and what did he give you?"

"I don't know who he is. He told me to give this to my uncle." She showed him an envelope that someone had written MAC's name on it with a thick, black felt pen.

"Lindy, put the envelope on the floorboard in front of you." Her grandfather's tone delivered a level of concern, leaving no doubt he meant business. She placed it on the floor and then pulled her feet up onto the seat, drawing them tight to her chest. Bella pulled her feet up like her sister had done. He placed a call to the Brookfield Police Department and stressed to the person who had answered that it was important he speak with Detective Marten.

When Mac's friend Jason Marten answered, the girls' grandfather said, "Marten, it's Thomas Donaldson. We may have a situation at the girls' school. A stranger passed an envelope to Lindy. It's addressed to Mac."

"Interesting development. With all the weird shit going on, I'm going to alert the hazmat guys to take a look. You stay put. Don't open the envelope." He ended the call.

Hearing what their grandfather had said, Lindy and Bella sniffled tears back.

Thomas called the school and told the receptionist to get an urgent message to the principal. He told her, "This is Thomas Donaldson, Bella and Lindy Donaldson's grandfather. I don't have time to go into everything. We're parked in front of the school. You need to get everyone away from us and leave the area. We may have an anthrax exposure. The police have a hazmat team on the way." He gave the woman on the phone a description of his truck.

When Thomas was on the force, anthrax hadn't been something he knew anything about—at least law enforcement in Brookfield didn't. He knew as much about the bacteria as the girls did, but he knew it could be fatal to humans.

After he ended the call with the school, he patted the girls on their legs and said, "Everything will be alright. Marten wants to assume the worst, but he thinks it's a note or something harmless."

Next, he called his wife. After explaining in as cryptically as he could about what was happening, he said, "Come to the school, please."

Wringing her hands, Bella asked, "Is she coming?"

"Yes, she is."

"Why can't we leave?"

Thomas looked at his granddaughters and felt an ache in his heart. In as gentle of terms as he could think of, he said, "You know, there might be evidence on it like fingerprints or particles of dirt. If whatever is inside has anything to do with your mom, even something as small as dirt could help lead your Uncle Mac to where she is. But if we drove away, dirt could fall off the envelope."

Both girls glanced down at it.

When they looked up at him, Lindy said, "Call Uncle Mac."

Mac answered, "Hey there, Thomas. Has something happen...."

Cutting him off in mid-sentence, Thomas chose his words carefully because of the girls, and updated him on the situation. As Thomas spoke with Mac, he watched the school principal through the windshield as she directed parents to leave the area. A custodian placed orange cones across the sidewalk and street at a suitable distance in front of them. Then the custodian did the same behind them. Next, in his rearview mirror, he saw the custodian walk to the intersection behind them and block the road leading to the school. In the distance, he heard sirens approaching.

After everyone secured their positions, per the emergency preparedness plan for potential anthrax contamination, an officer in a full, protective suit approached the passenger side of the truck. Both girls had scooted so close to their grandfather they were almost sitting on his lap. They were crying and had their eyes covered. The officer opened the door and took possession of the envelope. Leaving the door open, he took the envelope to a portable enclosure that officers had erected in record time, where a laboratory technician awaited the envelope.

It felt like hours had passed while Mac and Patti Donaldson stood at a distance from the old truck, isolated from everyone. Mac looked at his watch. It showed four-fifteen—the girls got out of school at two-twenty.

Patti looked at Mac. "I know. They've been sitting there for hours." Mac pulled her close to his side.

As quick as the scenario had escalated, it ended. The scientist shared there had been no anthrax or any other detectable toxin in the envelope. The officers pulled off the face masks. Mac and Patti ran to the truck.

Lindy jumped from the seat to her grandmother, Bella to her uncle. Lindy said, in Patti's ear, "I'm scared."

Patti whispered back, "Everything is okay now, sweetie. Grandpa was being extra careful. Let's go to the ranch."

For one of the few times Mac could remember, Bella said nothing. She cried on his shoulder as he held her tight.

Patti said to her husband, "Lindy's going to ride with me."

Mac leaned over to look at Thomas, then added, "And Bella can ride with me. We'll meet you at the ranch."

When Mac turned to head toward his truck, Detective Marten called out to him. Mac waited for him to catch up. "We're sending a sketch artist to the ranch to get a description of the guy who handed Lindy the envelope."

"Good plan. What's in the envelope?"

Marten hesitated. He glanced at Bella and said, "I'll send you a text. The officer will meet you at the Donaldson's ranch."

Thomas overheard Marten and shared, "I snapped some photos of the guy."

"Brilliant. We'll have the tech guys run those through the facial recognition database to see if anything pops." He looked at Mac. "Scratch the sketch artist. I'll send a deputy out to talk with Thomas and the girls about everything they saw."

* * *

It didn't surprise Mac when his niece, Bella, who normally talked his ear off, sat quietly in the seat beside him. From her perspective, all she knew was something terrible might have been in that envelope and the kids in the parking lot watched them as they sat in her grandpa's truck.

Mac glanced sideways at his niece. "Are you okay?"

"Yes." Her little chin quivered.

"Do you want to talk about what happened?"

"Do you?"

"I'd like to talk about it."

"Okay."

"Why do you think the police were at the school?"

"You said you wanted to talk about it…you tell me why they were there."

Mac smiled. She was quick for an eight-year-old. "Did you see the man give your sister the envelope?"

"Not really."

"Would you be able to describe him to the deputy?"

"I don't think so." She twirled her hair around her finger and looked out the side window. "Can we pickup Roxy?"

"Sure." He passed her his cell phone. "Text your grandpa and tell him we're swinging by my place and then we'll head to the ranch."

Bella typed the text with youthful speed and then set his phone on the console between them. Within seconds, his phone vibrated. Bella leaned over to look at the screen. "He did a thumbs up."

When the traffic light turned green for his lane, Mac did a U-turn. "Can we talk more about what happened?"

"Uh-huh."

"Have you ever seen the man who gave Lindy the envelope before?"

"No. Never. What was in the envelope?"

"A message for me." He couldn't tell her it was a photograph of her mother, dirty and bound to a chair in what looked like a warehouse with a message scrawled across it, "Better hurry."

"What did the message say?"

"A message about an investigation I'm involved with. I can't talk about it."

He breathed a sigh of relief when she didn't probe deeper. "Because grandpa used to be a police officer, he wanted to be extra careful and make sure he didn't disturb any potential evidence on the envelope."

He felt her gaze turn to him. "That's what he said."

Mac felt grateful he and Thomas had been consistent in their explanation for the girls.

As he turned onto his cul-de-sac, her attention went back to the road ahead of them. He pushed the button on his sun visor to open his driveway gate and pulled to the rear of his home. "We can't leave Comet home alone. She'll have to come with us."

"Yay!" She clapped her hands and then stopped, as if remembering the scene at the school.

"Do you want a snack or need to use the restroom?"

"No," she said, as she climbed down from his tall truck.

Roxy and Comet ran out the doggy door to the backyard. Roxy's big plume of a tail wagged with enthusiasm. Comet spun in circles and ran around the entire yard.

"You stay with Comet while I get Roxy into the truck."

Bella knelt and calmed Monica's wild-eyed Maltese. Mac gave Roxy some love, then hoisted her up and into the back seat, then clamped her collar to the seatbelt.

Next, Mac went to Bella. "You climb into the truck before I put Comet in or she'll take over your seat." Bella did as he asked. With both dogs in the truck, they were once again on their way to the Donaldson's ranch. Comet had made herself comfortable in Bella's lap. Bella clamped the dog's harness to the seat belt they shared.

"Hey, do me a favor. Text Monica and let her know we have Comet."

Bella grabbed his phone again and did as he asked. When she had finished, she asked, "Where's momma?"

"I don't know." He let that truth settle. "I'm doing everything I can to find her."

"Where'd she sleep last night?"

"We don't know. When I know an answer to your questions, I promise I'll tell you."

"I don't want to go to school tomorrow. All the kids are going to talk about the police and all."

"I'm sure if you tell grandma you don't want to go to school, she'll keep you home." Mac had already decided the girls should stay at the ranch until they found Maggie.

"When you saw the man approach Lindy, what did you notice about him?"

"Ummm, he looked like a jogger."

"Did he look like a jogger because of his clothes?"

"Yes." She stroked Comet's back as she spoke.

"Did you watch where he went after he handed Lindy the envelope?"

"He walked down the sidewalk until I couldn't see him anymore."

"You didn't see him cross the street?"

"No."

Mac turned onto the dirt driveway leading to the Donaldson's ranch. When he neared the house, he saw a patrol vehicle was already there—he assumed the cruiser belonged to the officer Marten had sent.

Bella waited for Mac to get the dogs out before she opened her door, then she jumped down. As she rounded the front of the truck headed for the door, Lindy opened the screen door and let the puppy out. The little dog ran to Comet. They sniffed each other and remained friendly. When the puppy approached Roxy, she snarled, which the pup respected and turned back toward Comet.

Inside, Mac introduced himself to the officer seated at the dining room table. "Marten told me to drop what I was doing and get out here."

"Thank you." Mac's emotions made the words hard to say.

The officer had his laptop open and had a notepad ready. When he showed he was ready, Lindy sat next to him.

He didn't want Bella and Thomas to hear Lindy describe what she'd seen, so the officer asked them to wait outside. Patti, always the thoughtful hostess, brought iced lemonade and homemade cookies to the front porch.

Inside, Mac sat at the table, ready to take notes.

* * *

Mac, his 10-year-old niece, Lindy, and the Brookfield Police Officer, Isaac, sat at one end of the Donaldson's oval dining room table. Lindy glanced at Mac and mouthed, "I'm scared."

Mac reached out and took her hand in his before he whispered, "You'll do fine."

Considering the ranch house always had people and dog sounds, the house was eerily quiet. When Patti Donaldson came inside through the front door, the wind from the opened windows caused a vacuum making the door slammed shut behind her. The sudden noise startled Lindy.

Patti hurried to Lindy, hugged her, kissed her cheek, and said, "I'm sorry, sweet girl."

Lindy straightened her posture. "It's okay, grandma."

Patti kissed her granddaughter again and said in a hushed voice, "I'll be right back. You all need some refreshments." She went toward the kitchen and returned with a plate of cookies and cold lemonade for the three at the table.

After setting the beverages and treats on the table, Patti pulled a chair around and sat next to Lindy. The look she gave the police officer rivaled what he may have experienced as a child in trouble. She told him in no uncertain terms, "I wasn't at the scene. I have nothing to contribute to help figure out what happened—I'll sit here by Lindy and stay quiet."

The tone of Patti's voice told the officer he wasn't getting rid of her.

Isaac grabbed a cookie, took a big bite, then placed it on a napkin. He murmured, "Mmm," then said, "I'm ready to get started." He placed a voice recorder on the table and pressed the record button. "Brookfield Police Officer Isaac Johnson, badge number 674, Tuesday, May 8, 2012, the time is fifteen-twenty, I'm with Mac MacKenna, Patti." He stopped and looked at Patti.

She said, "Donaldson."

He continued, "Patti Donaldson, and her granddaughter, Lindy Donaldson."

Patti held Lindy's hand while Mac readied himself to jot down anything helpful.

"Do you remember the man who handed you the envelope for your uncle?"

"Yes."

"What color was his skin?"

"White with freckles."

"Did he have tattoos?"

"Yes, he had an alligator wrapped around his right arm, a cross on his left arm on the underside of his wrist." She pointed to the spot on her arm. "And the word Jesus on the knuckles on his left hand." Again, she pointed. "That's the hand he used to hand me the envelope, so I saw the cross and letters then."

"Excellent, Lindy."

Patti patted her granddaughter's bouncing knee.

"Were the tattoos colorful or black?"

"Black."

"Did he call you by name?"

"Yes."

"How tall was he? Did you look up at him after he called your name?"

"Yes, he was taller than me."

"A lot taller?"

"Taller than Mac."

Isaac looked at Mac. "I'm six feet, two."

After Isaac clicked his mouse a few times, he said, "Close your eyes and see the man who handed you the envelope."

Lindy did as she was told.

"Look around him. Was anyone looking at him?"

"I don't know."

"Okay." Isaac took another bite of his cookie.

"What color were his eyes?"

"Can I open my eyes now?"

"Yes, I'm sorry."

"I think his eyes were green."

"That's good. Were his eyes wide open or sleepy looking?"

"Wide open."

"Did he have eyebrows?"

"Yes, bushy and red."

Isaac took a sip of his lemonade. "Do you want to drink some lemonade or to take a break?"

"No, thank you. I'd rather finish so Mac can go find my mom." A tear ran down her small cheek. Grandma Patti leaned over and hugged her.

"I'll speed it up. We know the man had a cap on. Did you see his hair under his cap?"

"No."

Isaac made eye contact with Mac before he asked, "You couldn't see his hair?"

"I think he was bald."

"Thank you for the clarification. You're doing good, Lindy."

She said, "He had a long beard."

"What color was his beard?"

Lindy squinted her eyes as if trying harder to see the man in her mind. "Sorta orange."

"Have you ever seen anyone else with the same color of hair? It could be a movie star or a singer, or someone you know."

"Jessie from Toy Story."

Mac looked at Isaac and gave a slight shrug.

Isaac said to Lindy, "Jessie is the best. Do you think she and Woody will ever get married?"

Lindy stifled a giggle. "They're cartoon characters."

Returning the seriousness to his voice, Isaac asked, "Did his orange beard look natural or fake like he had a hair stylist color it? Do you know what I'm talking about?"

"Yes, it looked natural."

"Do you remember what he was wearing?"

"Athletic clothes."

"Can you be more specific?"

She shook her head.

Isaac said, "Lindy, please answer the question with words."

"No, I can't be more specific."

Sensing her fatigue, Patti stood, "Time to lie down, Lindy." Without asking permission, she hustled Lindy out of the room.

Mac wanted to be sure to tell Marten that Isaac had done a fantastic job with Lindy. "Thank you. You did great with her. I hope we find out who this guy is."

"Would you ask Thomas to come inside so I can get his recollection? And I'm told he has photographs?"

Mac went outside and to the end of the front porch. "Thomas, it's your turn. I'll stay out here with Bella and..." he paused, looking down at the puppy chewing on a rawhide. "Does the puppy have a name yet?"

Bella giggled, then said, "Yes, she has a name. It's Pepper."

"Pepper? Like the old dog's name?" Mac asked, as he sat next to Bella on the porch chair Thomas had left.

"Grandpa said they name all their dogs Pepper."

Mac laughed, then scooped up little Pepper and placed her on his lap. Her black curls jiggled in response to her wagging tail as Mac scratched her behind her ears. A jealous Roxy tried to nuzzle in for Mac to pet her.

Inside, Isaac asked Thomas the same questions he'd asked Lindy, but in a more adult manner—recording everything they said. After Isaac transferred the photos to his laptop, they both walked outside to join Mac and Bella on the porch. Isaac stretched his back a few times, and bent over to touch his toes.

When Isaac rose from his position of touching his toes, he said to Thomas, "The tech guys will run the photos through the facial recognition soon."

Mac nodded. The puppy tried to open her eyes but failed.

Isaac went inside to retrieve his things. He came outside with his laptop case and another cookie. While holding the cookie in his mouth, he shook everyone's hand with his free hand, even Bella's. "Marten will let you know as soon as they have anything."

They watched Isaac drive away from the ranch. Mac hugged Thomas and then Bella for a few extra seconds—picking her up and spinning her around. "Gotta go, little one. Tell your sister goodbye for me."

With one hand steering the truck backward, with the other, he speed dialed Nico. Mac saw a tearful Bella waving as he glanced through the windshield. He waved back.

Nico answered, "Hey Mac, what's happening?"

"I want to find that punk, Anson. He's going to give up the name of the person who wanted the license plates or…" Giving the future interaction some consideration. "I can't predict what I'll do."

Chapter 24

Mac picked up Nico at the police station and they were on their way to Anson's grandmother's home. "Did you find out anything about Stockford's affair or a link to Maggie's abduction?"

"Some of the old guys in the conference room who're going through the case files remembered the affair. They said the woman, named Donna, was an emergency call operator. They also remembered Stockford's wife found out and demanded he dump the other woman for good or get out. He'd said if they divorced, she'd take half of his pension with her."

Mac said, "Sounds like the stereotypical 'scorned woman.' But that's not how Monica describes her. He was married once, correct? Did they think the affair had anything to do with the murders or with Maggie?"

"They had no clue how his affair so long ago could relate to his murder or Ann Sawyer's murder. As far as I know, he had one wife. Sawyer was two years old at the time of his affair."

Mac shook his head. Frustration quickened his heart-rate. They rode in silence until they parked in front of Glenda Mullis' home for the second time that day. Her minivan wasn't there. Instead, Anson's motorcycle sat in the driveway.

Glenda was no longer sitting on her front porch, but the front door was still open. The screen door stood between Mac and Nico and Anson's grandmother. Mac pounded on the door trim.

He saw Glenda shuffling toward them with the help of a cane.

"Hello, boys, nice to see you again. What's up? Am I in more trouble?"

As Mac opened the screen door, he said, "Glenda, come sit on the porch with us. Whether you're in more trouble depends on how you answer our questions."

Saying nothing more, she scooted to the same chair she'd sat in earlier. Mac stood in front of her, leaning his butt against the porch railing. Nico sat next to her and pulled his notebook from his pocket.

Glenda gave a sideways glance at Nico's notebook.

Mac started, "We met your grandson at his work."

"He told me."

"Did he tell you what we wanted from him?"

"He said a friend of his stole your narcotics and you're looking for him. I can't help you. I want nothing to do with narcotics."

Mac counted to three in his mind. "We didn't have any narcotics stolen. Your grandson lied to you."

Glenda's face registered disbelief. Mac continued, "Someone abducted my sister…"

"He told me you'd try something tricky to get me to tell you more about him." She crossed her arms.

Mac wasn't in the mood for niceties. "And the man who took her drove a utility-type van with your license plates."

"I don't understand." Glenda clasped her hands together on her lap, squeezing so tight her knuckles turned white.

"Let me break it down for you." Mac's voice had an agitated edge to it. "Your grandson took your license plates, sold them, or let someone borrow them for a price. Whoever has your plates, put them on a van and then abducted my sister using the van with your license plates. Clear enough?"

"Should I call a lawyer?"

Mac adjusted his stance. "I don't care if you call an attorney, a priest, or a TV repairman. We aren't here to arrest you. We are consultants with the police department, not officers. If you help us find your grandson, we won't call in to have an officer come here to read you your Miranda Rights and haul your ass to jail for aiding in the abduction of my sister."

"He told me you guys were coming for him and he needed to use the van to go to some guy's house who had your narcotics to get them back for you. He wants you guys to leave him alone."

"Now that you know his story is all bullshit, where do you think he is?"

"You're scaring me."

"I'm sorry, Glenda, I don't mean to scare you. But finding my sister is what's most important to me."

She relaxed her posture. "He said the guy with the narcotics was hanging out in some old industrial area outside of town. I didn't want to know more. He told me not to worry if I didn't see him for a few days."

Mac patted Nico on the shoulder. "Let's go." He bolted from the porch and tossed over his shoulder, "Thanks, Glenda." He stopped, turned around and added, "And Glenda, your grandson is a piece of shit, don't trust anything he tells you."

* * *

Driving away from Glenda Mullis's home, Mac punched the throttle, but then remembered he was in a residential neighborhood, with children around and there were speed limits. The last thing he needed right now was to hit someone or have a cop issue a speeding ticket.

"Do you think she's telling us the truth?" asked Nico.

"Who knows? We have nothing else to chase." Mac sped toward the only abandoned industrial area he knew of in Brookfield.

Industry in the United States hit its peak in the mid-1900s. The economy shifted from manufacturing to service-providing industries. As the U.S. entered the twenty-first century, manufacturers moved their businesses to other countries where they paid less to have their products made, and the end of an era began. Now, across the United States, if you looked hard enough, not on main thoroughfares, but in the seedier sections of towns, you'd find abandoned, industrial areas like the one in Brookfield.

Brookfield's industrial area used to include a thriving lumber mill, which Mac had been told had burned to the ground ten or more years ago. After the fire, one-by-one, the other businesses—a trucking company, an ice business, a truss manufacturer, an ironworks factory—all had closed. The land had become a multi-acre eye-sore.

Nico nodded. "Good point," he acknowledged. "There must be a link between the murders and Maggie's abduction. The more I think about it, I think you're right about the timing being too coincidental. In law enforcement, you're trained that there's no such thing as a coincidence, and this case looks like a prime example."

Mac considered what Nico said. "Then we figure out how they're related." He turned his blinker on to move into the fast lane.

Nico pulled out his notebook. "First killing. Retired police officer, Bruce Stockford. Age sixty-six, retired in 1996 with thirty years on the force—he could have a lot of potential enemies. Married forty-two years, one son, and two grandchildren."

Mac lifted his foot from the throttle as the speed limit dropped to forty miles per hour.

As they approached, they could see the remains of the old industrial buildings. For sale, and private property signs greeted them as they entered the area. Mac slowed the truck to a crawl as they drove around the dilapidated buildings. He saw a lot of corrugated metal, metal doors, roll-up doors, large windows too high to reach without a ladder, loading docks for pickups and deliveries.

The roads hadn't had a fresh coat of asphalt in so long there were more pot holes than not making it impossible to see fresh tire tracks.

Nico read from his notebook, "Second killing. Unemployed School Administrator, Ann Sawyer. Age thirty-eight, having an affair with Mayor Ozzy Eastland. Single, no children."

Mac said, "Keep your eyes open for Glenda's van or movement. Even a bird at this point might lead us somewhere." Mac continued thinking about connecting the crimes. He added, "If Stockford's killing has something to do with his affair all those years ago ..." He stopped mid-thought. "Do we know what Ann's mother's name was, assuming she's deceased?"

Nico jotted in his notebook. "I'll find that out, too."

"Also, check into whether Sawyer has an older sister. Maybe the 911 operator was young, like eighteen or twenty. Maybe Sawyer was the love-child he never knew about? Talk about gross—to have an affair with a woman you didn't know was your daughter." Mac shivered at the thought. "Do we know how old the other woman was at the time of the affair?"

Nico flipped through his notes. "I'll find out."

Mac's mind was running down a mental spreadsheet. "And who was Sawyer dating before the mayor? We should also look into the mayor's wife—but how would she or her life circle back to Stockford? While we're at it, Mrs. Stockford—Monica won't like it, but after what you heard about her temper and the ultimatum she gave her husband, we have to consider she may be involved. Could this be about people who cheat on their spouses? But Maggie's never ... Oh, shit. Remember the doctor she dated who said he was single, but turned out to be married, with children, and a habitual cheater who kept a secret condominium as his sex lair?"

Nico raised an eyebrow and looked at Mac. "His sex lair?"

"My point was—back then—she'd fit the definition of 'the other woman.'"

Nico made more notes. Then texted someone. After a minute, he said, "My friend at the FBI said he'd help however he could. Let's start with seeing what he can find out about Stockford's 'other woman'." After he sent his text, he said, "If this is all connected because of infidelity, I think they would have killed the mayor rather than his mistress."

"Fair point."

They cruised around the large, warehouse type buildings at a snail's pace, observing somehow structures had burned to the ground. Mac broke the quiet. "There are a lot of tire tracks through here. It wouldn't surprise me if teenagers come here to have sex."

"We should come back at night," Nico said.

Mac gave him a sideways glance. "You want to catch teenagers engaged in sex?"

"No, if Maggie's here, it's possible her captor comes at night to check on her."

"Good idea. You concerned me for a minute.'" Mac gave his friend a slight smile. "Let's go back to the first building you come to when you enter from the highway and see if we can get into the building to look around. We can check one building at a time to eliminate them one-by-one." He did a U-turn and went in the opposite direction from which they'd come.

"You sure you were never in law enforcement?" Nico asked.

"I'm sure. Growing up, I hung out at the Donaldson's ranch a lot. With Thomas being a deputy sheriff, he told us all kinds of crazy stories about cases. Bobby's mom would try to make him stop filling our heads with his work, but we wanted to hear all the gory details. You'd have thought the stories would've steered both of us away from violence, but Bobby followed in his father's footsteps and I joined the air force." Mac's voice trailed off at the end of his thought.

"My dad was FBI, and he never talked about work. And then I became an FBI agent like my dad."

"I didn't know your dad was FBI. You don't talk about him much"

Nico shrugged. "We aren't close."

Mac picked up on the hint that he didn't want to talk about him now, either. He parked at the first building and retrieved his handgun from the gun box behind the driver's seat.

Nico clicked the safety off on the weapon in his holster.

They approached what would have been the main door to the office area of the first building. Mac jiggled the doorknob. Locked. They moved along the loading dock. Mac bent down and grabbed the first roll-up door and heaved. Also locked. Nico did the same to the next one. Also locked. They tried all the roll-up doors. All locked. They retraced their steps and descended the steps to the asphalt.

Mac said, "You go one way, I'll go the other to see if there's an open window."

The windows on the first side appeared to be office type, and all were closed. They walked around to the back and side of the building. The large windows toward the roof were a pivot-type. If they'd left one open, the guys would need a tall extension ladder to get inside—but they didn't have one. And if they did, it would be a long drop on the other side.

Mac stopped and stared up at the window. "Let's move on to the next." He turned around and headed back to his truck.

They found an unlocked side door in one warehouse. It also had an open window on what looked like the second floor. Upon entering the building, they saw the interior was in shambles. Much of the roof had collapsed, making traversing the floor impossible. They doubted a captor would carry Maggie through the rubble. The building had become a home for several bird species, who they startled when they opened the door. They flew to the rafters for a safer vantage point. One, a nesting turkey vulture, made a loud squawk. The guys froze in place a second later, when her mate flew in through a hole in the roof. He landed on a tall pile of roofing material that gave him a full view of the room, his mate, and the guys. His wingspan looked to be close to six feet, his red face glared at them.

Mac tapped Nico's arm and whispered, "Time to go."

They stepped backward out of the building along the same path by which they'd entered, keeping their eyes on the male bird who kept his eyes on them.

Back outside, Nico said, "What the …That was one gigantic and butt-ugly bird."

Mac laughed. "I take it they didn't have vultures where you grew up."

"No, I've never seen one of those before."

His mind back on Maggie, Mac said, "No way would she have been in there."

"Agreed. Too undisturbed."

Mac's cell phone vibrated in his pocket. He pulled it out to see Monica's face on the screen. He answered, "Hey Babe. What's going on?"

"Mrs. Stockford said she'd answer your questions if you can come to the house now that the children are with their parents."

"On our way. Thank you." Mac looked at Nico. "We can talk with Mrs. Stockford."

Chapter 25

Mac turned off the highway and headed into the subdivision where the Stockfords lived. A sizable group of reporters had gathered near the entrance. A patrol car and two uniformed officers sat between the reporters and the road into the community. Not far down the road, they saw the yellow crime scene tape they'd strung from one giant redwood tree to its twin on the other side of the driveway. Next to the driveway sat a strange piece of metal art made from what looked like motorcycle parts.

Looking toward the art piece, Nico said, "Interesting."

A uniformed rookie stood guard, leaning against a tree. They'd caught the young man amid a yawn, which he attempted to stifle when he saw them. He didn't look old enough to drive, let alone wear a badge and carry a weapon. His slight frame seemed even smaller with the large duty belt and all its adornments wrapped around his thin waist.

Mac stopped the truck short of the tape and allowed the rookie to approach the driver's window. Saying nothing, Mac held out his police consultant identification. Nico leaned over and stretched his arm in front of Mac to show the officer the same identification.

"We're here to speak with Mrs. Stockford."

The rookie spoke into the radio attached to his vest. The person on the other end must've given permission. Without having said a single word to them—trying to look as macho as possible—he knew he'd never be able to lift the tape high enough for Mac's large truck to pass under so he removed the yellow tape from one side and walked it to the other so they could proceed down the driveway.

Nico quipped, "Friendly kid. He didn't look old enough to be a cop." Then he shifted his gaze to the wooded area on their left and saw the officers combing the woods. He said, "Looks like they think the shooter was out there. We can't see the house yet. It's a long shot to the house."

The driveway curved to the left, making the home closer to the area where the officers searched.

Nico calculated in his mind. "I'd guess two-fifty to three-hundred-foot shot. An expert marksman. Maybe ex-military."

Mac didn't see Marten's vehicle. He assumed they must be working the investigation from the 'war room' at the station. A few patrol cars were still on scene, nothing like Monica had described when she first arrived on the day of the murder. He saw Monica's jeep. Parked next to her sat an unmarked government vehicle. He asked, "Are the feds here?"

Nico glanced at the vehicle parked near the house. "Looks like it."

As Mac parked the truck on the gravel driveway aimed at the front porch and next to the unmarked government vehicle, Monica exited the house and walked toward them.

She said nothing until she was a few feet away, "Hi guys."

Mac and Nico said hello. Mac paused and peered into the sedan they'd assumed belonged to an FBI agent or two, noticing they had a laptop mounted on a bracket attached to the dash so the passenger could use it while the partner drove. A crumpled, fast-food bag sat on the floor mat, which he assumed had held their breakfast from earlier.

Even though she'd worn civilian clothes, Mac respected her as a police officer rather than his girlfriend. He followed her lead.

She hugged Mac, but didn't kiss him.

"Are the feds here?" Mac asked.

"Yes, they're out in the woods with our guys, looking for anything. One of them is supposed to be a renowned tracker."

Nico gave her a warm hug. "Quentin Reynolds?"

"That's him." She turned to Mac. "Please be gentle with Gretchen. She's been through a lot in the last few days."

"We want to know about rumors of an affair Bruce had years ago. I don't know if talking about it will upset her, but it's the one connection we've got to connect Bruce to Maggie. And it's not much."

"All I ask is try to be gentle."

Nico trailed after Mac, who followed Monica into the home. Gretchen was a fit, older woman, even more so when compared to Glenda Mullis. She sat in an over-sized chair. She leaned on the side arm with her socked feet curled under her. As they drew closer to the living room, the woman stood and outstretched her hand. "Hello, I'm Gretchen Stockford."

Mac, then Nico, shook her hand, introduced themselves, and then sat on the sofa next to her chair.

It wasn't a surprise to anyone that she looked pale and tired. Her short, graying hair seemed a common cut for athletic women—she had the muscles of a runner or a rock climber.

"We're sorry for your loss, Mrs. Stockford," Nico said, as if he'd said those words many times to grieving spouses. He continued, "Understanding this is a difficult time and knowing our questions may upset you. We want you to know we appreciate you allowing us a few moments of your time."

She nodded. "Please call me Gretchen."

Nico balanced the notebook on his thigh, ready to write as much as possible, regardless of whether or not it seemed important. He waited for Mac to take charge.

Mac started, "We don't want to further contribute to your pain, but we have a delicate subject-matter to discuss with you."

"With that introduction to your questions, I might need a cup of coffee and a box of tissues before we begin."

Monica jumped to her feet. "I'll get both for you. Hot or cold coffee?"

"Hot, please, with creamer."

Monica looked at the guys. "Would either of you like some coffee?"

They both asked for a hot coffee.

While Monica was out of the room, Mac refocused his attention on Gretchen. "Has Monica told you about my sister?"

She shook her head. "No."

With what had happened to the woman's husband, he felt she didn't need to know about Maggie, but he wanted to find out if she knew of a connection. "Did she tell you about Ann Sawyer?"

"Yes, she did."

Mac continued, "Yesterday, someone abducted my sister. She lives in Brookfield."

"Oh, my goodness, I'm so sorry. Do you think her abduction relates to Bruce's murder?" Her voice caught when she said her husband's name.

"To be honest, I don't know. I may be wrong to even consider the possibility, but I have nothing to go on."

Nico spoke up and said, "An old cop saying is…."

She finished the sentence, "There's no such thing as a coincidence." She slumped. "Bruce used to say that. Even to our son. One time he and a friend were hitting baseballs with each other and they broke the neighbor's living room window. The next day, a different neighbor told Bruce he had a baseball-size dent in the fender of his truck. Wyatt denied his involvement. Bruce told him the same thing…." Her sad eyes connected with Nico's gaze.

"Yes, all us law enforcement types say it or something like it now and then, when the circumstance fits."

Monica returned with a box of tissues, four mugs of steaming coffee and a container of creamer. Gretchen added creamer to her mug, Mac and Nico drank theirs black. Monica added creamer to hers as well. Nobody asked for sugar and nobody was saying anything either.

Mac broke the silence when he looked at Monica and told her what she'd missed. "I was telling Gretchen about Maggie and that we aren't sure if there's a connection to her husband's death."

She nodded.

Gretchen blew her nose. "I think I'm ready for your questions." Her gaze locked on Mac. "How can I help? I don't believe we've ever met your sister."

"You may have, but the meeting wasn't memorable. She works at the hospital in the emergency room." He refused to speak of her in the past tense. "Have you or your husband ever gone to the emergency room?"

"Of course, hasn't everyone?"

"When?"

"When have we gone to the ER?"

"Yes."

"Well, give me a minute to think about it." She sipped her coffee, then said, "One time, when Adler fell off his bicycle. Turned out he'd broken his arm. And once…."

"Who took Adler to the ER? You or your husband?"

"Both of us. Bruce had already retired, so we were both home when it happened."

"Another time, when Bruce was grinding some metal and a sliver of metal flew into his eye." She looked at him, expecting another question.

Nico looked up from his notebook. "Did he make the metal art we saw at the end of your driveway?"

Her posture softened. "Yes, he did."

Mac pulled a photograph from the chest pocket of his T-shirt. "Was he into motorcycles?"

"No, he wanted the parts for his art pieces."

He stretched across the coffee table and placed the photo of Maggie on the table in front of Mrs. Stockford. "Do you recognize her? Was she your nurse?"

She looked at the photograph of Maggie for a long second. "I don't recall." She placed the photograph on the table.

"Did your husband ever work on a detail at the school?" He took a big swig of his coffee, keeping his eyes on her as he looked over the mug.

She set her mug on the side table and rubbed her eyes. "He retired sixteen years ago. How could I remember detailed minutia about his job?"

He met her darkened stare with a twinge of frustration. "I'm sorry to ask questions you perceive as irrelevant or improper—I don't know what you know or don't know until I ask." He looked down at Maggie in the photograph he'd left on the coffee table, then looked up at her. "I'm desperate to find my sister."

"I'm sorry. I'm exhausted and feel depleted." She propped up her jaw with her hand—elbow burrowed into the arm of her chair. "Go on," she said, emotionless.

"We've heard there were rumors your husband had an affair. Did he?"

"Yes, it's true. He ended the affair and told me he didn't want to lose me—I told him I wouldn't tolerate infidelity a second time. Please don't tell me he had other affairs."

"We only know of the one affair. Do you remember anything about the other woman?"

She took a slow, thoughtful sip of her coffee. "I'm pretty sure every woman whose husband has cheated on them remembers the name of the 'other woman' if she knew it. Her name was Donna."

"Do you know Donna's last name?"

"Andrews."

Mac furrowed his brow. "Was she related to Coach Andrews?"

"I don't know."

"He was a coach at Blackstone Academy."

"Doesn't ring any bells for me."

"I'm sorry to ask. Do you know how long the affair lasted?"

"Several months."

"How did you find out about it?"

"A wife of one of the other officers. She said she'd want someone to tell her if her husband was having an affair, so she told me. In response, I told her about her husband's affair as she said she'd want to be told."

Monica took a slow swallow of her coffee.

Mac asked, "How'd she handle the news?"

"About as well as I did."

"What's her name?"

"Hmmm, I haven't thought about them in many years. I remember they divorced not long after the news of the affair came out. She moved away. He married the woman he'd been cheating with and they moved away too."

Nico's pen paused over his notebook, and he looked up at her. "Do you think there's a chance their adultery and you revealing it may have had anything to do with your husband's death?"

Gretchen looked at Nico for a few extra blinks. "I have no clue."

Nico jotted something down on his pad. "Try to remember their names and let Monica know."

She nodded.

Mac cleared his throat. "Did Donna Andrews move away after the affair ended?"

"I know she left her employment with the police department. She'd been an emergency operator. One time, Bruce and I went to Handley's Coffee Shop for breakfast on a Sunday after church. When we walked inside, Bruce and a server made eye contact. Her face showed some type of emotion—anger, love, hate, concern— I'm not sure which. Bruce turned me around and said he didn't want to eat there. When we were back in the car, he told me the woman in the coffee shop had been Donna. It was the first time I'd seen her. She was quite attractive."

Mac added, "Do you know if Donna had children?"

"No, I know nothing about her. I've chosen to know as little as possible about the whole affair. Bruce admitted he'd made a mistake and begged my forgiveness. He promised to never have a wandering eye again. I trusted him to be truthful. End of story."

Nico considered the information the older officers had told him from their recollection, which differed from hers.

"Can you think of any other relationships—even friendships— that come to mind? We may connect the smallest detail to your husband's death."

"You can say, murder. I'm not so fragile that I can't accept what happened for what it is. And I've told Monica and the two detectives all the possibilities I could think of."

"Thank you for your time."

"I hope you find your sister soon and unharmed."

"Thank you."

Mac, Nico, and Monica walked in a single file out the front door. Once on the porch with the door closed, Mac said, "There has to be a connection between the two killings and Maggie." He jabbed his thumb toward the front door. "She may know more than she's telling. Holding back to preserve what's left of his reputation. Has she said if he had other affairs?"

Monica said, "You say that like you know something, like he had more than the one. What do you know?"

"Nothing."

Monica pushed, "How could him having multiple affairs help find Maggie?"

"Maybe he had an affair with Sawyer and Maggie treated them at the ER after an accident and… I don't know." He rubbed his neck like he had a tight muscle.

"That's a stretch, but I'll try to get her to talk more about the affair."

Chapter 26

Maggie felt like an earthquake had awakened her. When she opened her eyes, she saw her captor. She knew she had to befriend him like Peyton had done, no matter what it took.

She gave him the most pathetic, facial expression she could muster—reminding herself he was dominate, her submissive.

He dropped a backpack on the floor and pulled out a water bottle and twisted the cap off. "Open up."

She tipped her head back and resumed the baby bird position, waiting for the momma to drop a worm into her mouth. He poured a small trickle of water and allowed her to swallow.

After she'd had enough, she said, "Thank you."

"Are you hungry?"

"Yes."

Next out of his bag of tricks was a mangled granola bar—he tore open the wrapper.

"Will you please loosen my wrists so I can feed myself? It's not like I can go anywhere with my feet strapped to the chair legs."

It appeared he gave this request some consideration, then pulled a razor knife from his backpack, and sliced the tie that held her right wrist to the arm of the chair. Then he handed her the granola bar.

"Thank you." She took a small bite, both savoring the morsel and wanting it to last for as long as possible. "How many days have I been here?"

"One."

She held in her urge to scream and cry at the same time. Thinking about the girls gave her strength. "What has to happen before you'll let me go?"

"I don't know. I do what I'm told."

She nodded while chewing a nibble. "Are you married?"

"No."

"Do you have children?"

"No. You ask a lot of fucking questions."

"There's no one else I can talk to. Do you have a pet?" She wondered if he had anything he cared about in his life.

"A cat."

"Aww, cats are so lovable. What's its name?"

"A black cat named Lucifer."

She took another small bite, thinking the name he chose for his cat said more about him than the cat which concerned her.

"How long have you had Lucifer?"

"Not long. He wandered into my apartment a couple of months ago when I left the sliding door open all night. He wouldn't leave."

"That's nice of you to take him in and give him a home."

"Now, I leave the door open so he can come and go. I don't want him shitting in my place."

"I bet he likes the freedom."

"I see what you're doing. Eating slow. I'm not stupid."

"It feels good to let the blood circulate in my arm. Of course, I want to move it as much as I can. I told you I'm a nurse. Would you be willing to release my other wrist so I can move my arm?"

"If I do, no funny stuff and I'm not releasing your legs, so don't ask."

Using his razor knife again, he cut the tie on her left wrist.

Swirling her left hand in circles and rotating her shoulder, almost felt orgasmic. "Thank you."

"Finish eating the granola bar so I can go."

She ate the remaining sustenance in two bites, leaving the empty wrapper on her thigh. "May I have some more water?"

He handed her the bottle. She gulped the entire bottle as fast as she could, then wiped her lips with the back of her hand. She handed him back the empty bottle. "When will you come back?"

Rather than continue the conversation, he pulled two zip ties from his pocket.

"Not too tight, please. If you make them too tight, the restricted blood flow will cause permanent damage to my hands."

It surprised her when she felt the binds were looser than he'd done them before.

"Thank you."

"Will you come back tonight and bring me food? I liked the hamburger you fed me… I don't remember when, but I remember it was good. Can you bring me another hamburger?"

Again, he ignored her questions.

From his pants pocket, he pulled out a syringe.

"No. Please. Don't." She shook her head violently. "You don't need to sedate me."

He flicked the barrel of the syringe twice to get any air bubbles to the top and then squirted a small amount of whatever was in the syringe out to clear the needle of air like he'd been in the medical field or an addict who had done that many times.

"Please, please don't do this. I won't scream. I've been good. Please, I'm begging you. Please." Tears streamed down her cheeks as he jabbed the needle into her arm. She watched the liquid leave the barrel of the syringe and then felt her eyelids drift shut.

She thought of her late husband. *Please, baby, show Mac where I am.* Then, hearing the footsteps walk away, she blurted out, "Please come back, please don't leave me here to…."

Chapter 27

It was two in the morning when Mac's phone vibrated on the nightstand. He saw Marten's name on the screen and grabbed his phone. "Hey. Please tell me you have good news about Maggie."

Roxy stood from her big, fluffy bed. She shook her head, making the dog tags on her collar jangle. Then she lumbered to Mac's side of the bed and laid her big head on the bed.

"I hope I don't have news about Maggie, but a local driving home from the night shift at an old folks' home spotted a woman's body by the swinging bridge and called it in. Her description sounds too much like Maggie. Can you meet me at the morgue? They're taking her there."

"I'll get there as fast as I can."

"And Mac, the officer said she has a medical symbol tattooed on her ankle."

"I'm on my way."

He jumped out of bed and turned toward Monica, and said, "Somebody found a dead woman's body and her description sounds like Maggie. And she has a medical symbol tattooed on her ankle," he said, as he rushed to the closet to dress. Poking his head out the closet door, he added, "Maggie has a caduceus tattoo on her ankle."

"Oh, no, Mac. It can't be her. You know she has more life to live. Stay positive. I'll take care of the dogs… Unless you want me to come with you?"

"Thank you. I've got this."

He tossed some water on his face, brushed his teeth, and dressed. When he went downstairs, Monica sat on the sofa with Comet on her lap and Roxy next to her.

"Call me when you know something," she said, as he bent down to kiss her goodbye.

"I will." Then he hurried to his truck.

Not expecting a response, Mac texted Nico and told him what was happening and that he'd connect with him later in the morning. Nico replied in an instant and said, *Pick me up. I'll be out front.*

Mac considered his options as he changed his course to head toward Nico's complex. If the body was Maggie's, she'd already passed. If the body wasn't Maggie's, then she was still alive and waiting for him to find her. In the end, he decided two minutes added to his travel time wouldn't make a difference.

Driving to Nico's, he tried to think about viewing the body. He couldn't relate the body to a person, not when the person might be his sister. He thought, *it isn't Maggie they were bringing in—it isn't.* Like Monica had said, Maggie had a lot of life left to live. The girls needed their mother. It's a mother's job to teach her daughter or in Maggie's case, her daughters how to cook, do laundry, shop for groceries, show them how to drive, talk about sex, deal with a break-up and what a broken heart will feel like when you're a teenager. Sure, their grandmother could teach them the basics, but not like a mother. He repeated to himself. "The body is not Maggie—it's not."

As he'd said, Nico stood at the curb in front of his apartment complex. Mac did a rolling stop and Nico hopped inside. He buckled his seatbelt as Mac drove away from the curb.

"Why are you up?" Mac asked.

"I couldn't sleep. Too much on my mind. I keep hitting replay, trying to see a connection between what little we know about all the recent crimes and Maggie."

Mac stayed quiet for a long minute, then said, "If it's her, the girls are going to be so scarred for life. Who'd raise them? Their single uncle or their grandparents?"

"Don't think negative thoughts. Stay positive."

"Monica said the same thing."

Mac parked the truck, and the guys ran to the rear employee's door. When it opened, Marten was on the other side. "They aren't ready yet."

Mac said, "Tell me everything you know."

"Someone beat her, raped her and then tossed her from a moving vehicle."

Mac steadied himself. He felt like he'd received a gut punch. "Raped?" he whispered.

"The responding officer told me there was a lot of blood on her and a large amount between her legs. It's an assumption."

Nico said, "If they tossed her from a moving vehicle, then there had to be at least two people in the vehicle. It's impossible to drive and toss a body from the vehicle."

Marten said, "I agree. There may have been more than one person and it's secluded there. Nobody would see them stop to dump her."

"Was she on our side of the bridge or the other?"

"Our side. What are you thinking?"

"I'm not thinking anything," Mac said, "Gathering facts."

Nico jotted everything in his notebook.

"Let's get some coffee while we wait." Marten turned and led them through the hallways to the familiar staff lounge in the police station. The overhead lights were dim in the hall compared to the brightness during the day, as were the lights in the lounge. A couple of officers sat at a table eating something out of takeout food containers.

Mac, Marten, and Nico sat at a round table near the coffee machine. Halfway into their cups of coffee, Marten received the notification that the body was ready for viewing. They dumped the remaining coffee in the sink and hustled out of the lounge.

Upon arriving outside the morgue, and because the woman inside had been the victim of a homicide, Marten asked the guys to put on personal protective gear.

When they were ready, Marten pressed the buzzer on the wall with the back of his gloved hand and the door opened. The three men walked into the sterile room. Their disposable gowns made swishing sounds as they walked. Mac saw the woman's body on the autopsy table with a sheet draped over her from head to toe, and his stomach did a flip. Bile shot up his throat. He swallowed it back down and inched toward the table.

Dr. Ian Gibson, the coroner, a short, bald man, also wearing protective gear with the added safeguard of a face shield, greeted them. "Hello fellas, sorry to get you out in the middle of the night, so to speak. I hope this person is not your sister, Mac." He looked at them as if expecting something in return. When nobody said anything, he followed up with, "Please touch nothing—the body, the cloth, the table—nothing."

With an emotional voice Mac croaked, "Her ankles. I want to see her ankles." His mind felt jumbled. He couldn't be certain which ankle Maggie had the tattoo on.

The coroner gave him a curious look and nodded his understanding. "The Staff of Aesculapius tattoo?"

"No, the caduceus. Maggie has it tattooed on the outside of her ankle."

Mac felt clammy and repeated, "I need to see her ankle. Now."

"I think you'll be relieved." With care, he folded the cloth to above the woman's shins and said, "This tattoo is a rough version of the Staff of Aesculapius—represented as a single serpent entwined around a rod wielded by the Greek god, Aesculapius...."

The doctor's voice faded away. Mac stared at the woman's ankle. He said with a faint, choked voice, "It's not Maggie." Then a little louder, "It's not Maggie. Thank God, it's not Maggie's tattoo." His knees buckled, and he dropped to the floor. He gulped for air, but had a hard time filling his lungs. "Holy shit, guys, that's as close as I want to come to thinking about my sister being dead. Thank you, Dr. Gibson," he said as he stood and rushed to leave the room.

When they were all back in the hallway, as Mac opened his mouth to say something, Marten gave him a tight bear hug. Then pushed away from him, still holding onto his shoulders. "That was a close one, brother."

"We must find her. What have you got—anything? Any connections between Maggie and the murders?"

"I promise, we are looking at every little detail no matter how insignificant it seems to find a link, but to be honest, the chief has the murders at the highest level for fear another may happen."

Before Mac could say something he'd regret, Marten continued, "Every person who's combing through Stockford's files and cases has Maggie on their mind. Finding a missing person is also important."

Mac looked at Nico. "Where are you going after this?"

"I thought I'd shower, then have coffee at Red's, see if she's heard any gossip. Did you have something in mind?"

Marten glanced at his wristwatch. "Guys, it's after four. I've got to run. I'll call you if anything breaks." Marten patted both guys on their shoulders as he turned to walk away.

"I need to call Monica, and I want to scour the industrial area for any further leads. How about I meet you at Red's at six?"

Nico sensed Mac wanted some alone time. He'd feel the same if he were Mac, given the emotional roller coaster he'd been on. "Good plan."

"I'll drop you at your place and then see you at Red's."

Chapter 28

After Nico showered, he drove to the outskirts of town to Red's Roadhouse. He arrived before the old codgers, who gathered there every morning. The smell of coffee brewing greeted him as he pushed open the large, heavy wooden door.

The lights were low, ideal for sleepy, old guys—in Nico's case, perfect for sleepy, not so old guys too.

Rinda pushed through the double doors separating the kitchen from the bar as Nico plopped himself down on a barstool. "Good morning," she said. "What got you up with the chickens?"

"Coffee first, please." A few sips later, he told her he had accompanied Mac to the morgue because someone had found a deceased female on the side of the road.

She listened with her hand on her heart as she waited in silence to learn if the body was Mac's sister.

He explained the difference between the caduceus symbol and the Staff of Aesculapius. "I know Mac. He's grateful it wasn't his sister, but she's someone else's sister, daughter, mother…." He stopped talking when a customer pushed in through the front door. It was one of the usual guys who headed straight to the Posse corner.

Following the regular customer was the man Nico had seen there before. Who he'd hoped to see—Albert. He sat, leaving two empty seats between them.

He looked at Nico and bobbed his head. "Morning."

Rinda walked back to Nico and the man with a fresh pot of coffee in one hand and an empty mug in the other. She stopped in front of them, looked at the man and as she filled his cup, said, "Morning, Albert." Then she looked at Nico. "Ready for a refill?"

He pushed his mug toward her. "Keep it coming."

After filling his mug, she put the pot down and asked, "How about some breakfast?" She jabbed her thumb toward the kitchen.

"One of your Denver Omelet sandwiches sounds perfect, thank you." Before he could ask her if she'd heard anything more from her customers, she turned and disappeared into the kitchen.

After dropping off a toasted bagel and cream cheese to one of the old guys at the end of the bar, she started another pot of coffee before returning to where Nico sat.

He wanted to ask her if she'd heard anything helpful, but hesitated with the stranger sitting so close.

Breaking the quiet, she said, "Do you remember the pharmacist in town who got caught dealing illegal drugs on the side of his legal drug business?"

He shook his head. "Must've been before my time. Why?"

"Rumor has it they found him murdered in Indonesia."

Nico paid close attention to the man two seats down to see if he gave away any clues he was eavesdropping on their conversation. The man held his coffee mug with his left hand and slowly turned the pages of the Mountain Tribune, the local newspaper Rinda subscribed to for her customers.

Nico said, "Indonesia? I didn't hear about that."

"Small-town gossip. When he heard the police had a warrant for his and his nephew's arrest, he hightailed it out of town."

"What happened to his nephew?" he asked.

She refilled his mug. "He was the head coach at Blackstone Academy. I bet Mac and the coach worked together. It's my understanding it all went down at the beginning of the school year, but I wasn't here either, so you'd need to ask him."

Nico sipped his coffee, and then said, "He should be here soon."

"Did they say how the pharmacist died?"

"Shot in the head."

"Does it seem weird to you someone killed three community members within the same week? His death was elsewhere—bad luck, strange coincidence, or part of a bigger plan?"

"You sound like an FBI agent." She winked at him and then grabbed the pot of coffee and two mugs before she walked to the end of the bar, where two more old guys had joined the group of friends.

Without looking away from the newspaper, the man seated near Nico asked, in a hoarse, whisper-like voice, "You're an FBI agent?"

Nico almost hadn't heard him. "Ex-FBI." He held out his hand to shake. "Nico Stark." The man didn't seem to notice the gesture, so Nico dropped his hand.

"That's good." The man stood. "Nice to meet you." Then he placed a ten-dollar bill on the bar and left.

As the new guy neared the door to leave, Mac came inside. Their paths crossed, and they looked at each other. The man nodded to Mac. As he skirted around him, he said, in a soft, non-threatening tone, "Excuse me, tough guy."

His comment seemed weird to Mac, like the guy was much older when he looked about the same age as Mac.

A bell sounded from the kitchen. Rinda went inside and returned with Nico's breakfast sandwich. "Here you go."

She watched him take his first bite. He stopped chewing to say, "Mmm, thank you. It's delicious."

Mac sat next to Nico and looked at the sandwich in his hand. "That looks good."

Nico said, covering a mouthful, "It is. You should have one."

"Monica made breakfast for me. Did your new best friend hear anything worth chasing?" He referred to Rinda with a head nod.

"Not much." He shrugged. "And probably not relevant, but she has some questions about a pharmacist who used to live here."

"The coach's uncle?"

Nico had pushed the last bite of his sandwich into his mouth. "Mmm hmm."

"What about him?"

Nico slid his empty plate forward. "Someone killed him in Indonesia where he's been living."

Mac said, "Until we find Maggie, everything's relevant."

Nico smiled. "Spoken like a true crime investigator."

Rinda arrived in front of Nico and Mac. "Hi, Mac. Nice to see you again." She held up the coffeepot. "Coffee?"

"No, thank you. Nice to see you too. Hey, what all do you know about the pharmacist's murder?"

"Nothing more than the guys told me." She pointed at the old guys down the bar. "They may know more. They seem to know a lot about a lot of things."

Mac stood. "Ready to go in five? I'll go chat with the guys."

Nico nodded.

Once Mac was into his conversation with the regulars, Nico asked Rinda, "How would a guy go about asking you to go on a date?"

"By asking."

"When aren't you working?"

"I can get away for a shift. I own the place, remember?" She smiled.

"Would you like to go for an afternoon hike and a picnic?"

"When?"

"Whenever you can get a shift covered."

As Mac headed toward the door, he waved his hand at Nico. "Let's go."

Nico said to Rinda, "To be continued."

Chapter 29

Mac and Nico pulled into Maggie's driveway seconds before Marten and Ruiz parked at the curb in front of her house. The men gathered on the front lawn under the old shade tree.

"How're you holding up?" Marten asked Mac.

"With my family, you know I've had some bad times—this nightmare is right up there with my grandfather's, and my parent's tragic deaths." He paused, picked up a twig the tree had dropped, and tossed it on the grass. He looked at Marten. "I'm scared."

"I know. Me too. It's been almost forty-eight hours." He didn't need to say more.

Mac flexed his jaw. "Let's go inside. I want to hear what you can tell us about what you've learned so far and we'll update our murder boards." He unlocked the door and held it open for the guys, then closed it and secured the deadbolt. "Are you connecting the two murders? Any evidence that points toward the shooters?"

Nico took his usual place, marker pen in hand, standing at the murder boards they had pinned to the dining room wall.

"Who wants coffee?" Mac asked.

Marten and Ruiz raised their hands.

Nico said, "I've already had a gallon."

He could hear the guys talking in the dining room as he watched the coffee maker. Shortly, he returned with two steaming mugs, placed them on the table, and then went back to the kitchen for cream and sugar for Ruiz.

Marten stayed standing while Ruiz sat at the table. He read the notations on the murder boards for Stockford and Sawyer. Then stared at the photo of Maggie that the stranger had given Lindy at school. Maggie's wrists were bound to each arm of a grimy, old chair and her ankles to the front legs. She looked dirty and drugged. It broke his heart to see his best friend's sister in this horrific situation. Putting his head back in the moment, he said, "The woman found at the swinging bridge was a local druggie. We're 99% sure she has nothing to do with the two murders or Maggie. Your information looks current."

Mac nodded. "Monica has been filling in the gaps for us."

Marten nodded. "Did she tell you we found Stockford's cell phone number on a sticky note at Sawyer's home this morning?"

"No, I haven't talked with her since she left for work. What did Mrs. Stockford say about Sawyer having her husband's phone number?"

"She said Sawyer had ordered a metal art piece from him." He shrugged. "Sounds reasonable at this point. Oh, and the mayor's wife left him. Not something that would go on your boards, but she's madder than a wet hen. And she isn't staying quiet about his infidelity. She gave a statement to the Mountain Tribune about how Sawyer had weaseled her way into her husband's pants because she was unemployed and destitute. If she's good at her word, the marriage is over."

Mac guffawed. "That's an issue of the newspaper I might buy."

Marten sipped his coffee. "If it makes it to print. I'm confident the mayor or the sheriff will put the kibosh on anything the wife says to their reporters. Not sure they have any pull with the news stations, though."

Marten's phone rang. He answered as he hurried out the front door, returning moments later.

"Anything new?" Mac asked.

Marten answered, "Nothing relevant." He sat down next to his partner. "The man or woman had to have been a pro. They took Stockford out with one precise shot. We've found very little hard evidence. The shooter's body weight pressed down on the mountain misery slightly, and they left the note. Otherwise, it's like they dropped out of the sky. The chief brought in a friend who's a tracker with the FBI."

Mac jabbed his thumb toward Nico. "We saw his vehicle at the Stockford's and thought it had 'feds' written all over it. It had a sweet laptop setup."

Marten, sounding weary, continued, "With Sawyer, the shooter used a large caliber weapon at close-range. And get this. The bullet exited Sawyer's skull, but we don't know the type of gun used because the team didn't find any evidence from the shot. The shooter left no trace of a print, no shell casing, no projectile, or anything for us to go on."

Ruiz added, "They somehow erased their tire tracks—left no footprints, broken pine needles, nothing."

Marten continued, "The tech guys are searching for other murders with a professional feel to them to see if there are potential connections based on the cleanliness of the kills."

Nico said. "Sometimes it takes very little to set someone off. Your average gun enthusiast rarely has the skills to keep the perimeter around the murder as clean as you say it was. It could be some angry dude who's out for revenge because Stockford put him in jail or prison and Sawyer failed him or his kid in school."

The three guys stared at Nico like they were at a law enforcement seminar on 'Persons of Interest 101' and he was the presenter.

Marten asked Nico, "Where would you look to find a connection?"

"I'd stop looking for the shooter. I'd follow the money paid to the shooter. It sounds like the shooter is top shelf—the good stuff—and they aren't cheap." Nico pulled out a chair and sat down. "I'd look on the dark web at the hired killer bulletin boards. My guess is the money came from someone who knows of or knew both victims at some point. There are ways to find IP addresses for isolated areas. Get your IT guys on the money hunt instead of the hunt for similar crime scenes. I believe this is less of a 'boots on the ground' investigation and more of a dark web deep-dive. The shooter and the client connected somehow—find out how."

Marten looked at Ruiz, who shrugged. "I hate the dark web. We need to talk to the IT guys."

"Thanks, Nico. We appreciate you pointing out a different perspective." Marten looked at Mac then. "I'll stay in touch. Let me know if you need any help with anything you find out about Maggie."

Mac had been thinking about Mrs. Stockford the entire time the guys had been talking. "Before you leave, why didn't Mrs. Stockford say something about Sawyer's connection to her husband when her murder hit the news?"

"Not sure. I'll ask Tanner to find out."

After the guys left, Mac turned to Nico. "That was cool."

"What?"

"You riffing about where you'd look and to follow the money. Your FBI skills were shining bright, my friend."

"Or my excessive inquisitiveness was shining bright." He laughed.

"Nah, you're better than you give yourself credit. Let's tap into your inquisitiveness and go out to the industrial area again."

As they gathered their gear, Mac added, "I want to swing by the old coach's house. All this talk about the coach and his uncle made me want to look at his place. I assumed the uncle inherited it and don't know how it will play out since he's confirmed dead now. I'm curious if it's sat empty since the drug bust went down."

Chapter 30

As Mac and Nico drove away from Maggie's house, Mac sighed. "I want to pick up Roxy and take her with us."

"Sounds good."

"I've been working on her tracking skills. I grabbed one of Maggie's sweaters." He pointed to the zip-type baggie on the backseat with a light-blue sweater inside.

"It'd be outstanding if she picked up her scent. There's never a good time to be held captive, but if Maggie is somewhere without heat and air conditioning, at least the weather is decent."

Mac gave Nico a sideways glance. "That's a positive take on the situation. I thought I was the positive one, and you were the dark side of this duo."

"Captives don't last long when the weather is less than ideal. Based on weather and nothing else, Maggie has good odds."

Mac turned onto his cul-de-sac. As usual, the neighborhood looked quiet. He pushed the button on the remote control to open the gate in his driveway.

Both dogs bolted out the dog door and into the fenced backyard.

"Are we also bringing Comet with us?"

"No. She's too distracting for Roxy."

After Mac loaded Roxy into the backseat of his truck, they were on their way to the coach's house.

Nico asked Mac for clarification, "So, let me get this straight—this local pharmacist was the uncle of the coach at Blackstone Academy?"

"Yes. The coach got mixed up in his uncle's illegal drug activity. I remember he had a weird relationship with his mother, who, from what I heard, was as mean as they come."

"You never met the mother?" Nico jotted down a note in his notebook.

"No, and I never met the uncle either. The mother and coach lived together. I think he was about my age."

He looked up from his notebook. "I love my mom, but I couldn't live with her—she'd still spit on a napkin and try to wipe my face." Nico looked at his notes for a moment. "There might be a connection between Stockford and the drugs or the drug bust and the coach's connection to Sawyer because they worked together—maybe the uncle's drug business is the link. Did Sawyer know about the drugs?"

Mac waited in his lane to cross the highway. "Nothing I saw to show Sawyer knew anything about the drug ring." The traffic light turned green. "I thought we could look downtown for Anson's grandmother's van. You never know, he may be bold enough to think we aren't on to him."

"Or dumb enough to be in plain sight." Nico checked his notes again. "And does it seem suspicious that the uncle's death happened about the same time someone killed Stockford and Sawyer, then someone snatched Maggie? I don't believe in odd coincidences. Someone murdered three people from little old Brookfield, and one person abducted all within one week."

"Damn, good thinking." Mac pulled over at the curb and grabbed his cell phone.

Marten answered on the first ring, "Do you have news about Maggie?"

"No. We forgot to ask you if it's true someone killed Coach Andrews's uncle who fled the US back when you guys busted him for selling narcotics?"

"Yeah. How'd you hear about that?"

"Nico heard it at Red's Roadhouse. Some retired cops get together for coffee in the morning. They were talking about the pharmacist."

"It's true. They found him face down on a massage table in a seedy whore house with a bullet in the back of his head. According to the business owner, the masseuse left the room to get warm towels. When she came back, she saw blood pooling under the opening in the table where your head rests. When she looked under the table, she discovered little of his face where it should have been."

Most of the downtown businesses weren't open yet. The few people Mac and Nico saw were older couples on their morning walk.

"Wow! Very graphic answer. Thank you. Do you think his murder connects to what's happened here?"

"Until we solve these crimes, we consider everything connected. What we need is the break to show us how they connect. Where're you headed?"

"We're taking Roxy to the old industrial area to look around some more buildings, but Nico wondered if the murders and Maggie's abduction were about drugs. What if Stockford had been into drugs? Perhaps Sawyer knew what the coach had been doing at school. I had a hand in stopping the drug activity at the school."

Mac could almost hear the gears in Marten's head turn. "Good thoughts, Nico. I'll pitch all of that to the team. Thanks, guys. Gotta go."

Mac returned his phone to a cup holder and left the quaint downtown area.

He turned off the highway into the subdivision where Coach Andrews had lived. He parked along the road near his house, at about the same spot where Mac had once spied on the coach. Mac relaxed in his seat. "It looks like someone lives there now."

Nico took in the house and the surrounding neighborhood. "Someone with a security team."

"Yeah, it's interesting. Like a celebrity or someone important."

They both watched as three men who could've been mistaken for secret service walked around the front area near some vehicles. Dark suits, holstered weapons, ear pieces, neat haircuts.

"Or someone with money. Wealth makes people paranoid, and wealthy people often have tight security for fear of being robbed or kidnapped."

"Why would a fat cat buy a house in Brookfield?"

"They like to hide in small towns where the community helps shield them because they become star-struck, so to speak."

As they watched, a man walked out onto an upstairs balcony. Nico blurted out, "That's the weird guy from Red's."

"I almost bumped into him at Red's earlier. He said, 'Sorry, tough guy.' Not sure what that was about."

Nico continued his train of thought as they watched the activity of packing things into an SUV. "Here's a weird comment he made to me right before you saw him. He sat a few seats from me. Rinda and I were talking about the pharmacist's murder and when I asked too many questions, she told me I sounded like an FBI agent. Then she left to tend to customers. After she walked away, the guy asked if I was an FBI agent. I said I was an ex-FBI agent. He said, 'That's good.'" Nico looked at Mac, expecting he'd see the weirdness.

When Mac said nothing, he continued, "Did the guy mean it's good that I'm an ex-FBI field agent versus an active one?"

Mac stared at the coach's old house. "It's an odd thing to say. You said he's weird. Was it an odd thing to say coming from a weird guy?"

"He also didn't shake my hand when I introduced myself. He wore leather driving gloves and never took them off, not even to drink his coffee."

Mac turned to look at Nico. "He wouldn't shake your hand?"

"I'm not sure. I attempted to introduce myself and offered a hand to shake, but he never looked at me, not even when he asked if I was an FBI agent."

"Sounds like he may lack social skills."

"You see some good in people I don't see. I assume the worst in people," Nico admitted. "That makes us a good team."

Mac looked at his friend. "Does this mean you're back to the bad cop and I'm the good cop again?"

Chapter 31

Monica entered Mac's number on her phone's keypad. It rang once and then she heard, "Hey babe."

"Do you have Roxy? I'm at the house and she's not here."

"Yeah. Sorry, I should have let you know. I wanted to see if Roxy would pick up Maggie's scent out in the old industrial area. Nico and I are going to look around more buildings."

"God, I hope she does. You've worked hard with her on the tracking. Anything new otherwise?" She scratched Comet's back.

"Nico had a hunch."

"Let's hear it."

"Remember the pharmacist drug bust in town?"

"Yes."

"His nephew worked at Blackstone Academy, and so did Ann Sawyer. What if we connect the drugs to Stockford? Did you hear someone murdered the pharmacist in Indonesia?"

"I heard about the pharmacist. Weird timing, don't you think? How'd you hear about it?"

"Nico heard it from the gal who owns Red's Roadhouse."

"There must be more to the story. Anyway, Marten and Ruiz told me about Nico's drug connection hunch. They've got the IT guys working on it. Meanwhile, we're still going through old files. With as many years on the force as Stockford had, we've got a lot of paperwork to look through."

"Hang in there."

"Between you and me, and I'm serious, do not repeat this."

Mac cocked an eyebrow. "You're on speaker and Nico's with me."

"That's fine. We have so many retirees looking through the files. Most are seniors—if you know what I mean—they lose focus and start reminiscing about 'back in the day.' I try to stay on top of them, but... On one hand, we have too many people digging through the files. On the other hand, we need all the help we can get. Sorry. I'm being petty—I'm exhausted, but don't you dare tell Marten."

Mac smiled. He knew she wanted to make a good impression with this opportunity Marten had given her. "You need to come home tonight to get some sleep."

"I'll try. Do you guys want an update on the mayor?"

"Sure."

"Hi, Nico."

"Hi, Monica."

"The chief is at the mayor's office a lot or he's here at the chief's office. Which leads me to believe the mayor is hiding out to avoid the press. And his wife is fit to be tied. She's headed down the path to ruin his reputation."

Mac shifted in his seat. "You can't blame her. Have you been back out to the Stockford's?"

"Yes. I check in on Gretchen throughout the day." Monica took the stairs to the bedroom she and Mac shared. Comet followed her every move. She flung herself backward on the bed. Comet jumped up and licked her cheek. "There's one drawer in a file cabinet in the Stockford basement I'd like to look through to confirm it's full of family photos like Gretchen says, but it's locked and she won't budge on letting me look through it."

"Marten said they found Stockford's phone number on a sticky note at Sawyers."

"Yeah, they asked Gretchen what she knew. She said Sawyer had ordered one of Stockford's metal art pieces like the one at the beginning of their driveway."

"Do you know if his type of art jives with Sawyer's decorating style? I've never seen her place."

"I don't know, but it's a good thought. I'll ask Gretchen what specific piece she ordered. It could've been for a gift."

"True," his voice trailed off. "I can't shake the question about why she didn't say something about Sawyer sooner. Sawyer's name was all over the news and the news spun her death as suspicious given Stockford's murder"

She told him she'd ask Gretchen more about Sawyer. "I'm going to take a quick shower and put on fresh clothes. If I learn anything new, I'll call you."

He thought about saying he loved her, but held back because Nico was listening. "Okay." He clicked off the call.

She ran the hot water until a good cloud of steam swirled in the shower before she added some cold water to get the right temperature. For what felt like minutes, she stood with her back to the spray and let the water pound between her shoulder blades. She could see Comet curled up on the bathroom rug, waiting for her to finish.

Marten had told her to dress in civilian clothes until they solved the case, or at least they eliminated Mrs. Stockford as a suspect. She liked this detective work and thought she could get used to not wearing a uniform and the heavy, duty belt.

After her shower, as she strapped on her ankle holster and secured her belt holster, she then put on a loose shirt and left it untucked to hide her weapon.

She wondered if Mac had checked his mailbox in the last few days.

Comet walked at a fast pace in front of Monica, with her leash stretched as tight as possible. The energetic dog ran straight ahead, and then zig-zagged, reminding Monica of water skiers who glided over the wake from one side to the other. But in this scenario, the skier pulled the boat.

They walked down the driveway to the front gate. Mac's place had a white picket fence around the front yard. The cul-de-sac looked deserted. At the intersection, Monica looked right, then left, expecting possible traffic, but like the cul-de-sac, the neighborhood lacked activity of any kind—human or vehicular. She remembered it was a weekday and children were in school.

Mac received mail in a community cluster box—six boxes wide by four boxes high. The post office mounted it on a corner at the opening of the cul-de-sac where his street intersected with others in his neighborhood. She didn't care for living on a cul-de-sac with one way in and one way out—she preferred alternate access points. Mac's box was in the upper left corner. Her years of police work made her stand to the side and open the mailbox with caution. When nothing happened, she looked inside. Mac had not checked the mail in days. He had several advertisements about recent home sales, envelopes with credit card offers, grocery store newspaper inserts, and a manila envelope that made the hairs on the back of her neck stand up. Someone had scrawled Mac's name on it with a black marker—no address, no postage.

Walking back to the house, Comet tested her strength again by pulling on the leash. Monica stopped walking. When Comet couldn't go any farther, she looked at Monica for direction. Monica stomped her foot. "Bad dog." Comet's ears drooped, and her tail curled between her legs. She looked away, not making eye contact with Monica. They continued walking back to Mac's place, as she called him.

"Hi, Babe," he said.

"Hi. I checked the mail and there's a manila envelope with no address or stamps. It has your first name written in dark, block letters on it."

"Not again. Treat it like it's an explosive or anthrax. Put it in the middle of the cul-de-sac, wait in the driveway as far away as possible, and call Marten. I'm on my way home now."

Chapter 32

When Mac and Nico neared Mac's neighborhood, the Brookfield Police Department hazmat crew were already there. An officer stood behind barricades, halting all traffic from entering the cul-de-sac.

The neighbors who were home stood on their front porches watching the activity with concerned expressions. Mac appreciated the response, considering everyone in the department was working overtime to solve the two murders.

Mac recognized the rookie officer at the barricade from the station. He'd said hello a few times as they passed each other in the main hallway. They approached the young man. "Well, what have they found?" Mac asked as he approached the officer.

"They're getting their gear on. Stay back," he commanded, expressionless, like he'd never seen them before. He held his hand up to stop them from getting any closer. Nico took hold of Mac's arm to keep him away from the cordoned-off area.

Mac saw Monica waiting on the front porch while the techs swabbed the envelope and screened for metals with a hand wand.

It took all the patience Mac could muster to stand by and watch as the techs checked the envelope's exterior. It felt like hours had passed before they it sliced open. Then they pulled what looked like another photo out of the envelope.

What if it had been an explosive that hurt Monica or worse? He thought about filing a complaint with the United States Postal Service because one of their carriers had to have allowed someone to put the envelope into his secure mailbox.

Extreme irritation had almost bubbled over the edge of his patience when Mac saw them swab the photo and then signal to him he could come see what it was.

He bolted past the young officer and grabbed the photo. Like in the last photo, Maggie sat on a decrepit-looking metal chair like you often saw in military offices. Her legs and wrists secured to a chair in the same dark and trashy setting. She looked dirtier than she did in the first photo, and her hair looked disheveled, like her captor had grabbed her by her hair more than once. He could tell she was high on something. Drool dribbled from the corner of her mouth, but she was alive. A vision of the woman in the morgue flashed through Mac's mind.

Whoever had left the photo for him had written in the same black marker as on the outside of the envelope, "It hurts when a loved one dies. Will you find her in time?"

Mac turned, slapping Nico's arm. "He's going to kill her." He sprinted toward his truck. Over his shoulder, he yelled to Monica, "I'll call you!"

"Hey, come back here." A tech yelled at Mac. "That photo is evidence. We need to maintain a chain of cust...."

Mac never slowed. He hopped into his truck, slammed the door. Nico got in on the passenger side. The tires squealed when making a U-turn to head to the highway.

Roxy, who'd been asleep in the truck—oblivious to the potential danger half of a football field away from her now sat up, startled and barked.

Adrenaline surged through Mac's veins. "What else do you see in the photo besides Maggie?" He thrust the photo toward his friend.

"Looks like a large industrial space or a warehouse. One of those pre-engineered, metal buildings like you find on rural properties where they keep tractors and farm equipment—like what Thomas has for Rhubarb but bigger."

Roxy paced from one back seat window to the other. She sensed the urgency in their journey.

"I think we've been looking in the right area, not the right building. I've felt her presence. Let's start at the back and work toward the highway instead of continuing to work from the front to the back."

Nico stared at the photo using the magnification feature on his phone. "I agree. And based on the cryptic message, time is of the essence."

Once at the area where the abandoned warehouses sat, Mac's memory flashed on an experience during a deployment when his team had to find two soldiers who'd lost communications after reporting they'd set off an Improvised Explosive Device—an IED. They weren't sure how injured the soldiers were or if they'd moved since they'd lost their communication with them. They moved fast and quiet to the last known location and found them there—alive. He had to be as successful in his search for his sister. Had to.

They parked near the farthest warehouse from the highway.

With Roxy at his side, he held out Maggie's sweater for her to sniff. When she began pacing, eager to get started, he pointed and said, "Go." She trotted toward the closest building, her nose to the ground. Mac and Nico ran behind her. She turned a corner at the rear of a building and went out of sight. When they caught up to her, they found her sitting, which was her way of saying she'd found something. They turned the corner and saw she'd found the charred remnants of a delivery van. For her to have stopped at it, she'd picked up Maggie's scent from it. Mac felt his shoulders droop as he stood frozen in place. He asked, "Is that Ms. Mullis's license plate?"

Nico referred to his notepad, then look at the charred license plate. "It is," he confirmed.

Mac pressed the speed dial to Marten. Before Marten could finish saying hello, Mac said, "We found the van. It's torched—the inside is a pile of ashes. Will you send a crime scene unit to see if they can find human remains inside?"

"Give me your location."

Chapter 33

She heard him coming, the heavy footsteps, the jangle of keys. She knew there was no other way than to try again to befriend him, become the submissive, become his possession.

Bile gurgled up her throat. Rather than pretend to need him, she wanted to scratch his eyes out. Thoughts of her girls drove her to do whatever she could to see them again. As much as she wanted to be fierce and try to overpower the guy, she knew she needed to be nice. She knew her girls must be so scared.

Her back was to the door, but she heard the door scrape open and knew he watched her. She felt exhausted and lethargic, but knew it was the drugs. She heard his heavy footsteps stop in front of her. "You came back. Thank you." She wished he'd have worn a mask. She had no experience with criminals. Like most people, she knew what she saw in movies. In her thoughts, him wearing a mask would've been a good thing because she couldn't have identified him—except, of course, for his large, unique tattoos.

He dropped his backpack. "Hungry?"

"Of course…." She scolded herself and knew she had to dial back the sarcasm. "Yes. Did you bring me a hamburger?"

"I did, but it's cold."

"That's okay." She didn't want to think about how long it had been unrefrigerated. "Thank you. Will you let me feed myself so my arms can move?"

"You try something stupid and I'll zap you." He pulled a stun-gun out from his pocket and clicked it a few times to scare her.

"I won't. I'm too weak anyway, and you're twice my size."

He cut the ties and freed her arms from the chair, but not her ankles. She swirled her arms above her head. "Thank you," she said, in the smallest voice she could muster, and then reached out for the food.

He paced around the room as she ate—eating as slowly as she could—she wanted to gobble the food down. She knew if she ate faster, she'd vomit after having an empty stomach for days.

"How's your cat?"

"You eat and don't talk about my cat."

She sensed something had agitated him and hoped it didn't mean bad news for her. His eye movements and pupil dilation told her he was high on something again.

"Are you alright? You seem angry with me."

"I'm not angry with you. There's a lot of shit going down."

She took another small bite and chewed. "What kind of shit is going down?"

"Nothing for you to know."

"Please don't hurt me. I have two daughters. Lindy is ten years old and Bella is eight. I'm a widow trying to raise two beautiful girls. Lindy is...."

"Stop!" he roared. "Stop telling me about your kids."

Tears ran down her cheeks as she took another bite of the burger. She swallowed and asked, "Are you close to your parents?"

"No. My old man is serving time in Pelican Bay and my mom left us when I was a kid, so no. I didn't have the perfect childhood like you did."

"I didn't have a perfect childhood, either. My dad was an alcoholic who abused my mother. He's also in prison, and I hate his guts." She lied. Thinking if she made their childhoods sound similar, she'd connect with him.

He stopped pacing and stood in front of her. "I thought your brother was a war hero."

"Mac?" She snorted. "He isn't a war hero. He ran away to the air force because if he hadn't, he might've killed our dad—he hated him that much. Then he didn't come home until long after dad went to prison."

He paced some more. She took a bite of the cold burger.

From across the room, he asked, "What prison is your dad in?"

"I don't know, and I don't care. I didn't go to his trial, and I never looked into where they sent him. May I have a sip of water, please?"

He closed the gap between them and snatched up the bottle from the floor near her.

She closed her eyes and braced for what he'd do next.

He held out the bottle. "Take it."

She guzzled the water, but then, without warning, he grabbed the bottle from her—splattering water on her face. "You'll have to pee if you drink too much."

"Why do you care?" She heard the snarkiness in her tone and forced herself to sound helpless. "I'm so thirsty and ... you know, I already wet my pants." She tried to look embarrassed.

He shrugged and handed her back the water. She downed the entire bottle, then shoved the last of the burger in her mouth.

"You can tell me what shit is going down if you want to talk about it. Who am I going to tell?"

"Do you want to know because you think you're getting out of here and you'll have something to tell the cops?"

"No. You look like it's bugging you and I think you're going to kill me, so what does it matter what you tell me?"

He stared at her for an uncomfortable minute. "I'm supposed to kill you today. The guy giving the orders says your brother is getting close to finding you."

She felt a zing of hope run through her. "Can't you move me? Do you have to kill me?"

"Those are my orders."

"If Mac's close to finding me, he's close to finding you, too. Wouldn't you rather they charge you with abduction than murder? If all you did was kidnap me, I can testify in your favor and against whoever is in charge. Let him take the fall, not you. I'll tell them you haven't harmed me."

Like a trapped animal, he rushed at her, making her flinch and turn her head. "Please don't hurt me."

From his pocket, he pulled zip ties and secured her wrists to the arms of the chair. "I ain't gonna kill you. If you die, it's on you."

She watched as he pulled a syringe from his pocket. Uncontrollable tears flooded her vision. "Please, please don't. I'm not going anywhere." She sucked in short bursts of air, trying to fill her constricted lungs. "Please don't." She squirmed and felt the jab.

He hurried out the door and locked it.

Chapter 34

While Nico and Roxy had guarded the burned van, Mac went to get the truck before the techs arrived. He knew Roxy had outdone herself and would need a nap.

Roxy fell asleep within seconds of Mac helping her up into the back seat of his truck. Now, Mac and Nico watched the crime scene techs brush at the ashes, looking for pieces of human remains.

The van reeked of gasoline, which someone had used to start the fire. Mac feared they'd find something to show Maggie had been inside the van. But he hoped she hadn't been inside when they torched it.

"While you were getting the truck, I sent the VIN number to my friend. He said they stole the van a week ago."

Mac looked at his partner. "That means whoever took Maggie planned it a week ago?"

"Looks that way."

They fell into a silence watching the techs work.

As if he'd read Mac's mind, Nico shifted his weight to his other foot, growing impatient. "People think after cremation the entire body turns to ash. Not true. Someone at the crematorium places the cremated remains into a cremulator which grinds the bone pieces into a fine sand and then they place it all in an urn for the loved ones."

Mac stared at him like he had two heads. "I think I felt better not knowing that little piece of trivia. And how do you know about cremulators?"

"Sorry. I took a Recovery of Human Remains course at the Body Farm during training. Their purpose is to study the decomposition and skeletonization of human bodies, not cremation, but," he shrugged, "I asked a lot of questions."

"What you're telling me is if Maggie was in the van when the person set it on fire," he pointed to the CSI team, "they'll find pieces of her?"

"Yes."

They became quiet, both in their own thoughts, waiting for anything from the van to help them find Maggie.

It felt like hours had passed when the team supervisor walked to Mac and Nico. He had a crime scene evidence bag in his hand. Mac took a deep breath.

One of the crime scene techs lifted his head from the van, then walked to where Mac waited. "No bone fragments, but we found some bits from a rug that must've had fire retardant on it, which kept it from disintegrating." He held the sealed bag up for Mac to see.

He took a quick look, and said, "The rug we believe Maggie's captor rolled her up in."

The supervisor said, "Good news." He gave them a thumbs up. "She wasn't in the van at the time someone set it on fire—and now you have a solid clue, her rug was in the van." He took back the evidence. "We've got more work to do," he jabbed his thumb toward the van, "I don't believe we'll have anything more than the rug fragments to help you locate your sister."

Mac thanked the man as he and Nico decided where to go from there.

Nico said, "Roxy did a great job finding the van. Let's see what else she might find."

The guys climbed back into Mac's truck and drove to the location near where they had parked earlier, deep into the industrial area. After they settled on a fresh location, Mac helped Roxy out of the truck and told her to sit. He hugged her, scratched her favorite spots and murmured, "good girl." Then he held out Maggie's sweater for Roxy to sniff before he released her, and said, "Go."

They followed again as best they could, monitoring Roxy as she darted in and out of the loading docks. She went up ramps and sniffed the roll-up doors. Her paws were up on walls, allowing her head more height to sniff toward windows that had once allowed fresh air into a building but now appeared to be rusted open about four inches.

Roxy carried her body low as she glided through the industrial area's nooks and crannies. They startled nesting birds as the three of them hung close to buildings. Trash had accumulated in corners, and evidence of drug use accumulated on the northern-facing sides where the sun never shined. People had tossed broken hypodermic needles and pieces of liquor bottles into make shift fires on loading docks under the overhangs where the addicts could stay out of the weather.

Nico panted as they jogged behind Roxy. "Looks like a good place to stay if you're homeless."

Mac was accustomed to running with Roxy and wasn't breathing hard yet. "We need to talk to the chief about cleaning up this area."

"I hate to be the voice of doubt, but good luck. It seems with smaller and smaller budgets, cleaning up places like this becomes less and less of a priority."

They found Roxy when they turned a corner. She had laid down near the door of a building—her signal to Mac she'd found what she thought he'd asked her to locate. The building, like all the others, looked abandoned years ago. A faded sign on the front of the building showed the previous tenants had been 'Tough Guy Ironworks.' In their excitement to break in to the warehouse, Mac and Nico hadn't noticed the sign.

Mac clipped Roxy's leash on her collar so she wouldn't wander off, praised her, scratched her neck, and gave her a treat. Then he and Nico pushed and pulled the heavy metal door, but it didn't budge. He cupped his hands and yelled into the air, "Maggie!" He waited and listened for a beat before yelling again and again. They heard nothing except birds fluttering away.

Mac looked at his friend. "I'm going to get my crowbar from the truck. I don't care if I'm charged with breaking and entering— Roxy says Maggie is in here or has been in this building and I'm going inside."

"You won't get any argument from me."

On the way to the truck, Mac called Marten and told him what they were about to do. He told Mac they'd never get a judge to sign off on a warrant to access the building based on Roxy's signal. "I'm going to pretend we never talked. And, Mac, if you find Maggie in there, you need to go through the canine certification program."

"I'll give it some thought." Although he hadn't given Mac permission to break into the building, he also hadn't told him not to. Mac knew Marten wanted him to find Maggie almost as much as he did. "Are you getting any closer to an arrest on Stockford or Sawyer's murders?"

"I wish. We're going live tonight on the news with a reward leading to an arrest."

"How much?"

"$20,000."

"That might get some tips."

"And a bunch of crazies, too."

"Yeah. Gotta go." Mac ended the call as he arrived at his truck. He grabbed the crowbar and hustled back to the warehouse.

Chapter 35

Across town, at the police station in the conference room where there were too many people combing through Stockford's old files, one of the retired officers stumbled on a business card from an adoption agency in Kentucky. He stood and stretched, then went to Officer Tanner. "Hey, Tanner." As she turned around, he held out the card for her to see. "Did Officer Stockford and his wife adopt their children?"

She looked at the business card. "They have one child, a son. He's not adopted, that I know of, but the subject never came up. I'll call Mrs. Stockford."

Tanner stepped out into the hallway and leaned against the cool, textured wall, waiting for Gretchen to answer her call. She nodded when a fellow officer walked past her and into the break room.

"Hello," Gretchen answered and was out of breath.

"Gretchen, it's Monica Tanner. Are you alright?"

"Yes. Hello, Monica. I'm fine. I left my phone in the living room, not expecting a call. I was in the basement. When I heard it ring, I ran to answer it. Have you found Bruce's killer?"

"I'm sorry to bother you. No, we haven't found the killer yet. I have a personal question, if that's alright."

Gretchen replied, "Do I have a choice?"

"Did you adopt Wyatt?"

"What?! No!" Her tone said the question had insulted her. "He's our child. I carried him to full term. Why?"

"We found a business card in one of Bruce's old files. It's from an adoption agency in Kentucky. Does that ring any bells?"

"No. Nothing. What's the name of the agency?"

Dodging the question, Tanner said, "Thank you, Gretchen. I'll call them and get back to you if it turns out to be anything."

The two women chatted about how Gretchen was doing before they ended the call. Tanner wondered what the woman had been doing in her basement.

She went into a small, windowless, empty office to use the desk phone. She flicked on the light and looked around. One desk, one chair and one telephone. No wonder it was empty—it felt more like a closet with a desk than an office. She opened drawers searching for a notepad and pen, then gave up as the empty room had an empty desk. Down the hall, she grabbed a notepad and pen from the conference room, told the guy who'd discovered the adoption agency business card where she'd be if anyone looked for her, and then returned to the makeshift office.

She knew she could hand this task off to the IT guys, but her ego pushed her to get the first solid break. Convincing herself to proceed, she thought you never knew if someone might remember Stockford. And you wouldn't know if you didn't ask. As she punched in the phone number, she felt hopeful. An older-sounding man answered the call with what sounded more like 'yellow' than hello.

"Hello. Is this the Kentucky Home Adoption Agency?"

"The what?" His voice cracked from lack of use. He cleared his throat and coughed.

Tanner spoke louder, "The Kentucky Home Adoption Agency."

"Is this a joke? Agnes, is that you?"

"No, sir. This isn't a joke, and this isn't Agnes. My name is Officer Tanner, and I'm with the Brookfield Police Department in California. Does this phone number belong to the Kentucky Home Adoption Agency?" Her voice had shifted from casual to authoritarian.

"Oh. No. This is Phil Little."

"Mr. Little, do you know of the Kentucky Home Adoption Agency?"

"No, I don't."

"Are you in Kentucky?"

"Yes, I am."

"Are you anywhere near Jamestown?"

"I'm not telling you where I live. What's this about? I watch the news. This sounds like a scam. How do I know you're a police officer on the telephone?"

"You're smart to be cautious, sir. May I ask how long you've had this phone number?

"Close to twenty years."

"Thank you, Mr. Little."

"Oh, I have to go. My supper is here." He hung up on her.

Tanner looked at her phone in disbelief and shook her head. She wanted to poke her eyes out with the pen she held in her right hand. This had been an unproductive waste of her time. She picked up her notepad and smashed a little spider, climbing the wall next to her with more strength than needed, given its size. She pulled a tissue from her pocket and wiped off the spider splat from the wall and the back of her notepad, then looked around for a trash can—there wasn't one.

She regrouped, looked up the information online and called the business licensing department for Fentress County. The person who answered in the County Clerk's office was as suspicious as Mr. Little had been. She explained who she was. Which prompted a similar skepticism to Mr. Little's.

"I'm investigating a murder and have questions about one of your local businesses."

After Tanner had given the adoption agency's name, the polite woman placed her on hold. Twangy bluegrass music played—too loud.

The woman had the information when she came back on the line. "We issued the Kentucky Home Adoption Agency a business license in 1975. They closed the business in 1997. I'm not at liberty to provide you with the contact information or name of the previous business owner without a court order."

"Can you tell me if the business owner held or holds any other business licenses?"

"Give me a minute." The phone switched to the same loud music loop.

The music stopped and a different woman spoke. She shared her name, Alice Rogers, and informed Tanner she was the supervisor of the records department in the county.

After Tanner explained why she had called and said she needed to know the name of the business owner and if that person had any other businesses in the county since the adoption agency had closed.

The woman said, "Yes, she has a family counseling business, but I can't give you the business name because it's simply her name."

"Thank you. You've been helpful."

After she hung up, she punched in a few numbers on the phone to reach Jamestown's information when the same retired officer who had given her the business card burst through the door. He stuck his hand out. "More notes on the adoption agency."

Tanner hung up and took the papers from him. The retiree ducked out of the room and closed the door.

She didn't know if there was anything to connect the adoption agency to Stockford's murder, but she felt a tingle and hoped this wouldn't take her down a rabbit hole. The notes were cryptic, perhaps scribbled in haste—"eight, boy, $10,000, name change, Donna."

Donna? Tanner thought for a moment—*the same Donna from years ago? As in Stockford's lover?*

Chapter 36

Tanner presented the information about the adoption agency to the chief. He called to obtain a court order for the Licensing Department in Fentress County, Kentucky, to release the owner's name and contact information for who had owned the adoption agency. He'd had to promise a bottle of the judge's favorite, single-malt scotch, a round of golf and dinner at the golf course club-house, but he approved the court order request.

Tanner felt like she and the retired officer may have their first lead. She knew from keeping her ears open that detectives never got excited about potential leads—at least it's what they said in the break room. But she couldn't contain her enthusiasm.

"Shit," she blurted out when she saw the time. Kentucky was on eastern standard time, and the County Clerk's office would close soon. There was no way she'd sit on this potential lead until tomorrow.

She ducked out the back door and stood on the concrete stoop to get some fresh air while she called Gretchen Stockford.

"Hello."

"Gretchen, hello, it's Monica Tanner. How're you doing?"

"What can I help you with, Monica?"

Gretchen had dodged the question again. Tanner wondered if Gretchen had a habit of doing that or was this new. "I'm calling about the adoption agency I mentioned earlier."

"What now?"

"The note found in Bruce's file doesn't make much sense to me. It says, 'eight, boy, $10,000, name change, Donna.'"

Gretchen went silent. Tanner couldn't even hear her breathe. "Does that mean anything to you?"

"No." She paused. "Perhaps the woman Bruce had an affair with may know something about it. We've been through this and I don't care to revisit the topic. I don't know more than I've told you."

"Do you remember Bruce ever going to Kentucky for business reasons?"

"Hmmm." She paused. "He may have. There were several times when he had to go out of town for business purposes. To be honest, he and I didn't talk about his work."

"Hang on a sec while I grab a notepad." Monica scanned her ID badge on the sensor and ran to her temporary closet/office. She all but fell into the desk chair. "I'm sorry to ask you to share what you recall about his trips, but it may be important to help solve his murder."

"Fine. I remember very little about it. As I already said, we didn't talk about his work."

"Do you remember when he went to Kentucky?"

"I'll need to look through our old files for an airline ticket."

"Is it possible he drove?"

"Anything is possible."

Tanner heard Gretchen tensing. "Do you remember if he was gone one day, several days, or a week?"

"Hmmm. When he left, I think he was gone several days."

"That would lean toward him driving. Any way of figuring out when he went if he drove?"

"Someone murdered my husband on our front porch. My grandson found him. I don't want to talk about anything to do with Donna anymore—it's ancient history. I don't see how any of this could be relevant. I want to be left alone to grieve. Please." Her voice sounded angry with a sprinkle of pain.

"I'm sorry, Gretchen. I know this is difficult. If I didn't believe it might help solve the murder, I'd never bother you with these questions."

"How do you know this is difficult? Have you had your husband gunned down on your front porch?"

Tanner felt like her mother had smacked her cheek for getting mouthy. She softened her tone and chose her words with care. "No, I haven't. Again, I'm sorry. I can't imagine what you're going through, and I'm sure this must be difficult for you."

Not hearing anything, she continued, "Do you know anything about her children?" Tanner felt like they both knew who she was talking about. At this delicate juncture, she thought it best to not say Donna's name again, for fear Gretchen would hang up on her.

"No. When I found out something was going on, I confronted him. He told me at first that he'd felt sorry for her because she was a single mother of twins. Then one thing led to another. He gave me a bullshit story about me working nights and he was lonely. Like it was my fault they'd had sex. I gave him an ultimatum—end it and stay faithful or I'd divorce him. We've already gone over this."

"And he ended it?"

"Yes. I kept a close eye on him after that. Once I learned he'd cheated on me, I never fully trusted him again."

"I'm so sorry to ask this, but were the twins his?"

She gasped. A quiet moment passed. "Not that he ever told me."

"Thank you, Gretchen. Again, I'm sorry. I hope you're hanging in there. Call me if I can do anything for you."

"You're welcome." The call disconnected. Monica felt bad for the woman, who seemed so gentle and kind.

One of the retired officers from the conference room pushed open the door. "Tanner, your warrant is in. The chief cleared everything with the Kentucky authorities, and someone from the Records Department is on the phone for you."

Tanner shooed him out the door and answered the call.

"This is Officer Tanner." She had her pen ready to write the information down.

"Hello, this is Alice Rogers, in the Records Department. We spoke earlier."

"Yes, Alice. Did you receive the warrant you requested?"

"Yes." Her voice wasn't terse, but not friendly either.

"Are you able to tell me if the person who operated the Kentucky Home Adoption Agency has had any other businesses in the county?"

"Yes, Evelyn Rycroft has a family counseling business." Then she provided the address and contact information.

"Have you ever met Evelyn or know of her?"

Her tone softened. "No, I'm sorry. I know nothing about her."

"If you wouldn't mind, please mention her name to anyone you think might've met her and call me if you hear anything. It's of the utmost importance. We're dealing with a murdered police officer, and she may have known him. Although she is not a person of interest, we need to investigate if her adoption agency has any ties to the person we are looking for."

"Oh, my gosh. I will."

After speaking with the supervisor, Tanner took a deep breath and called the phone number Alice had given her. Three rings and then a woman answered, "Hello." She breathed heavily, like it was hard to take a full breath. Tanner could hear the hiss of an oxygen concentrator.

"Hello. I'm Officer Tanner with the Brookfield Police Department in California. Is this Evelyn Ryecroft?"

There was a brief pause. "Yes."

Tanner thrust her fist into the air and felt successful. "I'm calling about your connection to the Kentucky Home Adoption Agency."

"I wondered if someone would call me about this one day."

Chills ran down Tanner's back. "Why is that?"

"Ask me what you want to know about the agency and perhaps you'll have the answer to your question. I'm an old woman. I have cancer and I don't have long to live. I would like to clear my conscience before I die."

Tanner had a pang of guilt and sorrow for the questions she was about to ask the woman. "I'm sorry about your sickness."

"Thank you, but my disease is not why you called."

"Does the name Bruce Stockford sound familiar?"

The connection went quiet except for the oxygen hiss. When the woman spoke, her voice quavered a bit. "Yes, and no. I spoke with Officer Stockford on the telephone many years ago."

"That's who I'm asking about. Officer Bruce Stockford. How did you two connect?"

"Through a friend who has long since passed. He, the friend, not Officer Stockford, arranged complicated adoptions."

"What is a complicated adoption?"

"In Officer Stockford's case, a mother who wished to relinquish a child."

"Why is that complicated?"

"She didn't want the child to know who his mother was—erase the paper trail, so to speak."

"And you handled those types of adoptions?"

"Not regularly, no. But I was desperate for money and those types of adoptions paid well."

"Do you know why the mother didn't want the child to know who she was?"

"No. Other than he was a twin and the mother couldn't handle having two children, so she relinquished one child."

"An identical twin or fraternal twin?"

The woman didn't respond right away. "You know...I never asked or I don't recall."

"Did your friend know the mother?"

"He never told me he did."

"What can you tell me about the child?"

"I remember he was eight, and quiet."

"Do you know who adopted the child?"

"Oh, yes, Mr. And Mrs. Patrone adopted him."

"Do the Patrones' have first names?"

"Irving and Milly—everyone called him Irv."

"Past tense as in he died?"

"Yes, so has Milly. They were older when they adopted the boy."

"Do you know when they died?"

"Last year, Irv died from a heart attack and the next month, Milly died from a broken heart. They did everything together. Rumor has it she never recovered from losing him."

"Is there anyone you can think of who might know more about the boy they adopted?"

"Milly has a sister. She lives in a retirement home here in town. She might know more about what you're asking. I don't know what her health is."

"Evelyn, you know what you did was illegal, don't you?"

"Don't judge dear. Desperate people do desperate things. I was a single mother and needed to provide for my child. Arrest me. The doctor hasn't given long to live. I'd rather enjoy the thought of the gossiping women all gathered at their monthly meetings talking about the crimes I've done. I can see them now—the garden club, the pinochle club, the luncheon at the senior center—what a grand ending for me." She gasped for air.

"It's not within my power to decide if the authorities arrest you. I'm required to brief my boss about our conversation."

"Fine with me. Would you be interested in the documents and audio tapes that I've kept about the adoption?"

Monica couldn't tamp down her eagerness, she replied with too much exuberance, "Yes," she stammered. "Yes, I'm interested in all the documents you have—forms, notes, audio tapes—all of it." Her hand shook as she scribbled notes on the conversation.

"Very well then. I'll ask my daughter, Lexie, to send them to you."

"Please have her overnight everything. The police department will reimburse her for the cost."

"Alright. I've grown quite fatigued from our conversation. I need a nap now."

"Thank you, Evelyn. Again, I'm sorry about your illness." Tanner felt sad for the old woman.

They said goodbye. Tanner headed to the chief's office with her notes. She felt it was best to have his approval before she called Mrs. Patrone's sister. As she hurried down the hallway, her thoughts were like a disjointed flowchart—how does the adoption connect to the murders and how do the adoption and murders connect to Maggie's abduction?

Chapter 37

Nico held Roxy's leash as Mac pried open the door to the warehouse where Roxy had picked up Maggie's scent.

The door scraped loudly against the floor as Mac tried to open it. He stepped back and rammed his shoulder against the door. It didn't budge. "Nobody's used this door in years. That's not a good sign."

They walked around the building and found another door on the opposite side. He looked at the worn and faded sign on the door. It read, "Tough Guy Ironworks. Business hours: Monday - Friday, 8:00 to 4:00." He elbowed Nico. "Look."

"Tough Guy Ironworks."

"That's what the weird guy at Red's said to me when we bumped into each other. He said, 'Sorry, tough guy.' I thought little of it then, but now I wonder if it was a clue." His words sped up. "Was he in on this?"

Nico replied, "It's time to find Maggie and then we can deal with the guy from the bar."

Unlike the first door, this door was wooden and had a padlock on it. Mac looked at Nico and pointed at the stoop. "Looks like recent shoe prints."

"It's hard to tell how recent." Nico worried about what they might find on the inside. He'd been called a pessimist a few times— by ex-girlfriends—he felt he was more of a realist. Plus, he'd seen a few dead bodies on the other side of doors in warehouses.

Nico held Roxy's leash while Mac used the pry bar to pop open the cheap padlock. He pushed the door into the abandoned space. Birds fluttered upward, sending a cloud of dust into the air toward a hole in the roof. A swirl of dank, stale air attacked their airways.

Mac sneezed. Then sneezed again.

Roxy pulled Nico into the dark interior. Her leash slipped out of his hand. She bulldozed into the space and began barking, causing a thunderous ruckus.

"Roxy. Stop," Mac said, as firm and quiet as he could, but he wanted her to hear him.

She froze, turned, and looked at him.

"Roxy. Come." he whispered, and slapped his thigh.

She complied and sulked back to him with her tail between her legs. Splashes of light filtered in through holes to lighten the darkness.

Mac wrapped the leash around his wrist a few times to reel Roxy in and keep her by his side. Once he felt he had a good grip on her, he turned on his flashlight.

Nico turned on his too and shined it on the surrounding floor.

Shining the light around, he saw the interior and suspected there were two floors above him, but the ceiling had large holes where the floor had fallen through. Between the dust and the powerful odor of mildew, Mac sneezed several more times in rapid succession.

"Your sinuses don't like it in here."

"I'll live. Let's see where Roxy takes us." Mac gripped the leash and patted Roxy on her large, hairy head before he let her smell the sweater again and gave her the command to find Maggie.

Roxy moved at a faster pace in one direction, which led them through the dim warehouse toward a far corner where they found another door that, based on the scrapes across the floor, looked like someone had used it recently.

Mac turned to Nico and asked, in a hushed voice, "Did we go in a circle and this is the door we came in?"

"I don't think so." He shined the flashlight on several oil drums near the door. "These oil drums weren't by the door we came in." Then he shined the light on the floor. "Look how many times the door has scraped here."

They shined their flashlights around the room, taking it all in. Roxy seemed less sure of herself than she had been outside. Mac knelt next to her and petted her thick coat. Her long tongue dangled out the side of her mouth, slobbering while she panted. "It's okay, girl," Mac said, with a soft voice next to her ear.

Mac spoke, in a hushed voice, to Nico, "My gut tells me this is it. Let's listen for a second."

As he stroked Roxy, her breathing slowed. He closed his eyes and focused all his attention on listening. He heard deafening silence. Then a faint scraping sound. "Did you hear that?"

Nico turned and pointed to the door, then put his index finger to his lips. "It sounded like it came from that direction."

Mac pulled open the heavy door, making as little noise as possible. Nico held his weapon at the ready. They peeked inside and saw what looked like the inside of a loading dock area. Large, metal roll-up doors rattled as the door they'd breached flew wide open and slammed against a wall.

Mac grabbed Nico's sleeve and reeled Roxy's leash tight. "Listen." He motioned for the dog to sit.

After a second or so, he heard the scrape again. He couldn't determine if it sounded closer or farther away. They shined their flashlights around the room and landed on another door on the far side of the cavernous space. "Over there." Mac aimed his light, and they made their way to the door.

They shined their lights on the floor and both noticed the dusty debris littered the area had what Mac wanted to say were recent shoe prints.

The door opened with ease. On the other side of the door, the room appeared to be an office. Four old desks, one in each corner with papers rotted on top of them.

"This place never ends. I'm lost now." He sighed in frustration. "I can't say if we're moving closer to or farther away from the sounds we heard."

Nico lowered his voice. "We keep looking."

They continued in the direction they had been going, making a grid-like search of the bottom floor as best they could, given the limitations of walls and the amount of decaying material.

Mac heard the faint scraping sound again. He pointed in the direction he thought it came from. Nico nodded in agreement. They both readied their handguns.

Chapter 38

In her drugged sleep, Maggie and Bobby were at his parents' ranch, sitting on the front porch. They talked of plans for their wedding. She smiled at the memory. She wanted a small wedding. He wanted a large one. He rationalized his position because his father's law enforcement friends would want to attend. Her logic centered on the cost. Her parents couldn't afford to pay for the wedding as is customary, and she didn't want nor expect his parents to pay for what her parents couldn't. He argued. *"Then we get married in Las Vegas."* This made her laugh out loud waking up their old, blind, black Labrador, Pepper. Pepper stood and stretched out her front legs, then plopped back down onto the porch. She watched Bobby scratch Pepper in a place so pleasing her hind leg thumped against the porch boards. Then Bobby stood, turned, and placed his hand on the screen door handle and said, "Maggie, yell."

"What?" she asked, her head tilted to one side.

He looked at her again and said with force, *"Maggie, yell!"*

She tried, but her throat was too dry to make more than a faint, croaking sound. As Bobby placed one foot inside, she tried harder to scream. He looked back at her, then disappeared from her sight. She struggled to stand. In her thoughts, she yelled, *"NO! Bobby, don't go. Come back, Bobby, please, come back."* Tears ran down her cheeks. There she sat, stuck on the front porch all by herself. Even Pepper had gone with Bobby.

Her mind seemed scrambled. Her head listed to one side. She felt too tired to hold it up. The hamburger had filled her tummy and, like the quiet time after Thanksgiving dinner when the elders often napped, she, too, wanted a nap. Her breathing slowed.

Then she thought she heard it again, her name. She thought her cruel imagination had played another trick on her. When she blinked her eyes open, the reality of her location triggered a feeling of dread in the pit of her stomach. Bobby wasn't here. Mac wasn't here either. Not even the man who had snatched her was here.

She wiggled in her seat and scooted her chair around to face the door. "Help!" Her voice was dry and strained. She glanced all around her, hoping to see something to use as a tool. All she saw was the same thing she'd seen every time she looked—rotting vines that had crept in through the walls to escape the scorching sun and then shriveled from lack of sunlight. Cobwebs hanging from the high ceiling, broken glass panes on windows too high to reach, rusted metal tables bolted to walls. For a long moment, she fixated her focus on the broken glass panes and considered the shapes the light made as it streamed through the window. Forcing her mind to look at her lap, she thought she saw the threads in her pants moving like worms headed for her knees. She didn't like how she felt—and she felt so tired. It took all the strength she could muster to scoot her chair around.

Panic slapped her in the face when she realized someone was approaching the door. This time, the sounds from the other side of the door were different—it wasn't her captor. Fear surged through her body like an electric shock. She sat still, listening. Now she knew, the person walked quietly. Her captor walked loudly, clumsily. It had to be the boss guy. He planned to kill her himself, since the other guy couldn't do it. Her head drooped—it felt heavier than a bowling ball. Tears filled her eyes and her bladder released. She didn't care. The quiet tears wouldn't stop. She whispered, "I'm sorry girls, mommy is so sorry. Bobby, I failed our girls. I'm sorry, babe."

Lost in her disappointment, she knew firsthand from working in the emergency room at the hospital that life wasn't always fair. Her girls lost their father to a violent act and now a similar demise for their mother. It's not fair.

She wondered if her adult girls would remember her. Would they see her in their children's faces, mannerisms? Would they tell their children about the grandmother they had never known? What job would the girls gravitate toward? Would one or both become a nurse like their mother? Maybe one would become a doctor. This thought made her smile. Bobby's parents will raise them. The girls like being at the ranch. Bobby loved growing up on the....

The door scraped open. She couldn't lift her head. She wouldn't look. She wanted it to be over.

Mac yelled, "Maggie!"

Lifting her head, but prepared that this too was a hallucination, she looked up to where she heard her name and there he stood, at the top of the stairs—her brother. Hysteria overtook her, her voice had returned as sobbing grunts and dry groans.

He went to his sister and hugged her while Nico cut the ties that bound her to the chair. "You're safe now. The girls are safe. Let's go to them." Roxy pranced around and kept trying to lick Maggie's face.

All she could do was nod. Her emotions had taken over. She sobbed on his shoulder as he carried her like a child. She whispered, "You missed Bobby. He just left."

Nico stayed back and photographed every inch of the area where they'd found her.

With Roxy, Maggie lay on the backseat of Mac's big truck, curled into a ball. The dog kept licking her arms and smelling her soiled pants. She didn't care—she hadn't died. She hadn't let the girls down or Bobby. The girls' future included her.

Chapter 39

Soft music played as the crowd filed into The Pavilion at the fairgrounds. Mac sat next to Nico. It had been three days since they'd found Maggie. Both had sat without saying much since they'd taken their seats. Mac's thoughts kept landing on how he could've been attending Maggie's funeral.

There were two sections of folding chairs allowing room on each side against the wall and a path down the center from the main door leading to the stage. Soft music played while the large screen at the back of the stage area showed photographs of Officer Stockford. Mac watched as photographs of him and his family faded in and out for all to see—him in uniform, on duty, in a patrol vehicle, fishing with a young boy, on a cruise ship with his wife….

Monica had told Mac prior to the service Mrs. Stockford had requested a flag to be draped over her husband's closed casket. She had declined the local bagpipe honor band, who as a custom performed for fallen officers or firefighters.

The investigation into Stockford's and Sawyer's murders had stalled. A witness offered information about Stockford coming and going from Sawyer's home. With no other leads, Monica struggled with the possibility that Gretchen may have been involved in her husband's death.

Mac looked at the mayor, who sat on one side of the stage next to Police Chief Contee and other dignitaries, who Mac didn't recognize. The mayor looked haggard. Mac recalled when he'd attended Blackstone Academy's fund-raising gala in the fall. It was then he saw firsthand that Sawyer and Mayor Eastland were sneaking around like teenagers meeting in the parking lot before the Gala began. And now, someone had murdered Sawyer and the mayor's wife was making her husband pay for his wandering eye.

Few seat options remained available in the spacious room. Mac busied his mind calculating the occupancy—he hated funerals. He counted ten rows on each side of the room. Twenty or so total people per row landed him on about two hundred people on each side. He guessed—based on the square footage of the room and the number of exits—the maximum capacity was around four hundred and fifty people.

Activity at the entrance door caused heads to turn. Officers in full dress uniforms from both the Brookfield Police Department and the Brookfield Sheriff Department marched inside and formed lines along the side walls. Officers from nearby agencies were also among the officers. The conversations became hushed as everyone's attention focused on the officers. All wore a black band on their badges.

Mac caught sight of Monica marching into the room. It had been over a year since he had retired from the air force, but when a group of soldiers, or in this case law enforcement officers, marched into a room, he felt his military training to his core.

After all the officers lined both walls, as practiced to perfection, they snapped their left foot away from the right ten inches and moved their arms to their backs, open hands crossed in an X formation, right over left, right thumb over left, and kept their eyes looking straight ahead appearing to stare at nothing. Standing at parade rest, they awaited further commands.

Mac thought Monica looked mighty fine in her dress uniform. As he watched her standing still beside her fellow officers, he felt he loved her, but also felt nervous about what came next in their relationship.

Once the officers were in place, two officers escorted Stockford's wife, Gretchen, their son, his wife, and their grandchildren from a side door in the front to the front row—they all wore black. After the family members sat in their seats, the music lowered to soft background music, and all conversations ceased.

Mac's childhood friend, Detective Jason Marten and Detective Dan Ruiz, both were also in full dress uniforms, entered the stage from the same side where the dignitaries sat. They went to the empty podium. The photos continued to play behind them. Marten tapped the microphone and said, "Hello. I am Detective Jason Marten and my partner, Detective Dan Ruiz." He swiped his hand in Ruiz's direction. "We're with the Brookfield Police Department. We did not have the honor of working with Officer Bruce Stockford, but we're overseeing the investigation into his death."

Gretchen Stockford bowed her head and sobbed. Her son wrapped his arm around her shoulders.

Marten continued, "It's important for us to assure our community we will find those responsible."

In true Ruiz style, he said nothing. Marten continued, "To the Stockford family, distinguished guests, officers," he nodded to both sides of the room where the officers stood, "loved ones and friends. Today, we gather to honor Officer Bruce Stockford. To lose a fellow officer to an act of violence, whether it be in the line of duty or otherwise, is the hardest part of the job we in law enforcement must endure." He paused and looked down at the podium. Ruiz put his hand on his partner's shoulder.

"Officer Stockford wore badge number four-three-five for thirty years before he retired. He enjoyed sixteen years of retirement, spending time with his wife of forty-two years, Gretchen, their son, Wyatt, his wife, Isabel and their children, Sasha, and Adler." Marten paused and nodded to the Stockford family.

Mac noticed Adler hadn't looked up since he'd sat down. Sasha leaned his way and held his hand.

Marten continued, "In the front row are the remaining members of Officer Stockford's graduating class forty-two from the academy. Since they graduated, a drunk driver killed one officer in their class. Five passed from health issues, and seven are with us today." Again, he paused and nodded to the men in the front row. "Retired Officer Beckam would like to say a few words about Officer Stockford."

A man from the front row stood, then walked with a slight wobble. Before he took the stairs to the stage, he shuffled to the family where he shook each family member's hand—including Adler. Upon arriving at the podium, Marten and Ruiz shook his hand and then stepped aside.

"Thank you," he said to the officers, as he pulled a folded piece of paper from his pocket. "You learn a lot about your fellow recruits when you're at the academy. Life goals, hard times, good times, hobbies, and personalities. Bruce always talked about his family. The life he wanted to provide for Mrs. Stockford and his son."

Wyatt wiped away tears with a tissue his mother handed to him.

"They say there's one family member who is the glue that binds the family together. Bruce was the glue that held our class together. When one of us felt we wanted to quit, he'd point out why we were all there. He also made us laugh to lighten the load during the difficult aspects of our training. Although his antics sometimes resulted in extra physical training for all of us, we still appreciated his friendship. Bruce was an excellent police officer. He had the right amount of compassion and kindness, yet he'd take a perp down in a heartbeat. He seemed to be a natural, and he was an excellent marksman. In 2009, I remember attending a fallen officer's funeral with Bruce. He told me he had big plans to spoil his grandchildren and travel the world with Gretchen. Three years later, we gather here to mourn him. At that funeral, he told me to enjoy life now because we can be gone in a blink." He smoothed his folded paper, refolded it, and returned it to his pocket.

"I'm certain Bruce had more to do, and more places to see with Gretchen."

Mrs. Stockford blew her nose and dabbed at tears.

"Whoever did this need to be brought to justice…" his voice cracked and raised to an angry tone. "Someone knows something."

Detective Marten stepped forward and placed a hand on the retired officer's shoulder.

He appeared to bring himself back from the anger inside him and concluded his comments. "The community of Brookfield needs to come together and solve this senseless crime." He went to Mrs. Stockford, bent over, and hugged her before returning to his seat. You could hear sniffling throughout the audience. The slide show of photos continued—wedding photographs, graduation from the academy, Wyatt in his father's arms, Stockford in dress uniform— the same style Monica wore today.

Detectives Marten and Ruiz returned to the podium. A baby made a brief fussing sound as they approached. Marten said into the microphone, "Wyatt Stockford would like to say a few words about his father." Marten and Ruiz stepped backward.

When Wyatt, a lanky man stood and took a few strides with his long legs to reach the podium, his daughter, Sasha, jumped from her seat next to her mother to the empty seat next to her Nana. Wyatt stood still as he looked out at the people. "Thank you for being here today. We're broken. Without my father, without the kids' Pop-pop, we are on a sailboat at sea, drifting without a means to go anywhere."

Mac watched Gretchen Stockford looking at her lap or the floor.

"We'll be able to continue sailing through life, but we will forever readjust our sails to account for losing this vital person whom we loved more than words can express."

Wyatt's daughter, Sasha, and Gretchen Stockford embraced one another.

"My father supported every crazy notion I had growing up. Friends thought he must be a strict disciplinarian because he was in law enforcement. I can't speak for how he was on duty, but off duty—much like the retired officer had said—he was the glue that held us together. My dad loved having the grandchildren stay at their lake house. He taught Adler, our ten-year-old, how to play cribbage when he almost couldn't hold the cards in his small hands. He was the type of grandfather who sat for an hour while our daughter, Sasha, put girly hair clips all over his hair. Picture that big, strong guy you've seen on the screen today, but with pink butterflies and flowers clipped in his hair. He always kept his hair short, so the clips made it look like he had on a colorful wig." Several people let out a giggle.

"He attended every game I played in, from T-ball to high school sports. After I married my beautiful wife, Isabel." He looked at his wife. "On his days off, he went on countless sailing trips with me when he should have been doing things around his home." He paused. "He said he didn't want us to grow apart."

Wyatt looked around the room, then turned and appeared to watch the photographs of his father fade in and out. When he looked back at the gathering, he had tears in his eyes. His voice cracked. "We aren't sure how to move forward without him. Thank you for joining us today. We're sure you all meant as much to him as he did to you." He left the podium.

Many people were crying, blowing their noses, and rustling in their seats.

Marten returned to the microphone. "Police Chief Contee." He fanned his hand back toward the chief, who stood and straightened his uniform before proceeding to the podium.

The chief's voice thundered through the audience, "I'd like to repeat, there are no worse events than to lose an officer, retired or active, to violence. When we swear an officer in to serve his or her community, they know they're on duty or on call twenty-four hours a day and represent the department three hundred sixty-five days a year. They may be on vacation in another country, but if an emergency arises, they flip the switch from vacationer to law enforcement officer and respond in any way needed. They may retire from duty, but they never retire from their oath. Officer Stockford was and will forever be one of our brothers and we stand united in our appreciation for all Officer Stockford gave and sacrificed to serve our community." He paused, looked at the officers along one wall and nodded. Then he did the same to the officers along the opposite wall. "Officers. Ah-ten-shun!" he bellowed into the microphone before he took one step back, stood at attention.

In a blink, all officers clicked their left heel to their right, straightened their stance, lifted their chests, arched their backs, squared their shoulders, and stood at attention. In a synchronized fashion, all officers snapped their flattened right hand to their forehead, elbows aligned with their shoulders, and held the position. The chief did the same.

Mac knew what was happening. He'd attended too many soldiers' funerals.

Everyone in uniform saluted, including the chief.

The sound system crackled, followed by a female's voice. "Dispatch to 435." A moment of silence followed. "Dispatch to 435." Another moment of silence. "Dispatch to Officer Bruce Stockford, badge number 435." A long moment of silence passed. "We thank you for your dedication, loyalty, and for years of exemplary service to the Brookfield Police Department and the citizens of Brookfield. We will not forget your sacrifice. End of watch, May 2, 2012, 'four-three-five' rest in peace." The sound system did a few more crackles before it became silent.

From the moment the police chief stepped back from the podium and the sound system crackled, the attendees had hushed to a level of quiet beyond any church service Mac had ever attended. Respect for law enforcement and the murdered officer rippled through the room.

The chief stepped into an 'at-ease' stance. The officers followed his lead and did the same. He returned to the microphone and directed the officers along the walls to make their way to the exit and outside.

The chief's voice reverberated through the room, "The family thanks you all for attending today and requests privacy at the graveside service."

Chapter 40

Mac and Nico waited for Monica, Luke and Rinda to join them for a late lunch at Brookfield Bar and Grill. They both sat lost in their thoughts after attending Stockford's funeral.

It had been a long three days since Mac and Nico found Maggie in the old, abandoned warehouse. She hadn't left the Donaldson's ranch or the girls since the hospital released her. The exact purpose of her abduction remained unknown. If the purpose was to scare Mac—point taken. The message on the photos rattled around in Mac's thoughts—"It hurts when a loved one dies. Will you find her in time?"

Mac considered everything that had transpired from when he'd first agreed to work at Blackstone Academy. His gut said his military life had nothing to do with Maggie's abduction. It had to be connected to Blackstone Academy. Had he known when he agreed to work undercover at the school that Maggie would get dragged into trouble because of his connection to the school, he'd have said, "Hell no!" Nothing mattered more to him than Maggie and the girls. He knew leaving the school was the right thing for him to do. And he felt confident Luke would be an excellent replacement. He'd even heard from Roni that Luke had put a stop to the bullies who hassled Teddy. Score one for Luke.

The server brought him out of his thoughts. "What can I get you to drink?"

"Beer for me," Mac answered.

Nico ordered coffee with cream and sugar.

Looking around the restaurant, Mac noticed the lunch crowd had dissipated, leaving a few people at the bar enjoying an afternoon cocktail, but otherwise, an almost empty restaurant. A glance at his watch explained why—it was three in the afternoon, late for lunch, early for dinner.

Staring out the window, he felt tired. He said to Nico, "They arrested Anson."

"Good. Based on my experience, that little shit has trouble written all over him."

Mac smiled when he saw Monica pull her jeep into a parking space. He pointed for Nico to look out the window. "She's too much of a perfectionist."

Nico looked in the direction Mac had pointed and saw Monica back out of her parking space to straighten her approach. She opened her door and leaned out to see the parking stall lines, backed out once more and brought the Jeep to the center of the space, perfectly parallel between the lines, then hopped out of her vehicle. Nico said, "It'll give her an ulcer one day, or drive her to drink."

"I'll help her learn to relax," Mac replied, and then his thoughts went back to Maggie. "Maggie's going to sell our parents' house and buy one in Blackstone Estates because they have security."

"Can she afford that?"

"They have some smaller homes sprinkled in the development. She said too many bad things have happened at the house. She also said she did a lot of thinking while in her drugged state. Our childhood home has few happy memories—growing up with an alcoholic parent can destroy a child's early years. We have happy and sad memories about our grandfather living with us, then our parent's death, and now this. The Donaldsons said they can stay at the ranch until they find a house to buy."

"You can't blame her. She should also see a therapist to help her sort through the trauma."

Mac nodded his agreement and then watched Monica. As she came into the restaurant, a customer leaving recognized her. They stopped and talked. He watched her approach their table. After she sat down, he said, "You changed. I wondered why you were taking so long to get here."

"I'd like a beer and I can't drink alcohol while in uniform."

He patted her thigh and waved at their server.

"Hey, changing subjects." She said, "Did you stop by Maggie's neighbors like you promised and give them an update?"

"I did. Are you alright? You must be exhausted."

"I've been better." She scanned their immediate area and then leaned in toward the center of the table.

The guys both leaned in as well.

"After the service, Gretchen pulled me aside and told me she needed to confess something. For real confess something, like go down to the station, confess." She stopped talking when the server walked toward them. "Beer, please."

After the young woman walked far enough away, she continued, "I called Marten and Ruiz over to where she and I were. She told them she knew the drill. It blew my mind—what the hell had she done?"

They all sat up straight when the server brought Monica her beer.

Leaning in, she continued, "Marten told me I was too close to Gretchen and needed to step away to keep the discussion with her by the book."

"What the ..." Mac's brow wrinkled, and he shook his head.

She continued, "Plus, the whole adoption thing with Stockford, it's hard to learn an officer did some shady shit."

"I get it. There were some unscrupulous guys in the air force, too. When they didn't return or I got orders to go elsewhere, I never much thought about them again. I hope Stockford will fade for you as well."

Nico added, "We had a few rotten apples in the FBI. They're in every type of job."

"It's awful that we have them in our military and law enforcement."

She leaned in again and lowered her voice. "How do you guys feel about the chief putting a lid on the fact that Stockford's murder looks like revenge for his role in the black-market adoption?"

"The case is still open, right?"

"Yes. They have no solid evidence to show who sought revenge, no paper trail, no money trail—nothing to present to the district attorney. Perhaps the mysterious twin brother who their mother had relinquished had someone murder Stockford—the person who facilitated the black-market adoption. And someone mysteriously murders his uncle, the pharmacist whose drug business played a role in the man's twin brother's death in Indonesia within a few days of Stockford's murder." She took a swig of her beer, then continued, "They also have zip to show he had anything to do with Maggie's abduction, but you know he had to be behind it."

Mac put his arm around her shoulders. "I'm thankful he or whoever was behind this revenge killing didn't kill Maggie."

"A warning maybe?"

"But a warning for what? His brother is no longer at the school, his..." She looked around, then bent forward and lowered her voice again. "His nephew is no longer at the school." She looked at Mac. "Correct? The custodian was the coach's nephew?"

He nodded. "Yes."

Before she got more amped up, Mac said, "It sure helped Maggie that her abductor had a heart. The truth will come out one day."

The server approached. "Are you ready to order?

Nico replied, "Let's start with a platter of chicken nachos to share. We're waiting for a couple more people." Everyone in town knew Brookfield Bar and Grill had the best nachos.

The server headed back to the bar, where she seemed too interested in the bartender.

Mac said, "I can't stop thinking if I hadn't agreed to the job at the school, Maggie wouldn't have gotten mixed up in this."

Nico shook his head. "Don't blame yourself. If we question every decision we make for fear, something bad may result. We'd do nothing."

"If all of this is true, Maggie got mixed up in this twisted logic because of me then she's lucky to be alive when you consider the revenge plan against Stockford for his role in the adoption, Sawyer for her role as the coach's boss—I guess, — and the pharmacist for getting his nephew involved in the drug ring. Whoever was behind it didn't show mercy to any of them. I get Stockford and the uncle, but Sawyer must have been involved in the drug ring, or why else was she included?"

Monica answered before Mac could. "Since you asked, I think Sawyer may have been a warning—to the mayor. A power move. When they found out about the mayor's affair, it made sense to take out Sawyer—because she didn't manage the school well which if she had would've kept coach out of trouble—so then why not take out the mayor's mistress and create havoc for the mayor? What better way to feel powerful?"

Nico shrugged. "That's a possibility." He looked out the window. "Hey, did Mac tell you I invited Rinda to lunch?"

"No, he didn't." She looked at Mac.

Their server slid the platter mounded high with tortilla chips, cheese, chicken, and all the usual goodies onto the table with smaller plates for each person.

Mac shrugged. "Sorry, we've been busy."

Nico stood when Rinda approached the table, smiling at him. He introduced her to Monica, then they settled in. He hadn't seen her outside the bar. She wore blue jeans that showed off her tiny frame and had pulled back and braided her long, thick, red hair.

Last to join the group, Luke arrived a minute after Rinda. Mac introduced him to Rinda. Monica and Luke already knew each other with him temporarily staying at Mac's place. Nico had met him when he first arrived in town. Mac gave his friends some of the history he and Luke shared from their time in the air force.

Rinda ordered iced tea and Luke ordered water, then Mac told the server they needed more time before they ordered food.

Eventually, they all ordered and talked while they ate. Everyone seemed comfortable sharing stories as they got to know each other better.

Mac was silent for a few moments, watching his friends. It felt good to be home, back in Brookfield, where he'd been born and raised. Watching his air force buddy share embarrassing stories of Mac. With his soft-spoken, easygoing manner, he knew Luke would be good for the school, which solidified his decision to join Nico in the private investigator's business. He also knew he'd always be available should the school or Luke need him.

Monica leaned toward Mac and said, "I'm so spent. I need to go home and sleep for a week."

Mac waved for the server to bring him the bill. "As fun as this has been, we're going to head out. We need to do this again soon."

The server scurried to the table. She smiled as she said, "A man at the bar paid your bill."

Mac and Nico both jerked their heads toward the bar.

The server said, "He asked me to wait until he had left to tell you." She appeared to have picked up on their concern.

Mac looked at the bill. Someone had written on it, "See you again, tough guy. Keep your loved one close." He pushed Monica out of the booth and ran outside to the parking lot.

Chapter 41

That night, while Monica took a hot shower, Mac sat on the back porch drinking a big glass of iced water and enjoyed the cool spring breeze. Roxy and Comet were on the lawn, gnawing on rawhide.

He heard the back door open and close, then Monica sat beside him on the top stair of the porch. "It's a nice evening. Where's Luke?"

"He's working out at the gym."

They watched the lights from the downtown buildings come on as the sky darkened.

She stretched out her long legs in front of her. "Evelyn Rycroft from the adoption agency passed away. It's like she'd been waiting to release some skeletons in her closet before she died. Her daughter texted me."

Monica's phone buzzed. She looked at it, then at Mac with wide eyes. "It's Marten."

"Well, hello," she said. "Please don't tell me you need me." After listening for a moment, she said, "Can I put you on speaker so Mac can hear the update?" She added, "It's just the two of us." She pushed the speaker button on her cell phone.

"Hi Buddy," Mac said to his friend. "You must be a zombie by now."

Marten admitted, "I'm tired. But criminals don't care about law enforcement working overtime. They keep on doing illegal shit."

Monica interjected, "You said you have an update?"

The dogs continued to chew on their rawhide, unbothered by the phone call.

Marten began, "Thanks to Gretchen Stockford, the guys in IT found the connection between Stockford and Sawyer on a dark web website where a shocking number of people were soliciting hitman services. Gretchen lied to us about why her husband's phone number had been on a sticky note in Sawyer's home. Sawyer and Stockford were romantically involved …"

Mac and Monica shared a look.

"She knew her husband was cheating on her with Sawyer?" Monica's expression of shock mixed with disappointment prompted Mac to rub her thigh.

"Yes. She said, when she figured it out, she lost it, but decided she'd rather him die than embarrass the family again. Half of his retirement pension wasn't enough of a consequence for him." He took a breath.

Monica needed to confirm she'd heard him correctly. "Gretchen, had her husband killed? And she thought she'd get away with it?"

"She didn't say whether she thought she'd get away with it or not, but she confessed to soliciting a murder-for-hire."

Mac asked, "How does that connect to Maggie's abduction?"

"The plot thickens," Marten said in jest. "The IT guys saw two separate conversations about killing Stockford."

Mac asked, "Two different people were looking for someone to kill Stockford?"

"Correct."

Monica said, "Indeed, the plot thickens."

Marten sounded more tired as he went on with the update. "The IT guys saw Gretchen had inquired about someone to kill her husband and a woman—Sawyer. Another person responded and told her they knew someone who could take care of it for her. That person and a third person believed they were in a private chat space. Mostly, they were—the IT guys got into the chat space in stealth mode and read what led them to believe the two people had worked together before. The person who had connected with Gretchen mentioned another 'assignment' to the third person. Hang on."

It sounded like Marten covered the phone and spoke to someone, then he came back onto the call. "Sorry. There's a lot of shit going down right now. The feds are here in force …" He stopped. "Since it appears to have involved the Internet, the crimes are now federal, but they say they'll work with us. Anyway, I'm getting ahead of myself. Back on the dark web, one person told the other there was an interested party who wanted two people killed in the same town. It would be double the price. Here's the kicker. He also said she had offered too little for the job. Then the guy went shared a quote from John Dryden, a poet from the 1660s, 'Beware the fury of a patient man.' He told the hitman he'd been watching the same two people for a long time. He'd waited for the right opportunity to have them killed for their involvement in his brother's death. The guy offered to pay three times his usual fee for the short notice—again like they'd done business before."

When Marten took a breath, Monica spoke up, "Are you serious?! Stockford helped his lover, the dispatcher, relinquish one of her sons and now that relinquished son is behind this?"

"Yes. All paths lead to Coach Andrews's relinquished twin brother. And before I forget, your excellent police work in finding the woman who handled the adoption helped pull this all together."

Monica said, "It was teamwork. Let me see if I have this straight so far. Stockford, years ago, facilitated the illegal adoption of the twin brother. Stockford broke his fidelity promise to his wife and had an affair with Sawyer. Mrs. Stockford wants her husband and his lover killed at the same time the relinquished twin wants Stockford killed for his role in the adoption. How am I doing?"

"Good. Keep going."

"I can't connect Sawyer to the twin," she admits.

"Remember the coach's uncle and the drug bust, him fleeing the country, and his murder that coincided with Stockford's and Sawyer's murders?" He didn't wait for an answer. "We believe Sawyer was involved in the drug activity at the school. We've subpoenaed personnel documents from Blackstone Academy to see if there's anything to support that theory."

Mac and Monica remained quiet, listening, and watching the dogs, who were done with their rawhides, and now chased each other around the backyard.

Marten continued, "The IT guys connected the same unidentified man to contracting with a hitman in Indonesia to take out the uncle."

Mac jumped into the conversation, "Because the uncle corrupted his nephew—the twin who the mother had kept—and if he hadn't corrupted him, the twins may have been able to be together again?"

"Bingo. Or at least it fits. Now, gathering the documentation to get an indictment will be the challenge. We need to secure a federal warrant on the dark web website where the IT guys found all the connections. Easier said than done, because if they suspect a warrant is in the works to get some of their data, they'll shut down the site, wipe the data, and be in the wind."

Mac asked, sounding fatigued, "How does all of that tie to Maggie?"

Marten let out a big sigh, "We think, and it's an educated guess at this point. Maggie's abduction was a warning to you. The police chief tasked you with ridding the school of a drug problem, and you did. In the wake of that, we arrested his brother and his uncle. Because of all that you uncovered. The brother is dead. None of what happened was your fault, but the twin may have felt you played a role, and if you hadn't been involved, perhaps the coach would still be alive."

Mac asked, "Have you located the twin?"

"Yes, and no. He bought the coach's old home, but he's a few steps ahead of us. He's on his private jet, headed to an island that he owns."

"He owns an island?" Monica blurted out, then took a sip of Mac's water.

"Yes, he owns an island. It turns out he's quite wealthy, and has an army of lawyers—or so I'm told. He lives on the island in a villa—fully powered by a commercial-grade solar energy system—has a small, private airstrip. He may never come back to the states. But if he does, we've issued an arrest warrant."

Mac and Monica wait for more information.

"I know. I know. It's frustrating. Right now, we can't get him while he's there, and he knows it. When the adoptive parents died, he inherited everything."

Mac tossed a ball for Roxy to retrieve. "Maybe someone should look into how his parents died."

Monica changed the subject. "Somebody paid our bill this afternoon at Brookfield Bar and Grill. And wrote a message on the bill to Mac that read, 'See you again, tough guy. Keep your loved one close.'"

"Well, shit. I'll ask the owners for the security video to see if we can get something to show who wrote the message."

Mac chimed in, "It looked like the same handwriting as what's on the photographs of Maggie."

Marten took a deep breath and exhaled. "A handwriting analyst determined the revenge note and the messages on Maggie's first photo were not from the same person. We assume at Stockford's the shooter wrote what he was told to leave at the scene and then either the twin or an accomplice did the others. We may never tie her abduction to the murders, but we might charge him with her abduction if we catch him on the security video at the restaurant. It's a stretch and up to the district attorney."

Mac looked at Monica, shaking his head.

"I'm sorry, Mac. I wish we had a more concrete case, but...." He stopped talking.

Mac and Monica heard paper riffling sounds.

"Ruiz handed me information about someone finding a man's dead body down at the river. His description matches what Maggie said about the man who took her and held her. And it matches the description Lindy gave of the man at the school who gave her the envelope."

Monica said, "He's tying up loose ends."

"Looks that way."

After the call with Marten ended, Monica said, while still watching the dogs play, "That was a brilliant idea to research how the twin's adoptive parents died. Isn't there a new private investigation business in Brookfield? Might be an excellent first case for them." She leaned over and kissed his cheek.

* * *

Thank you for reading Unknown Revenge. I hope you've enjoyed reading the story as much as I enjoyed writing it. If you would be so kind, I'd appreciate you leaving an honest review wherever you purchased or borrowed the book. The Marshal Series will return— with a new Marshal at Blackstone Academy—Luke Lang.

Mac and Nico have opened their private investigation business, Two Guys PI. Mac bought Trav's Donuts. He and Nico have turned the back area into the office for the Two Guys PI and Nico moved into the upstairs apartment. Don't be sad about Mac leaving Blackstone Academy. He's not leaving Brookfield. Should Luke need Mac's help, he's a phone call away.

Watch for Two Guys PI - coming soon.

If you haven't read Unknown Threat, Book 1 in the Marshal Series, it's available for free wherever to purchase books as well as at RobinLyons.com.

UNKNOWN THREAT

This famous quote by Andre Malraux defines several of the characters in Unknown Threat, "Man is not what he thinks he is; he is what he hides."

Sergeant Mac MacKenna retires after 20 years as a pararescueman in an elite special ops unit in the U.S. Air Force and returns to his hometown. Aiding others at all costs is what the air force trained Mac to do—it's all he's known for his entire adult life.

He admittedly knows nothing about children or school other than he remembers being one and attended as a kid.

When the police chief asks Mac to pose as a marshal at Blackstone Academy to rid the school of crime—he accepts the mission. Soon enough, Mac's former life of loaded weapons and death-defying rescues is replaced with tangled webs of deceit, twisted wealthy and powerful people, murder, and a dangerous den of corruption disguised as a prestigious academy.

Unfortunately for Mac, meddling with the rich can have deadly consequences.

Continue for an excerpt of Unknown Threat.

And remember to watch for more of Mac MacKenna as he and Nico Stark open their *Two Guys P.I. - Private Investigation* business in the back of Trav's Donut Shop in Brookfield. New series coming soon.

UNKNOWN THREAT – CHAPTER 1

The morning began with a hike in Desolation Wilderness. Mac MacKenna and his dog Roxy, a long-haired black and tan German Shepherd rescue, hiked at 7,000 feet above sea level.

Twin Lakes trail head begins and ends just after the Chappell Crossing Bridge. Mac had enjoyed going to the peaceful and quiet mountaintop escape since he could drive. On this day, a Tuesday, he and Roxy had the trail all to themselves. As a form of therapy, Mac often rose early to hike up the mountain and catch the sunrise. Roxy tagged along sniffing trace scents from everyone and everything that had come before them.

Sometime around noon, they arrived back at Mac's truck feeling refreshed. For several years the area had experienced severe drought making it possible to hike in April.

Mac gave Roxy some water and let her sniff around while he stripped off his flannel jacket and tossed it onto the passenger seat. After ample time to cool down, he hoisted Roxy up onto the backseat, mindful of her breed's tendency for hip issues. Besides, he was in no hurry. Since his retirement from the U.S. Air Force, he took life one day at a time.

Mac found retirement a bit boring compared to the military. He'd torn down the wall between the kitchen and living room to open up the space and install hardwood floors in an old Victorian house he'd purchased in his hometown of Brookfield, California. Remodeling his home gave him something to do.

As he headed west on the highway, Mac's cell phone rang. It was his longtime buddy, Jason. They'd both joined the air force while in their senior year of high school. Jason stayed in eight years and then returned home to become a police officer.

Mac pressed the call button on his steering wheel, "Hey, Jason, how's it going?"

"Can't complain. Do you have a few minutes to talk?" he asked.

"Sure. Roxy and I just finished hiking up at Wright's Lake. We're headed back to town. I'm about to pull into Handley's to pick up cinnamon rolls for Maggie and the girls. What'd you need?"

Mac's older sister Maggie and her two daughters lived on the other side of town in the home where she and Mac grew up.

"Did you see any snow up there? Feel free to drop off some cinnamon rolls here at the office; they're the best."

"I just might. No snow, not even in the shady spots."

Mac waited in his lane to turn left into Handley's parking lot.

"It's gonna be a bad fire season. Do you have plans to leave the area anytime soon or are you sticking around?" he asked.

"That's pretty vague. What's up?" Mac was intrigued.

"I have a job for you if you're interested. To tell the truth, I need your help."

"Keep talking," Mac said as pulled straight into a parking spot near the front door.

"Blackstone Academy has a serious drug problem. In fact, over the weekend, the mayor's fourteen-year-old son overdosed and almost died. He's in the hospital recovering. Heroin, we think. Lucky for him, his older brother found him and called 911 shortly after he went unconscious. The police chief and the school board president want someone on the inside to help identify the source of the drugs. Somebody's getting rich over there and the next time there's an overdose the kid might not be so lucky."

Jason paused, took a drink of something.

"I'm not sure how I can help." Mac watched the lunch crowd pile into the coffee shop.

"They want someone outside of law enforcement so that nobody will tag him or her as an undercover cop. I suggested you. Everyone in town knows you're ex-Air Force. The chief thinks you're the right guy for the assignment."

"He doesn't know me. Am I supposed to pretend to be a teacher or something?"

Mac glanced in the rearview mirror and saw Roxy was still asleep.

"He knows of you. Small town chitchat. No, the board wants to hire a marshal to watch over the students and staff because of the increase in school violence across the nation. The Chief thinks it's the perfect cover. The superintendent and other school board members won't be privy to your real purpose. But they're in agreement it's time to hire a marshal."

"I don't know shit about kids, or about schools. I don't see how I could be the right man for the job."

"Your military experience with air force special ops trumps your lack of experience with kids."

"Is there some training?"

"As a matter of fact, California recently began a marshal program like the one Texas has had in place for many years. The Chief thought you could do it over the summer and be ready to roll when school starts."

"What about training on how to deal with kids? What age kids are we talking about?"

"Kindergarten through twelfth grade. The young ones are on one side of the school and the older students on the other."

"So, I'd need to deal with all ages is what you're saying? And what about the parents? I'm not the best people person." Mac paused. "How long will the job last?"

"You'll mostly deal with the older students. On occasion, the younger ones. But they aren't bringing drugs and weapons into schools. At least not yet, anyway. It's a public school, but some parents act like they own the place, they can be a little territorial at times. Not sure if they'll like that you're there or not. I can't sugarcoat any part of this for you. How long depends on how long it takes you to figure out who's dealing the drugs."

Mac fell silent.

"Mac, are you still having nightmares about the sandbox?"

"I know where you're going with that, Jason. The kids playing near the car when the bomb went off. We wanted to help, but weren't allowed to."

"That's it," Jason said, "It haunted me for a few years. The time I've spent giving back to the community has helped me feel like a better person. I seldom have nightmares anymore. Maybe the marshal gig will help you push past it. Another thing to consider, Maggie might shift the girls to Blackstone for high school. Better to clean up the drugs before they get there."

"That's hitting below the belt."

"I'm just throwing it out there for you to consider." Jason continued his pitch, "And, it's a paid position."

"You do know I receive a pension from the air force, right?"

"We all know the retirement pay's shitty. You could pay for the remodeling of your house, pay off your truck, and travel when school isn't in session."

Mac exhaled loud enough to cause Roxy to open her eyes and glance up to be certain all was well. "I'll give it some thought and get back to you."

"That works. You'll see this will be a good assignment for you. You may not know it yet, but you're the perfect guy for this job."

"I haven't said yes yet."

"The school board will approve your hiring at their June meeting. You should plan to attend and get a feel for how it works. Remember, nobody must know what you're doing there. Trust no one other than me, my partner Dan Ruiz, Chief Contee, and the school board president Michael Stromberg. Also, the Chief spoke to the school board about hiring a marshal. And whether or not he or she should carry a weapon. They agreed to amend their policy that prohibits weapons on campus by excluding the marshal."

"Jason, I haven't said yes yet."

As Jason had suggested, Mac went to the June school board meeting to see how things worked. He wasn't sure if he was ready for more bureaucracy.

"Psst, mister," the small brunette seated to Mac's right patted his thigh, "would you like a sign?" She smelled of too much perfume which failed to hide the hint of booze on her breath.

Expecting him to accept, she pushed a cardboard sign at him, the homemade poster board kind with a tongue depressor-style handle. It resembled the ones seen at high school sports events that say 'Go Team Go.' Except this one had a photo of a pistol inside a circle with a dark line through its center. Written above the crossed-out handgun photo was 'NO GUNS,' and beneath it, 'At Blackstone Academy.' Moms and dads, but mostly moms, held similar signs face down on their laps.

"No, thanks," Mac said.

She gave him a puzzled look and waited for him to change his mind.

The meeting room had theater seating with ten rows of forty seats and an aisle down the middle leading to the podium. Each row sat higher than the one in front, giving everyone an unobstructed view.

Of the two hundred or so people in the audience about half held protest signs. Only a few of the brave, well-dressed men and women ventured to the podium. They spoke into the microphone with quivering voices. None had been happy, but all were polite and courteous. Unlike the man currently at the podium. This guy was one smug son of a bitch. He looked about Mac's age, short by anyone's standards, he had dark hair and was clean shaven. And if Mac were to wager a guess, the man's suit cost more than his first airman's paycheck.

The crowd was amped up, feeding off the speaker's hostility. A man in the audience yelled, "No guns at school." Heads turned toward him.

"Order. Order." Michael Stromberg, president of Blackstone Academy's school board, banged his gavel on the square of wood.

"Order in the boardroom." He continued to pound his gavel until all voices quieted.

President Stromberg leaned closer to the microphone. His posture stiffened. He said in a booming voice, "Randall, if you cannot refrain from using profanity while addressing this board, you'll need to leave the room."

President Stromberg was a large man, not so much in size as in presence. He was older than Mac by a good ten years; his skin appeared weathered from too much time in the sun. A tall man, he spoke with a deep baritone voice and gave off a Hollywood mobster, kingpin vibe. Not someone Mac intended to cross. His signature cowboy hat hung alone on the coat rack in the corner. He'd worn a similar one two weeks prior when he'd offered Mac the marshal job. The silver and turquoise collar tips on his fancy white shirt matched his bolo tie.

Marlene, the superintendent's administrative assistant, told Mac, President Stromberg was a modern-day cowboy, a local cattle rancher who'd done quite well. That explained his deep tan and premature wrinkles. Marlene, a sweet, older lady, gossiped a bit too much for Mac's taste.

No sound from the other board members. The three men and one woman's nameplates all included the title 'Doctor' in front of their names.

Mac's phone was on silent. He typed a text to his sister.

Mac: *Are you still up?*

Maggie: *Yes. How's the meeting?*

Mac: *A jackass is speaking at the podium. Parents are waving signs that read, NO GUNS.*

Maggie: *Not feeling the love?*

While President Stromberg continued to admonish the speaker for his use of profanity, the fragrant woman to Mac's right patted his thigh again. She leaned his way and whispered, "Do you have kids at Blackstone?"

He stared at her for a long moment. She was about his age, wore too much makeup, had fake fingernails, and an unnatural looking tan. "No," he said.

"Are you from the newspaper? Why are you here?"

"To observe."

"Observe what?"

He returned his attention to the front of the room. In his peripheral vision, he saw the woman lean over to the lady on her right and whisper.

In the front of the room, each board member had a microphone and a laptop that sat lower than the table giving them a clear view of the audience. The blue hue from the screens in front of them illuminated their faces. At the far right, Marlene took notes. With lightning speed, she clicked on her keyboard.

"Randall, California's schools, are beginning to employ marshals, or resource officers on their campuses whether you like it or not. We received a grant to participate in a state-run marshal pilot program like the one in Texas. It's a done deal. On behalf of the board, we thank you for sharing your thoughts and opinions. Now sit down." President Stromberg dismissed the speaker with a flip of his hand.

The man didn't budge. He leaned in so his mouth almost kissed the microphone. "That's it? That's all you have to say?" He pounded his fist on the podium. "Not acceptable. You need to explain to all of us why you morons think we need a guard with a loaded gun on our campus. To hell with the state program. To hell with the program in Texas. I want answers, and I'm not sitting down until I get them."

A rumble rippled through the audience members. Several people waved their signs in the air. The inquisitive woman on Mac's right waved hers with great enthusiasm.

President Stromberg banged his gavel in rapid succession until the audience quieted down and signs landed on laps.

The speaker gripped the sides of the podium, as though he were about to go for a bobsled ride. His elbows extended out from his body. "Our school hasn't had problems. We don't have gangs, the kids don't do drugs, and they come from good homes. An armed guard standing sentry like they're entering a prison sends the wrong message to our kids. We pay a lot of money for our kids to attend school here. Excuse me; we donate a lot of money. So unless you want a serious hit to your pocketbook, you better reconsider." His voice cracked and squeaked like a thirteen-year-old boy's.

"You don't intimidate me with your threats, Randall." President Stromberg jabbed his gavel toward the speaker. "Listen up folks. A committee made up of parents and staff decided we needed a marshal. They developed the job responsibilities for the position. The committee also screen the applications and narrowed their selection to three candidates. Superintendent Sawyer and I made the final decision."

The speaker waited his turn to speak. "Gosh, Michael, that sounds so professional. Thanks for sharing, but I doubt the parents on your damn committee knew you planned to allow the person to carry a loaded gun."

President Stromberg motioned with his gavel to include the four other board members. "We discussed the final candidate at length before offering the job. And for the record, we are fortunate and honored to have someone as experienced as our finalist. He's a decorated Chief Master Sergeant retired from the U.S. Air Force Special Operations. He's undergone emergency medical training and is a weapons specialist. He fought in Iraq during Operation Desert Thunder and Desert Fox. His unit also helped rescue and treat victims of Hurricane Katrina. I could go on, but you look as if I were boring you, Randall. One last point, he's already scheduled to attend an 80-hour Marshal training course during the summer. 'We'…" again he motioned to include the board as a whole. "Approved the marshal to carry a loaded handgun." A collective gasp rippled through the audience. "Police Chief Contee supports our decision. The marshal won't be prancing around the campus waving a gun. If there were a real threat, I'd want him to protect your kids and the staff. Should a threat present itself, we expect him to use his weapon only when necessary."

Like zombies, the four other board members lowered their heads and shifted their attention downward to their laptop monitors. A loud rumble spread through the quiet room. Signs bobbed up and down.

The speaker opened his mouth to respond. Before he said anything, President Stromberg held up his hand to stop him.

President Stromberg waited for the room to quiet again before he continued. "I'm not going to engage in further conversation with you about our new marshal's employment. Furthermore, Randall, if you or the other parents have a problem with our decisions on how to keep your children safe while they're on campus, then I suggest you run for office in the November election. Your three minutes were up ten minutes ago. Step away from the podium and either leave the room or take a seat and be quiet."

The harsh, overhead fluorescent lighting, spotlighted President Stromberg's red face. His jaw jutted out, and a vein bulged across his forehead. He looked like he needed to loosen the slider on his bolo tie.

The speaker left the podium in a huff and went to a small woman sitting in the front row. He pulled her to her feet by her arm and yanked her along as he stormed out of the room.

"If anyone has a comment we haven't already heard, please step up to the podium," offered President Stromberg.

The audience sat frozen. Heads turned right then left. Nobody stood. No signs waved in the air.

The woman seated to Mac's right whispered too loud to the lean, athletic-looking woman on her right, "My kids have never seen a real gun. I don't like this. At all."

"My son hasn't seen a real gun, either. I'm undecided how I feel about it. I want to see how it plays out once school starts."

"Well, we'll see about the ridiculous notion that a glorified security guard should carry a loaded gun. I know people," the alcohol-fueled woman said, as she crossed her arms and straightened her posture.

Mac was like the proverbial fly on the wall. The hot topic of hiring a marshal had lasted about an hour. Of the parents who'd spoken on record, there'd been a common theme of dissension concerning him carrying a loaded gun. The school board understood disallowing him to carry a weapon would nullify his acceptance of their job offer.

President Stromberg banged the gavel hard, twice. His face glowed red. "Is there a motion to approve hiring Mac MacKenna as our new marshal?" he asked, through his teeth into the microphone.

"I move to approve the new marshal," Dr. Littleton said, a small, meek-looking man with gray hair combed over a balding head.

Another man leaned in and seconded the motion. President Stromberg banged the gavel again. "All those in favor?"

The three male board members plus President Stromberg leaned in and said, "Aye." Stromberg stared at the lone female board member, Dr. Ward, who'd said nothing.

"Those opposed?" asked President Stromberg glaring at the woman.

Dr. Ward leaned into her microphone without looking at the school board president and said, "Nay." Most of the audience jumped to their feet and applauded.

"Are you serious, Wanda?" He continued to look at her, as he banged his gavel and said, "Motion carries."

Wanda ignored him.

President Stromberg banged his gavel hard and bellowed into his microphone, "Order. Order. Order in the boardroom."

UNKNOWN THREAT – CHAPTER 3

Mac woke early on the first day of school. Even though the job was more a favor for Jason, he felt a bit excited and maybe a little nervous. Not that he'd admit either to anyone.

He checked himself in the mirror. He'd visited the barber on Sunday for a haircut and shave. He asked for his hair to be left a little shaggy and to leave some stubble on his face. He'd had his last buzz cut a month before he retired. It felt liberating to no longer have rules to follow, dictating his appearance and behavior.

Since his weapon was a heated discussion at the June board meeting, he decided to use a concealed waistband holster attached to the belt on his jeans. Leaving his t-shirt untucked should help hide his controversial handgun.

Roxy knew something was up. An anxious habit, she paced in the kitchen while Mac made his lunch. When Mac looked at her, she tilted her head one way and then the other trying to understand what was happening.

"No girl, you stay here," he said.

She flopped down with a thud onto her cushioned dog bed in the corner of the alcove off the kitchen.

"Roxy, it's okay."

On his way out the door, he scratched her big hairy neck to ease her nerves. When the back door shut, she followed by way of her giant-sized dog door. She stood in the fenced backyard and watched him drive away.

Anticipating a hot day, Mac rode his motorcycle to his new job. He had arrived an hour before school started. There were a few other early-risers parked in the staff parking lot across from the school's main entrance.

Mac flashed his ID badge at the scanner, and the main door slid open. He stepped inside and paused. The school was quiet. On the way to his office, the third door on the right, the one with the large bold word 'SECURITY' written on it, sat Marlene, sentry to the boss.

"Good morning, Marlene."

"Right back at you," she said, as she popped her gum. "Are you ready for the kiddos and their parents?"

"I'm as ready as I can be, never having dealt with kids before."

"If you have questions or concerns, come see me. And, you let me know if anyone bothers you." She winked and returned her attention to her computer screen.

Dismissed by Marlene, Mac swallowed hard and went outside to the front of the school. Part of his job required him to watch the kids as they arrived.

The clasp on the flag clanged against the metal flagpole. Reality washed over Mac. He was about to enter a foreign world. Kids. Busybody parents. Politics.

Parents started to park across the street and walk their kids to the school.

"You must be Mac?" Someone said from behind him.

He turned to see a tall young lady with a bouncy ponytail walking toward him.

Mac thought she might be a student. She was at least twenty years younger than him.

"I'm Roni," she said, thrusting her hand out to shake. "I'm your partner in crime. Just kidding. I have monitor duty before and after school too, sort of like your assistant. Is it true you were…"

"You." a woman screeched from the direction neither Mac nor Roni faced. They both spun around to see who made the fuss.

"Good morning, Mrs. Ross," Roni said with a cheerful voice.

The woman ignored Roni.

Mac recognized the woman he'd sat next to at the board meeting in June.

The mother held her little girl's hand tight. Mom on a mission, she stormed straight toward Mac and Roni. Her son followed. She was quick to send her son and daughter into the school. She stood before Mac with a hands-on-hips, feet-planted stance.

"You. *You're* the new marshal. Why did you pretend to be from the newspaper at the board meeting in June?" Her bare chest was crimson and blotchy; the redness spread up her neck.

Roni looked confused.

Mac's hand went up to stop her in her tracks. "Whoa, wait a minute, lady. I didn't pretend to be from the newspaper," he replied. "I said I was there to observe and that was the truth."

She squared her shoulders and planted her high heels. Again, she wore too much perfume, and maybe a possible faint hint of booze.

"Do not speak to my daughter," she said waving her index finger in his face.

"Okay," he said.

"I don't want you anywhere near her. Do you understand?" she said.

"Okay."

"I mean it," she said.

"Okay."

She turned and stomped back to her Jaguar.

Mac shrugged at Roni.

The front of the school buzzed with kids and parents. Moms, dads, nannies, and chauffeurs dropped off their darlings on the sidewalk before speeding off to do whatever they did while their kids were in school.

Family cars of the rich looked the same on the inside as everyone else's. Strewn about were candy wrappers, fast food remnants, and empty water bottles. Animated movies played on six-inch screens nestled into the backs of headrests. Stained car seats, toys, and other kid stuff cluttered the interior.

The younger boys scanned Mac up and down. The girls looked and giggled. All students wore blue and white uniforms and approached at a brisk pace from all directions. The older kids, boys, and girls alike, didn't pay much attention to the new marshal. Almost all said hello to Roni.

The young kids also said good morning to Mac, and more parents than expected introduced themselves. Ten or so even thanked him for his service to the country.

By lunchtime, those who ignored Mac on the way into school asked him questions. Did he wear a gun? Where was it? Where did he learn how to be a marshal? Why did the school need a marshal? What was a marshal? Would he be at the school every day? The standard interrogation.

Savannah Ross even said hello to Mac. Her demeanor was much more calm and polite than her mother's. She asked him if he was married and if he had kids or pets. She squealed when he told her about Roxy. She said they had a dog and a cat.

Nothing could have prepared Mac for the auditory assault brought on by hundreds of kids confined to one area.

Teddy Ross stopped Mac as he left the cafeteria. "Mr. Mac, what types of markets do dogs avoid?" His face looked serious as he peered over the top of his glasses.

"I'm not sure Teddy. What types of markets do dogs avoid?"

"Flea markets. Hahahaha." He chuckled and then laughed so hard he bent over slapping his leg. It took him a minute to pull himself together. "Get it? *Flea* markets."

"I got it. That's funny Teddy. You're quite the jokester." He couldn't help but smile because of his vivacious personality and a mass of brown curls that went every which way. Teddy also differed from his mother. His eyeglasses seemed to spend more time on the tip of his nose than on the bridge. Parts of his shirt hung out of his shorts, and he had a big Band-Aid on one knee.

"What'd you do to your knee?" Mac pointed.

Teddy looked down at his leg. "Oh, that. I rode my bike too fast downhill. My bike got the high-speed wobbles. When I tried to round a curve, I crashed into a bush. It's nothing." He shrugged.

By early afternoon, the noise level had given Mac a headache. He was more than ready for the day to end. Roni stood next to him in front of the calm school while they waited for the dismissal bell to sound.

"Is it true you were in Special Ops in the Air Force?" Roni said.

"I was."

"The single teachers are already talking about how handsome you are, wait until they hear that."

Across the street in the visitor parking lot, fathers waiting for their kids exchanged head nods with Mac. Mothers smiled. Mrs. Ross slammed the door of her Jaguar and marched toward them. The perfume assault arrived before she did.

"Did you speak to my daughter today?" she said with the same hint of booze on her breath. Sweat beads formed on her nose.

"Your daughter spoke to *me*."

"I told you not to talk to her."

"She approached *me*."

The bell rang, and kids exploded through the main door.

Other parents observed the confrontation unfold as they hustled their kids past Mrs. Ross and Mac. Roni stood her ground next to Mac in a show of solidarity.

Mrs. Ross jabbed her index claw toward Mac's chest. "I'm serious when I say you aren't to converse with my daughter. You're the adult."

"Mrs. Ross, have I offended you? You seem angry with me."

She poked her finger at him again. "Stay away from my daughter. I mean it."

"Look, Mrs. Ross. We're going to have to figure out a way to get along. I was..."

Savannah bounced out of the building toward her mother. "Hi, baby. How was your first day?" She knelt down and hugged her daughter.

Dr. Jekyll and Mrs. Ross.

Mac stayed at the front of the school waiting for stragglers to leave. He received a text from his sister.

Maggie: *How was your first day?*

Mac: *Remember the woman at the board meeting? With the protest sign?*

Maggie: *Yes.*

Mac: *She forbade me from speaking to her daughter.*

Maggie: *Because?*

Mac: *Unhappy they hired me. She accused me of posing as a reporter at the meeting in June.*

School had been in session for one week. Every morning Mac heard fifteen-second snippets of conversations about homework, or lunch or going to practice or piano lessons after school. Most parents said *'I love you'* as their offspring hustled away from them. A few moms planted a kiss, their sentiment filled with sweetness.

There were a handful of parents who appeared loveless, at least in public, anyway. Then there were a few parents who seemed downright mean to their kids. Kevin Jackson's father, the parent who'd asked the school board members at the June board meeting, which moron thought they needed a guard with a loaded gun, was one of those parents.

Mr. Jackson stopped his fancy red sports car at the curb. Kevin flung open the passenger door and hit the sidewalk running. Mr. Jackson slammed the transmission into park and thrust himself out of the driver's seat with the speed of a tiger. Not a single strand of his perfect hair style fell out of place. He yelled to his son, "Kevin, come back here." He smoothed the seatbelt creases from his suit jacket. Kevin had almost made it to the school entrance when he turned and walked back to where his father's car sat idling at the curb.

Mac took in a slow, deep breath and watched the parent-kid interaction before glancing at his wrist watch. Time was ticking, and the disturbance was holding up the drop-off routine.

Roni leaned toward Mac. "He's such a jerk. He does this almost every day. What's his problem?" she whispered, as she bobbed her head toward the Jacksons. "And Kevin creeps me out."

In Mac's peripheral vision he saw someone headed his way, he knew by the fragrance in the air Mrs. Ross was about to stage another attack. She shooed Teddy and Savannah toward the school entrance.

"Well, Mr. Marshal, start marshaling and make Mr. Jackson stop bullying his son. Why do the rest of us have to hear their family squabbles every morning?"

Mr. Jackson appeared to have overhead Mrs. Ross and changed his focus from Kevin to her. "Anna Beth, our 'family squabbles' are none of your business. Shut the fuck up."

Mrs. Ross gasp and put her hand to her chest as if she were to have said, *'Who, me?'* His brashness stunned her. She turned and retreated to the safety of her car.

Mr. Jackson returned his attention back to his son.

There was a tug on Mac's pant leg. "Mr. Mac?"

Without looking, he knew by the distinctive sing-song style with just enough nasal whine that it was Jillian, his little first-grade gal pal.

"Good morning, Miss Jillian. How are you this morning?" he replied without shifting his gaze.

She tugged on his pant leg again and dismissed his inquiry. "Did that big boy do something bad?" she asked.

"I don't think so, Jillian. Go on inside before the bell rings."

She held her ground, her concern evident by her stubbornness. Mac looked down into her golden-brown eyes and turned her shoulders in the direction of the school entrance.

"Please go inside before the bell rings."

Jillian turned back toward Mac and then looked at the scene the Jacksons were making.

Roni placed her hands gently on Jillian's shoulders and turned her toward the school entrance. "Go inside Jillian," Roni said.

Jillian did as Roni told her to do. When she crossed the threshold of the school, the first bell sounded signaling school would begin in five minutes.

Kevin's father clenched his jaw. His face reddened. He wasn't much taller than Kevin. An inch, maybe.

Kevin stood an arm's length from his father.

Mr. Jackson took hold of his son by the lapels of his shirt and yanked him close.

"I hate that he yells at…" Roni started to say.

"Hey," Mac pushed off from the brick wall and yelled at Mr. Jackson in an authoritative voice that made stragglers stop and look.

Mr. Jackson looked at Mac. Kevin looked also.

At this exact moment all around the world, parents were abusing their kids. At this time and place, it wasn't happening on Mac's watch.

Mr. Jackson pushed Kevin away like he'd launched a boat from a dock. Kevin's slight body stumbled head first, but his over-sized feet caught up with him after a step or two. He hurried toward the school.

While pretending not to look at the Jacksons, parents scurried along the sidewalk with their kids in tow. Kids gawked at the Jacksons. Parents turned their sons and daughters away from the confrontation and told them to hurry along.

The chatter from kid to parent and vice versa had gone quiet.

As Mac walked to the fancy red sports car, he said, "You don't need to get physical with your boy. You're upsetting the other kids. It's time to move on."

Mr. Jackson walked toward Mac.

"Mind your own fucking business," Mr. Jackson said.

"Move your car. You're holding up the other parents."

"I'll move my fucking car when I'm ready to move it." He stood like a statue.

"Your son has gone inside. You have no further business here. It's time to leave," Mac said, as he turned around to walk away.

"You've made a big mistake," Mr. Jackson said.

The next thing Mac heard was the slam of his car door. Then his car sped away from the curb and almost hit a parent and kid in the crosswalk.

"Wow, Mac, that was excellent and long overdue," said Roni. "I've never seen anyone stand up to that jerk."

"Talking like a dick's one thing when he got physical with Kevin, he crossed a line," Mac said.

Across the street, in the visitor parking lot, fathers who'd been standing guard gave Mac an approving nod before they drove out of the lot.

As Roni walked inside the school, Chuck Andrews walked out. Chuck taught physical education and coached most of the sports offered at Blackstone. He didn't look like a hardcore athlete. He looked more like a teacher who fell into a cushy gig. Everyone called him Coach. So far, he'd been welcoming and cordial.

Mac had spent a good amount of time perusing through the Blackstone Academy archives, yearbooks, and remembrances. Years ago, Coach fit the profile of an athletic coach. Stress and time had not served him well.

"Mac. Mac. Mac. What's this I hear about Mr. Jackson giving you a hard time?" Coach said.

"It's all good for now. What can you tell me about Kevin and his father?"

Coach and Mac talked for a few more minutes. Mac wanted to learn more about Kevin.

Coach and Mac walked into the school together. Coach asked Mac if he played golf. He needed a fourth for a round at the Country Club after school.

Mac accepted Coach's invitation. When they were inside, Coach went toward the gymnasium and Mac to his office. While he watched the security feeds fade in and out showing the many views of the campus, he texted Maggie.

Mac: *WTF. The crazy woman came at me again this morning demanding I break up a father-son conflict. The father went off on the crazy woman who ran to her car like a scalded dog.*

Maggie: *Sounds like she now sees that the school needed a marshal after all.*

Mac: *I think that revelation may have fallen short with her.*

Maggie: *LOL. Come for dinner tonight.*

Mac: *Can't. Playing golf with one of the teachers. Tomorrow?*

Maggie: *Golfing with a teacher? Ooh la la. Tomorrow's good. See you then.*

Unknown Threat is available at www.robinlyons.com and wherever you purchase or borrow books. The eBook version is free.

ROBIN'S READER CLUB

What do you get when you join my reader club? Free books, exclusive giveaways, book recommendations, author updates, and behind the scene on what's happening at the ranch, where I live. My weekly newsletter arrives in your email inbox every Saturday morning. It's a great way to start your weekend—your favorite morning beverage, and a glimpse into my country life.

Email addresses are never shared. I value your privacy as much as mine.

Join the club at: https://www RobinLyons.com

AUTHOR'S NOTE

For many years, I knew I wanted to write fiction. After a deranged man gunned down a colleague, an elementary school principal, a man I considered a friend, in his office, I knew I wanted to write the Marshal Series. This truly horrific event changed many lives, mine included.

The Marshal Series began as my way of raising awareness about crimes occurring at schools.

I've had the pleasure of working with many outstanding teachers and school staff. And I've met many awesome parents, and watched amazing children grow and succeed. Nothing I write is in any way meant to cast doubt about public schools providing a quality education. When I write about school trauma, students, parents, and/or staff, I write about the 1% who have ill intent.

Thank you for reading *Unknown Revenge, Book 4 in the Marshal Series.*

-Robin

ABOUT THE AUTHOR

I live in the beautiful foothills of Northern California on a cattle ranch with my husband.

With close to thirty years working in public education, the tragic loss of a beloved colleague to workplace violence inspired me to write the Marshal series.

Connect with me on my website or through social media, I respond as fast as possible to posts, messages, or email that aren't spam.

WEBSITE
https://www RobinLyons.com
BOOKBUB
https://www.bookbub.com/profile/robin-lyons
FACEBOOK
https://www.facebook.com/robinlyons.author
GOODREADS
Https://www.goodreads.com/robin_lyons
INSTAGRAM
https://www.instagram.com/robinlyons_author
PINTEREST
https://www.pinterest.com/robinlyons